ROCK & ROLL
NEVER
FORGETS

ROCK & ROLL NEVER FORGETS

DEBORAH GRABIEN

Thomas Dunne Books/St. Martin's Minotaur New York

This is a work of fiction. All of the characters, organizations, and events portrayed in this novel are either products of the author's imagination or are used fictitiously.

THOMAS DUNNE BOOKS.
An imprint of St. Martin's Press.

ROCK & ROLL NEVER FORGETS. Copyright © 2008 by Deborah Grabien. All rights reserved. Printed in the United States of America. For information, address St. Martin's Press, 175 Fifth Avenue, New York, N.Y. 10010.

www.thomasdunnebooks.com
www.minotaurbooks.com

Book design by Spring Hoteling

Library of Congress Cataloging-in-Publication Data

Grabien, Deborah.
    Rock & roll never forgets : a JP Kinkaid mystery / Deborah Grabien.—1st St. Martin's Minotaur ed.
        p. cm.
    ISBN-13: 978-0-312-37999-5
    ISBN-10: 0-312-37999-4
1. Rock musicians—Fiction.   2. Guitarists—Fiction.   3. Multiple sclerosis—Patients—Fiction.   4. Murder—Fiction.   I. Title.   II. Title: Rock and roll never forgets.
    PS3557. R1145R63 2008
    813'.54—dc22   2008012482

First Edition: July 2008

10 9 8 7 6 5 4 3 2 1

For a beloved ghost, gone too soon.
And for Nic, who's right here with me.

ACKNOWLEDGMENTS

If I thanked all the readers who held my hand through this, I'd need a separate volume. So, I'll keep it short: from Ita, who allowed me to fictionalize her on the condition that she got a great bodyguard's wardrobe, to Amy Garvey, from Hillevi Wyman to Anne Weber, from Marlene Stringer to Stephanie Lang, from Matt Hayden to Beverly Leoczko, from Sandra Larkin to Alexandra Lynch, from Cynthia Bossi to Barbara Ferrer, and every other reader who helped me on this one, as JP would say: Cheers, mates. Brilliant job.

Kate McKean, nice sharp incisive agent lady.

Jay Thomson, Gene Clark, Mark Jacobs, Craig Juan, Mike Urban, and you know who else, for providing me with the soundtrack by which I was able to write this series.

Michelle and Jeannette, Pete and David, and some other cool people, for letting me come back again. You know what I mean.

Julian Dawson, excellent biographer.

And to Bob Seger, for the title song.

ROCK & ROLL
NEVER
FORGETS

PROLOGUE

"*Good evening, Wembley!*"

The houselights came down. The house crew, up in the rigging and at the boards, brought up the stage lights: our band's thirty-year signature opening lighting, pale yellow ringed with a shimmering sort of dark moon effect, flooding the back third of the stage.

We stood in the wings, the five of us. This was how the show always started. We could do it in our sleep; knowing Mac, our lead singer, I suspected he'd sometimes done just that.

"*Ladies and gents, it's the final night of a long, long road trip, so please give a warm London welcome to Blacklight!*"

Right. Showtime.

We stepped into the shadows onstage. The crowd, about eleven thousand of them, responded in the appropriate way—they went nuts. Screaming, stamping, a thousand or so points of light that were actually disposable lighters, individual voices in the crowd shouting for various members of the band: *I love you, Mac! Luke rocks!* One young female voice near the backstage door, startling me, yelling, *Take me home tonight, JP!* That brought my head around—I rarely get that sort of comment. Actually, considering all our ages, it never ceases to surprise me that any of us get hit on anymore. But there's something about rock and roll.

I glanced behind me. My two Gibsons, a tobacco sunburst 345 and a Les Paul gold-top, sat in their stands. The guitar around my neck, my favourite Les Paul Deluxe, seemed heavier than usual. This had been a long tour, nearly a month on the road, twenty dates spanning most of Europe.

We were ending this leg of it in London. That was a smart move, nice for the rest of the band, since they actually live here. The scheduling didn't work nearly so well for me. I live in San Francisco now. The end of the tour, for me, just meant one more plane ride before I was home.

The truth is, I was exhausted. Multiple sclerosis and the nonstop grind of a major tour are a piss-poor mix.

Another glance, making sure that the low-backed stool I needed during gigs these days was in place. Yeah, right where it was supposed to be; the roadies had never forgotten that yet, bless them.

A roar of vocal thunder from the crowd shook the building. Mac the Knife—Malcolm Sharpe—our frontman, had stepped into the spotlight.

I looked over at Luke Hedley, our lead guitar player. We'd worked out a series of nearly invisible signals, me and Luke, for nights when the illness wasn't letting me do some of the fancier stuff I used to be able to do. He'd learned every guitar part of mine he might ever need to cover, visiting San Francisco for a full month, and we had it worked out. It had been tricky for Luke, getting my parts down; I'm a blues player at the core, less rock and folk than where Luke's musical thing comes from. Besides, he's used to doing it his way, since he writes damned near all the music for the band. But he'd done it.

So far tonight, it felt as if things would be doable. I was tired, yeah, but I could at least feel my fingers. That wasn't always the case; some nights I'd end up with my fingers doing what they did through memory, and not much else.

I shook my head at him slightly—my signal for *No, don't need help yet, it's cool for now*—and gave him a thumbs-up. He nodded and edged toward me. We'd stay close during the rest of the gig, using each other's energy for support. Same thing Calvin Wilson and Stu Corrigan, our bassist and drummer, would do, holding down the bottom. It was all about the onstage support, taking the energy from each other, from the crowd, making it happen, making it real, making it music, and then giving it all back, to the crowd, to each other.

By this point in the tour, any tour really, we were all pretty exhausted and edgy. It wasn't so bad as it might have been, this time. The pace of the tour had been pretty relaxed, fewer dates than usual and longer rest breaks between dates.

Even so, people were tired and cranky and bored with being cooped up with each other. Fortunately, rehearsals for the American leg of the tour weren't due to start for another month. I was pretty sure everyone wanted the break as much as I did. I hadn't mentioned it, but I didn't have to. I've been a member of Blacklight for nearly thirty years. I know the drill.

"The lady had issues, she took a little ride. . . ."

Mac hit the opening vocal perfectly. The band came in behind him, slamming into the song, because this is rock and roll and you have to cook from the first beat. I stitched a hot pulse in straight A, walking up the Paul's neck as Luke walked the

3

call-and-response line down his Strat. Moments like this, with the band's lighting moving around us, Luke looked really young; he's got that sort of colouring, used to be blond and now he's just pale, skinny enough so that the years don't show so easily. He and Mac are a type, you know? Long and lean. It's a good physical type for a touring musician to be. Hell, I'm a bit of a rail myself. Pity I didn't get their height along with it.

Behind Luke's shoulder, Calvin and Stu had already locked in and the bass was burning it up, hot and cold. Blacklight's rhythm section calls itself the Bunker Brothers—it's the name they use when Blacklight's off the road and we're all off doing other projects. For them, that means producing some of the high-quality industrial techno stuff they seem to like. But when they sync up onstage for Blacklight and lay down the rhythm that keeps the rock and roll in place, it's fucking amazing, just gorgeous, how much in step they are.

Stu must have got that I was watching him, because he suddenly caught my eye. He was grinning, nailing the drums, slamming the rhythm down. He's a bit easier to piss off than the rest of us—Irish Catholic raised in East London, so no surprise about him being touchy—but tonight, last night of this leg of the tour, he was right there in it, just thundering away, and Cal's bass was right there with him, cooking it. It was going to be one of those shows that got remembered by fans, twenty years down the line. I could already feel it.

"She traded in her Harley and she offered up her pride. . . ."

The part of my head, the bit I've trained never to get lost in the joy of the music, relaxed. This was all about playing. Mac was pure sex up there, and I'm damned if I knew how he maintained it in his mid-fifties, but he did, hot as the surface of Mercury. Half the women in the building, and quite a few of the men, would have loved to rip his clothes off. He thrives on that, too. It's not my thing, never has been; I never wanted that rush, to be needed that way. But Mac did, and does, and the fact that he does helps keep this band going as one of the most successful touring acts in rock history.

"Shadow on her shoulder, she took a little breath. . . ."

The wings offstage were crammed solid with our people, family and close friends, Blacklight staffers from the corporate office in London. This was a treat for most of them, getting to actually see a live gig by the band they work for. There were our roadies and techs as well, brilliant at their jobs.

There was also the usual group of hangers-on and total strangers backstage. I recognised a few members of the local press. There were Wembley house people. There was Domitra Calley, Mac's official—and the band's unofficial—bodyguard. Her eyes kept circling, looking for trouble to prevent. She had an extra reason to be vigilant; Mac had got hit with a paternity suit, and the girl's boyfriend had made threats. There were a lot of people I didn't recognise, but then, there always are.

Our road manager, Ian Hendry, was front and center. Ian was probably even happier about the upcoming rest break than the rest of us. He had extra stuff on his plate at the moment—our longtime manager, Chris Fallow, was into his seventies and had been in hospital for a while, battling cancer and emphysema and a few other miserable things. So Ian was doing Chris's job as well as his own. Stu and Calvin's wives were there, still digging it after all these years; Luke's teenaged daughter Solange was there, dancing, in high heels and leather. She looked exactly like her mum had looked, twenty-odd years ago, before she married Luke and got cancer and died of it. It was spooky. Déjà vu always is.

"Lady's gone dancin' with the kiss of death!"

Halfway through the evening, my body let me know just how long the show—how long the tour—really was. I signalled to Luke, who'd been watching for it—*It's okay, I can play, but my legs have gone*—and headed for my stool. The soles of my feet felt like I'd got them off one of those fire-walking people, and my shoulders had gone shaky with the weight of the Paul.

Next song, I thought, I was changing over to the 345. It was a much lighter guitar, hollow-body, and I didn't need the signature sound of either of the Pauls for the next few numbers, anyway. All I had to do on those was rhythm work—they'd been written by Luke, and there was a lot of hard rock lead in there. That was Luke's thing more than mine. Sitting, shifting the weight off my feet, I glanced into the wings.

Solange Hedley seemed to have brought a school friend with her, a pretty girl with long legs and a cloud of dark red hair. There was something about the girl that got to me, even through the music, the audience, the reality of the live show, and I suddenly realised what it was. Maybe it was the hair, or how young she was, but for a moment, I was nearly thirty years younger, and the girl in the wings, watching me, her eyes on me, was Bree. And that meant that if I looked just beyond her, I'd see another woman, another face, the woman I'd come in with. . . .

Vertigo washed over me and left me dizzy and sick at my stomach. I closed my eyes again, my fingers blessedly remembering what they needed to do for the song in progress, Luke taking up any slack. When I opened them again, I glanced back at the wings. The girl was still there, and she was staring at me. Not at Mac—at me.

Déjà vu. I looked away.

Two hours, two hours ten. We hit the closer, kicked it up a notch, let it explode out over the crowd, and headed offstage for five minutes of towelling off sweat and rehydrating. I don't drink alcohol, haven't since the early eighties, so I sucked down a bottle of mineral water instead. Someone had brought the dregs of the preshow goodies up from the dressing room; Mac grabbed a bottle of unopened champagne and prepared to douse the first few rows with it.

We let the audience tension build up, chanting, screaming, rising in pitch, for about five minutes. Back out onstage for the two-song encore. A nice moment, when we joined arms and took the edge of the stage and bowed to the audience. Wave to the crowd, tell them good night, acknowledge the cheering, the stomping. Offstage, houselights up, and done. It was time to go home, and thank God for that.

At first glance, everyone backstage was doing their usual post-gig thing. Mac was energised, bouncing about, dancing in place, as if he could have done another hour out there. Luke had sprawled out on a sofa, eyes closed, looking wasted, and I didn't blame him. Just watching Mac jump around was enough to leave me exhausted as well.

Ian was deep in conversation with Stu and Cal in one corner of the dressing room. Whatever it was they were talking about, neither of the Bunker Brothers looked too happy about it, and Ian looked worried.

He looked up for a moment and saw me hunting for my coat. "When's your flight, JP?"

"Carla booked me a red-eye. I need to be at Heathrow in about ninety minutes, so that's me out. There should be a car outside." I lifted my voice to get everyone's attention. "Oi! Cheers, mates. See you all in New York next month."

I grabbed my Les Paul case, left the equipment and the rest

of the instruments for the roadies to deal with, and headed out, picking my way through the backstage cavern and out, through a maze of road cases, unused amps, packing crates with BLACK-LIGHT stencilled on the sides.

Just as I got to the door to the backstage alley, a voice stopped me: young, light, nervous. It was the same voice that had called out an invitation to me just before the show started: *Take me home tonight, JP!*

"JP?"

I turned around and faced her. It was Solange Hedley's friend, a schoolgirl really, seventeen or eighteen, maybe. Bree had been not quite seventeen, but this wasn't Bree, even with the same cloudy auburn hair or the legs that went up and up. Bree was American, and Bree's voice was deep, and Bree hadn't begged me to take her home with me.

"Yeah, I'm JP." I glanced at my watch. "You're a friend of Solange Hedley's, yeah? I saw you earlier." *Heard you earlier, too, but not going to bring that one up.*

"That's right—I'm at school with Solange. I'm Suzanne McElroy."

She looked at me. There was glitter on her eyelids, and she'd carefully let a bit of lacy bra show. Those long legs were bare, her red-painted toes hanging over the lip of shoes that were all wrong for her feet. I felt very sorry for her, and of course telling her that would just about kill her.

"Nice to meet you." I gave her a smile and glanced at my watch again. "Sorry—I have a flight in just about three hours, and I need to go. My car's outside."

"I think you're very cool." Her inflection hadn't altered at all, but her eyes—she suddenly looked, I don't know, hungry, desperate, as if she thought she had an open place in her that an aging musician with a debilitating disease could fill. And me filling her, that was just what she had in mind. Bloody hell. Flattering, but not my thing, not at all. "I think you're very hot."

"Ta." I smiled at her and reached out to touch her cheek. She shook a bit when I did that, and I wondered how much virginal terror the glitter and the high heels and the obvious invitation to sex was supposed to be covering up. "That's kind of you. Hot? Maybe. Thing is, I'm also married." I heard myself pause, couldn't help it. "I have an old lady."

"It doesn't make any difference to me." Hunger, hope, something else, but I'm damned if I know what. I've never understood what drives people. What drives me is music, and I care fuck-all about most other things. "That you're married, I mean. Your old lady. I don't mind. She's not here, is she? It's okay. It doesn't matter to me."

I'd told Bree I'd ring home when the show was over. What time was it in San Francisco, three in the afternoon? Right. She'd have her cell phone turned on. I could phone from the car, on the way to the airport.

Suzanne was looking at me, hungry, scared, whatever. "It matters to me," I told her. "Nice to meet you," and headed out into the night, into the limo, to the airport, and, finally, home.

CHAPTER ONE

There are days when I honestly think there's no escape from rock and roll.

The limo from the airport had dropped me off at not quite four in the morning. The lights in the hall and the front room were on; I'd have been willing to bet that Bree hadn't been to bed at all, hadn't slept except for short naps. I'd also have laid odds that she'd kept the status of my flight up on her computer in the kitchen alcove, tracking it as it made its way across the Atlantic and over Canada.

By the time I'd hit the bottom stair, she was waiting for me at the top, with the door open and the cats wreathing around her ankles. This, Bree within touching distance, was what I'd been looking forward to, consciously jonesing for, for at least a week; she'd welcomed me back off the road so many times over the last twenty-five years that this homecoming had the feel of an old bathrobe, something you slip into because it's so comfy. Coming home to Bree, it always feels like that, you know?

This time was no different. First words out of her mouth—after I'd dropped the guitars and kissed her for about three minutes, and after she got her breath back—were an announcement that there would be nothing happening before noon. I thought about teasing her over it, she sounded so fierce, but I was too tired and too dragged down. She kissed me again, fussed over me as if she'd been ten years my senior instead of eleven years my junior, fed me some light gorgeous soup and homemade bread and my nighttime meds, and even managed not to ask how I was feeling. Once I put the spoon down, she had me upstairs, into bed, and unconscious.

I've known Bree since she was a dewy-eyed teenager. That's a quarter-century of knowing, and she's always been the wrong person to argue with. Besides, she's so often right, especially about what masquerades as my health, that I usually do what she tells me and I don't go on about it. I don't lie to her about what my health is doing, either. My old lady can be fierce, when the spirit moves her. I find it's a lot easier to be up-front with her, and avoid pissing her off.

Problem is, even Bree can't control the outside world, though it's not for lack of trying. So when my cell phone rang at twenty of nine the next morning, she'd got it and taken it into the hallway, ready to verbally rip whoever was calling this early a new one, before I could get my eyelids unglued.

It was just as well, since ungluing the lids was likely to take a while. I don't do mornings very well in any case; I don't mean to go on about the MS, but it's worst during that first hour of the day. I've tried telling Bree that it's just nature's way of reminding me to take my morning pain meds, but she doesn't seem to find that funny.

This morning was worse than usual. Jet lag's always a drag,

but it's a lot worse coming late to early in time zones; San Francisco to Europe, I take a nap and my body adjusts, but this direction, it's just bloody miserable. Makes it tricky for a touring musician, you know?

I lay in bed for a few minutes, eyes closed, feeling sunlight coming in through the bay windows, and trying to pinpoint where the biggest problems of the day were likely to be. *Sole of the right foot*, I decided; it was tingling and wanting to cramp.

I flexed both legs, nice and slow, trying to be careful, keep the stabs at bay; that didn't work very well, and I bit back noise. *Right quad, bloody hell, shit*, that was going to be a drag—the entire muscle was yelling, and those are big muscles, the quadriceps. The hands, mercifully, seemed fine. It's not easy being a guitar player with a disease that can take all the sensation from your fingers without prior notice. Tonight I was due for my weekly shot, the drug that keeps me out of a wheelchair, and that was completely cocked up already, what with my internal clock thinking it was eight hours ahead and still on London time.

It was right around then that I finally started paying attention to Bree's voice, drifting in through the closed bedroom door. There was a familiar note in it, exasperation, but more than that—it was mixed up with something else.

". . . Carla, why the hell . . ." Silence. I could almost imagine the staccato rapping of Carla Fanucci, Blacklight's imported–from–New York publicity handler and American operations manager. Bree's voice came again, this time with something new in it—anger, or disbelief, maybe. ". . . biographer? No, he didn't say anything to me, not a damned word. Of course I'm sure! Carla, I don't know what you're talking about! You want John to do what? No way. No. I said, *no*. Not a chance in hell he's going to—no, I really don't care whether—"

Silence, this time far too long. Bree, woken too early or,

worse yet, thinking I'd been woken too early, would be quiet this long only if something was wrong. And Carla, well, if Carla was demanding I do something and ringing up this early to say so, it had to be something major. She knew just how late I'd got to bed last night.

I got to the door just as Bree was opening it. The brief push-me pull-you would have been funny, if the look on her face hadn't killed any desire to laugh. She had this bleached, lost look on her face, and I felt my own stomach knot up; Bree only ever looked that way when one particular subject was on the table. That subject's name is Cilla. I'm married to her.

"Here." Bree handed me the phone, not meeting my eye. Her mouth was twisted down tight. *Shit.* She was swallowing tears; Bree doesn't cry in front of me, never has done. This had to be something huge. What in hell could Carla have said?

"Bree? . . ."

"It's for you." Bree's voice was bleak. "Carla. Something about a biography, a personal history of the band. She says you know all about it, and that it's important, and that it can't wait. Here. Take it, please."

I opened my mouth to answer, to say *Look, love, I haven't got a clue what you're on about,* but I didn't get the chance. She turned on her heel and went, heading down to the kitchen. I heard water running: coffee? Filling the cats' dishes? Trying to smother the sound of crying? I stayed where I was. Bree wouldn't thank me for intruding right now.

"JP? Are you there?"

"Yeah." Her voice was a bit sharper than usual. So was mine. "Yeah, I'm here. Bloody hell. I didn't get home until four this morning, Carla—you already know that. The European tour ended yesterday, remember? Whatever this is about, couldn't it have waited a few hours?"

"Sorry." That was bollocks. She wasn't sorry. This was her

13

job, and she was damned good at it. "But no, this really couldn't wait. And what do you mean, whatever this is about? It's about this biography. I wouldn't have dragged you out of bed this early for anything else."

"What biography?" I was dizzy, a bit off, and my jaw was tingling. That was typical for not enough sleep, but it was also an indicator that I might want to start thinking about bracing myself for an exacerbation of the MS. Not a good sign. "What are you on about?"

"Oh, damn." Her voice had changed. "I called Ian about this yesterday—you guys were onstage playing. He was supposed to tell the entire band about it. No wonder Bree's so pissed off. I'm sorry, JP. Ian did say he'd tell everyone."

"Yeah, well, whatever it is, Ian didn't tell me. Maybe he told everyone else, but this is the first I've heard about a biography. Telling the entire band, was he? Have I been given the sack from Blacklight and no one's told me yet?"

For some reason, I was feeling pissy, right at the edge of being insulted. If that was what Stu and Cal had been looking unhappy about after the gig last night, Ian had had plenty of time to fill me in before I left, and he hadn't done it.

Carla picked up on it, of course. She's razor-sharp, that girl is, but she'd have had to be completely dim not to suss out that my silence was because I was narked as hell and didn't want to snap at her.

"You must have left for Heathrow before he had it together." Her tone had changed again. "Damn. Sorry, JP. I really didn't mean to cause a situation here. I assumed you knew about it already. To be fair to Ian, I sort of dumped it on him in mid-gig, and he had a lot of stuff going on. I'm really sorry. Apologise to Bree for me, will you?"

"Yeah, I will. Look, hang on a moment, will you, please?" I covered the phone and gave in to a jaw-cracking yawn. "Sorry,

I'm dead on my feet. Okay. Since Ian didn't tell me, maybe you'd better do it. What's all this about, Carla?"

"There's an unofficial biography and history of the band in the works. I got the early word yesterday." I could hear her sucking down air. "The guy writing it? Perry Dillon."

"Shit!"

Bree's reaction—that miserable lost look of hers, her silence, her refusal to meet my eye—had suddenly become entirely appropriate to a simple phone call. There were biographers, and then there was Perry Dillon.

"Perry Dillon." I sat down hard. "The same bloke who writes all those knife-in-the-ribs exposé books? The one everyone's afraid to turf off the premises when he slithers in, because they're afraid of his tactics once they can't keep an eye on him? That Perry Dillon?"

"That's the only Perry Dillon I know about." This time, Carla actually did sound almost apologetic. "You get now why I woke you up? Sorry it upset Bree, JP. I wasn't trying to. But we need to tackle this, like, now. We have to decide just how we're going to handle it. This guy isn't going to just go away. I was hoping you'd have a few ideas of your own about it, but I guess I'm the bad-news girl on this one."

"Jesus." This was a hell of a way to wake up, having to try to wrap my head around the idea of Blacklight being targeted by Perry Dillon, a world-class sleaze making million-dollar advances off "histories" that were at least half full of every unsubstantiated rumour the man could find.

What a mess. No wonder Bree was downstairs in the kitchen, crying. This was going to be ugly, if the bloke couldn't be handled properly. "Carla, please tell me you haven't told him I was willing to talk to him. You haven't, right?"

"I haven't told him anything at all, JP. He hasn't called me yet. I got this one nice and early, strictly backchannel, which is why I called Ian as soon as I confirmed the rumour. It's also why I took the chance and woke you up, and no, by the way, I haven't forgotten what time you got home. I'm the one who booked your flight back from London, remember? The thing is . . ."

". . . you want to get to him before he gets to us. That it?" I got off the bed, trying to shake the needles and cramps out of my feet. No good—the body was doing its own thing. I went and sat in Bree's rocking chair.

"Of course. Grab the offensive first, and maybe we can get some control on the spin. If we can spike the bastard's guns, I say we do it. But . . ." Her voice trailed away. I knew what she wasn't saying.

"But, I'm the one most affected. What with having hooked up with Bree when she was technically too young to be with me legally, even though I didn't know it at the time. Wouldn't want Perry Dillon making me out to be a statutory rapist. And of course, there's my bloody wife, and my drug bust, and the fact that I was deported. And, since I'm me and not Mac, I actually give a shit about hanging on to some privacy, what with Bree being damned near pathological about it. So I'm the first one you rang. Of course. Right. Got it."

I honestly didn't think my voice came out any different, but I could almost hear Carla flinch. "JP, look—"

"No, you're right." Of course she was right; she was brilliant at her job. That's why Blacklight—the corporate entity rather than merely five dinosaurs who'd toured sold-out venues all over the world for thirty years—paid her such a spectacular salary. I was seriously tempted to have a few pointed words with Ian, though; for some reason, his not including me in that "entire band" thing was rankling more than it should. "Not your fault. You're right, we need to deal with it. What do you want me to do?"

She told me. A few minutes later, I clicked the phone off,

took a very fast shower and my morning meds, got dressed, and went downstairs. I'm being honest here: I didn't much want to. Bree gets upset about very few things in this world, but there was no way I could pretend that the situation, at least the way Carla'd spun it, was going to be anything other than miserable.

She was in the kitchen, surrounded by cats. Our senior cat, Wolfling, was curled up in her lap. For all that I'd rescued him as a tiny tabby kitten from a shoe box at the local market, he'd become Bree's self-appointed comforter over the past ten years. Her Siamese queen, Farrowen, was on the table, her tail curling around the bottom of Bree's coffee mug; right now, she was staring at me, not blinking, making me feel guilty. Our teen-aged moggy, Simon, ignored us both. He was busy chasing dust motes.

"Do you want breakfast?"

Her voice was neutral. *Damn.* I knew what that careful tone of hers meant: She'd already decided to bite the bullet and make it easy for me, which effectively meant I couldn't bring it up with her. Of course, if I went along with it and let her make it easy for me, I'd lose all right to deal with any of the fallout. As nice as it is having her smooth my path, there are times when I'd like to thump her.

"Bree, listen—"

"You should eat," she told me. Same damned flat unin-flected tone. "I'll make you some breakfast."

"Sod breakfast." I perched on the edge of the table. "Look, love, I don't want to make light of this, all right? And no, I didn't know a damned thing about it until Carla told me. She rang Ian about it last night, probably while we were in the middle of the show closer, and he didn't bother telling me before I left for Heathrow. And believe me, I'm planning on having a few choice words with the lad. Anyway, Carla wants to try to minimise the damage before this bloke ever gets started. Thing is—"

"I know. Fat chance. Believe me, I know." Her face had gone stony. She was putting up her usual Brave Little Woman walls, and kicking them down was going to take as much energy as dealing with Perry Dillon. Bloody hell, why couldn't she understand she was making it harder for me, not easier?

She was also refusing to meet my eyes, and that was worrying. Bree has very few feelings that I can't read in her face, but she wasn't letting me see her face, and that meant there were things she wanted to keep hidden. "I do get it, John. Is there any way at all you can at least demand some control over what questions he asks?"

"Haven't got a clue, love. We can try, and we will, you know that. I trust Carla to put the hammer down about what's off-limits. Whether it works . . ." I leaned over, ignoring protest from my jet-lagged muscles, and laid my cheek against her hair. I can't do that unless she's sitting—she's nearly two inches taller than I am. "I'm sorry, Bree. I'll do my best to keep this from getting out of hand. We'll get through it."

"You think so?" She looked up at me finally, and I felt my heart stutter a bit, the beat accelerating, trying to catch up and stay even. I've got a heart condition, something the doctors call arrhythmia, which means my heart does these bizarre little speed-ups. Some days, I felt like I was keeping the local casualty ward—the emergency room, right, I was a California resident now, not a Londoner anymore—in business.

I met Bree's eye. Her own were remote; something about the way the muscles of her face were working, I could see the pain.

Maybe she'd sensed that bit of heart action, because she tried for a lighter note. "We could sic Mac's bodyguard on him."

"She'd probably love that." The picture of Domitra wiping

the floor with a shadowy Perry Dillon—using every one of her martial arts skills and maybe a few bits of weaponry just for a lark—was too lovely to pass up. "Hell, *I'd* love that. I'd do it in a heartbeat. Bree, listen. This Dillon bloke, he's in Los Angeles at the moment. That means I'm up first—it'll be down in Carla's office. I'll ask once, and only once: Do you want to be there when I talk to him?"

"No!" It was pain, all right, and maybe panic, too. "Dear God, how could you think I'd even consider being there? Twenty-five years together, you don't know me better than that? That's not what I want at all."

"Then what do you want?" Here we went again, Bree with the walls that were supposed to protect me, and all they ever did was keep me out. "Tell me what you want."

She got up, too fast; Wolfling slid off her lap onto the floor.

"Invisibility," she told me quietly, and left me standing there.

Two days later, walking into Blacklight's Los Angeles offices, I was already edgy.

It wasn't just the prospect of the interview with Perry Dillon that was worrying me. I'd flown down from San Francisco the night before, still jet-lagged and achy as hell. I'd also come down without Bree. She'd opted to stay home entirely.

That surprised me, and it worried me, as well. Bree loves L.A., the shops and restaurants, the feel of the city itself. We'd been there a few times together, when I was doing California tours with my pickup band, the Fog City Geezers, and she always has a good time.

So I'd expected her to come down and wander around while I was working, the way she always did. Instead, she'd muttered something about not being able to find someone to watch the cats. That was complete rubbish. We were only going to be gone a day and a night and anyway, we've got a bloke called Sammy who keeps house for us when we're on the road. But it was obvious she didn't want to be within a hundred miles of this interview, and I hadn't pushed her. That comment of hers—that she wanted to be invisible—had planted itself in my head, and it was sitting there, next to my own pissiness at Ian. It wasn't a comfortable feeling.

"JP! Oh, good, you're nice and early. I meant to ask you to do that."

Carla got up from behind her desk and hugged me, hard and fast. She still called herself a New Yorker, but I'd have bet that was more stubbornness than anything else. Between the ultra-short spiky haircut, the tattoos, and the Rollerblading to work every morning, she looked, and vibed, almost completely L.A. to me. "I told Dillon eleven, which means he'll get here at ten thirty, and hope to beat you here so that you won't have time to talk to me first. I'll bet money on it."

"I got your message, about when to get here. And I wouldn't take that bet, you know?" I glanced over her shoulder, through the open door into the office's conference room. There was a coffee machine with a pot of hot coffee already made, and cups set out. "Right. You're putting us in there, then?"

She nodded. "I've talked to Cal and Mac. Depending on what happens with you, they're up next, but of course they're at home in England. If he wants to talk to them, he gets to fly there. I haven't been able to reach Stu and Luke yet. Your bad luck, JP, living in America—you go first."

"My bad luck. Right." I met her eye. "Carla, I want something understood, okay? I'm not answering any questions about my personal life. That's not negotiable: not word one, fuck-all, nothing. Maybe Mac doesn't mind watching his private life smeared all over the tabloids, paternity suits and that lot. I don't want that kind of PR, and Bree absolutely doesn't. I'm not answering any questions that aren't specifically about music. No exceptions. Are we clear on that?"

"Oh, hell yes." She obviously approved. "I've already told Dillon that, and he's been faxed over the list of what's off-limits, but there's nothing to stop him asking. You're going to have to be on your toes for this, JP. He's going to try sneaking in things, catching you off guard. Remember his Elvis biography? The one he got sued over?"

"I remember it." I did, too. My friend Kris Corcoran, the bassist for a band called the Bombardiers—his wife, Sandra, is in publishing. I remembered her talking about it, using language a lot more colourful than she'd usually go for. "That's the one where he interviewed about three dozen people, twisted half the quotes and put everything out of context. I heard he made so much money off it, he settled the lawsuit and didn't change a word. I'll be careful."

"Cool." She patted my arm. "I've also told him you're just off the road, and that he only gets one hour. With any luck, we'll have you out of here in time to have a big yummy lunch with Bree at that Beverly Hills deli she likes so much."

"Bree's not with me." Even to my own ears, my voice sounded shut down and chilly. "She stayed in San Francisco. She's not happy about this biography, Carla. Neither am I."

"None of us are, JP. Ian's tearing his hair out over it. And you should have heard Mac on the subject, when I finally got him on the phone and confirmed who was writing it. Some of the stuff he mentioned wanting to do to Perry Dillon were right out of a bad slasher movie."

Something caught her attention; not having stood in front of a Marshall stack for thirty years, her long-distance hearing was a lot better than mine. I watched her go from friend to PR heavy in the blink of an eye. Scary, really. "And there's the elevator. Get your game face on, JP—it's showtime."

21

I'd never seen Perry Dillon before. I had no clue what to expect, and frankly, I could have done quite nicely without ever setting eyes on him. I suppose there was an image at the back of my head, a face to visually match the sleaze of what he did for a living. Sort of like Jethro Tull's Aqualung, you know?

I certainly wasn't expecting an aging surfer boy, in what Carla told me later was "casual Friday" dress for an office somewhere. If the look was supposed to catch his victims off guard, it didn't work with me. In fact, a few more alarm bells went off in my head.

"This is such an honour." He was smart enough not to offer a hand. Damn. Bloody sharp, Mr. Perry Dillon was, sharp enough to cut. "I've been a fan of yours since your solo album, back in 1971."

I caught Carla's eye over his shoulder, and saw the warning in her face. He was trying to disarm me; that album, *Blues House*, had sold about a thousand copies total, and had gone out of print almost immediately. A year later, the only place you could have found it was at my local record shop, down in South London. Hardly anyone knew about it.

So yeah, it was the best butter, that choice, but I was damned if I was going to bend over and let him grease me with it. Of course he'd know about it. He'd have researched me top to bottom, all the better to dig the pit he wanted me to tumble arse over teapot into. . . .

"So, you don't mind if I have the recorder on, do you?" I'm not good with accents, especially American ones, but for some reason, I thought it was Chicago I was hearing. "For accuracy?"

"I'd prefer it, actually. In fact—" I nodded at Carla, who had come in behind Dillon's chair. "It's a very good idea. We're going to record the entire interview, as well."

He smiled at me, and that smile? I saw a predator. Not a pleasant one, like one of our cats; this was sharklike, or possibly a barracuda, something with small sharp teeth, too white and too many of them. "Cool," he told me. "So, we've got one hour? Let's get started."

The first questions, about my early years as a solo guitar player on the early seventies London circuit, were harmless. They were standard, bland, the same rubbish anyone might have asked me. As we went on, though, I began to suss out why he was so damned dangerous: He was a good interviewer, a great one, actually. He made every question sound fresh, even though I'd already answered these questions a hundred times in other interviews. Yes, I'd jammed with Syd Barrett as a teenager, back in London. No, that session hadn't been recorded. Yes, David Carnwell, the producer, had been present for that, and yes, Carnwell had got me my first solo guitar gig at the old Marquee Club in Wardour Street. . . .

". . . and you met your wife, Cilla, at the Marquee, that was in 1972. Is that right?"

Carla, hovering just outside behind Dillon's back, snapped her head around hard. I'd already seen the snare.

"That question's off-limits, Mr. Dillon." I heard myself in full ice mode, totally parky; it gobsmacked me, how English I could get when the need arose. I sounded like bloody Winston Churchill. "You have the list we sent you, of things you can't ask about. It's right there at your elbow. Did you want to take a minute to look it over? I don't mind waiting."

"Sorry." *Right*, I thought, *bollocks you're sorry, you miserable little shit.* "Let's move on."

More questions, innocuous, taking me through the sold-out gigs at the Marquee, Carnwell getting interested in my career, setting me up as a session player, live gigs to keep me in the public eye, the offers to record with the Stones and Bowie, my decision to spend time as a session guitarist instead, the work I did with Jack Featherstone . . .

". . . you and Cilla were married in 1973. How did she feel about your decision not to join any of the major groups? I've been given to understand that she was very ambitious for you—"

"Bloody fucking hell!" I got up so fast, I smacked both thighs against the table. The pain might have been barely noticeable on any other day, but today, it was excruciating; stress brings the damaged nerve endings right to the surface. The pain added an edge to my temper, and I decided to use it. "That's the second time you've tried slipping in a personal question. Want to try convincing me to give you a shot at a third? With the understanding that you not only won't get an answer, you'll be turfed out on your arse?"

"Okay, okay, I get it, I believe you." He held up a placatory hand, but his eyes were calculating. Barracuda, definitely. "I figured it was worth a try. Let's talk about how you ended up joining Blacklight. I mean, at that point they were already well on their way to becoming one of the most successful stadium acts in rock history, and a lot of people were really surprised that they'd ask a session guy to join. I've heard that at the time, some major names were being considered. . . ."

"Yeah, well, you heard wrong. They weren't considering anyone at all, including me. It happened organically—I'd worked with them, second guitar on some of the bluesier stuff on their fourth album. They weren't looking for a second guitarist, not actively. I was there already, as a session player, and we just happened to be a perfect fit." I glanced at the clock, and then at Carla. She gave me a tiny nod, showing me she understood the look: three quarters of an hour gone. I had only fifteen minutes to get through. When that clock hit the sixty-minute mark, Mr. Dillon was done and out. She wasn't going to let him hang about.

I had a moment of wishing I'd had Dom with me. I'm not

physically impressive, but Domitra in full on-duty regalia, even just standing there, would have had this bloke sweating and on his best behaviour. It was a pity that, right now, Mac needed her more than I did. . . .

". . . at a charity event in 1979. Is that right?"

"Yes, I—"

I stopped.

Shit.

Too late. I'd let my mind wander, and blown it—Blacklight had played only one charity event that I could recall in 1979. I wasn't likely to forget it. It was the show where I'd met Bree, and the events that had followed that show, that meeting, had changed the course of my entire life. I hadn't heard the first part of the question, but my stomach was telling me what it must have been. And I'd answered it. Bree was going to flip her shit.

"Out." I was on my feet. Carla was right there, one hand on the office recorder. "Get the hell out of here. Pack your tent and bugger off back to whatever sewer you crawled out of. And if you use one word that deals with my personal life, I'll bloody kill you."

"Thanks for your time." He was grinning, gathering his fancy tape recorder and putting it away. "Have a nice day."

I wasn't looking forward to confessing to Bree that I'd cocked up the meeting with Dillon. She surprised me, though. She took it well enough, very calm.

"Oh, well—no use crying over spilled milk. Don't worry about it, babe—the fucker's a pro. Getting information from people that they don't want to give, that's his speciality. And it doesn't sound as if you really told him anything about me at all. I'm just glad you're done with him."

She kissed me, a quick peck, and picked up my overnight

bag. There was a pile of suitcases and three guitar cases as well, at the other end of the hall; they'd delivered my luggage from the European tour. Bree would be doing laundry for days, unless I put my foot down and had it sent out.

"I don't suppose you brought me back a hot pastrami sandwich from Nate'n Al's? No? Ah, well. John, how about having some friends over, maybe tomorrow? I was thinking some food, make a little music—you know. I was on the phone with Katia earlier, and she says the Bombardiers are gearing up for rehearsing stuff for a new CD. They've got a new frontman. But it's your call. If you're too tired, or just not up for company, we can put it off."

"What's today? Wednesday?" I didn't have a clue why she'd suddenly gone all relaxed—I'd expected a meltdown and then a shutdown, knowing Bree—but I was too relieved to care. "Right. Love to see Tony and everyone, but let's do it at the weekend. And oi! Lady! You call that a kiss? Put that damned bag down and come back here and do it properly."

"Oh, yeah, like I'm going to say no to that demand." She grinned back at me, and dropped the bag. She has amazing eyes, big green headlamps. They get very green when she's turned on.

She kissed me, long and deep. I got one arm around her waist. This was the kiss she hadn't offered up yet, not since I'd been home from the road; Carla's phone call had crimped a few things. Perry Dillon had a lot to answer for.

"Well." She pulled back, but only a bit. I still had hold of her, and I wasn't planning on letting go. I could see the gold flecks in her eyes now. She looked like one of the cats. "So. What do you want to do? Should we lock the cats in the basement for an hour, or would you rather have some food first? Dinner's ready whenever you are."

"Yeah, I guessed that." The house smelled brilliant; the

moment I'd walked through the front door, it was obvious that Bree had worked off some tension and worry doing what she does best, which is cooking.

It's a pity I've never been much into food, because Bree's a trained chef, and damned good at it, too. Most of my tours, she stays home, freelancing with some of the best caterers in the area; she says it's the best of all possible worlds for her, because she can pick and choose and not be booked up more than a few days at a time. Since my diagnosis of MS, eight years ago, she's pretty much had to balance every job she takes with how I'm feeling, and when she thinks I might need her to be there. But she picks up new tricks from the rest of the local chefs, and new recipes that way. Right now, most of our neighbours were probably sniffing and drooling; the weather was gorgeous, and she had windows open. Right now, though, as good as the place smelled, I had other priorities.

Maybe it was relief that she wasn't upset over the Dillon thing anymore, or maybe it was that kiss. Whatever it was, it suddenly hit me that what I wanted was Bree. I'd been on the road for close to five weeks now. But I was home, finally, and that was my own bed upstairs and not a hotel bed in Paris or Frankfurt or Rotterdam, with Mac and some little starfucker half his age wrapping her legs around him and moaning in the suite next door. That was my old lady standing there, letting me rub her bottom with one hand, with her eyes going greener and clearer by the moment, and that meant I wasn't the only ready one around here.

She was watching me, and I came to a decision.

"Right," I told her, and pulled her up to me, hard and close. "I'm ready, all right, but not for food. Let dinner wait. Cats in the basement, and sod everything else. Food later. Can you put things on simmer, or something?"

"I'm *already* on simmer, damn it!"

27

Maybe I'm wrong about there being no escape from rock and roll. For the next hour, while the cats prowled around the basement and dinner stayed warm on Bree's big six-burner stove, we escaped everything and everybody. Bree has a sort of magic trick when sex is involved, a way of kicking the universe out of doors. Somehow, there's nothing and no one out there but the two of us. Everyone else just disappears, ceases to exist. I haven't got a clue how she does it.

"Hello, darling." I was sweaty and shaking a bit, getting some breath back, listening to my heartbeat doing a wicked little samba. It was bouncing around, trying to regulate itself back to an even rhythm, and not doing a very good job of it. I made a mental note, same as I'd been doing the entire tour: get in to my cardiologist bloke and have him sort it out.

I tried to steady my breathing, to not let her hear that I was having difficulty. I got lucky; her eyes were clouded and elsewhere. She can go on for hours, and it takes her a minute to get her non-bed legs back under her, so to speak. "Nice to be home, lady. Very nice indeed. Anyone would think you'd missed me, or something."

"Who, me?" She sounded stoned.

We lay there for a while. This always happens when Bree and I come together—I find myself thinking, remembering a girl with long legs and green eyes, and the first time I saw her.

It was June 1979, and Blacklight was winding down the North American tour for their fifth album. We were playing stadiums, mostly, and larger arenas generally; the album, *Pick Up the Slack*, had gone platinum before it ever shipped, and the tour had turned into a monster. We'd sold the first American leg out completely, going mostly east to west, starting with two nights at Madison Square Garden, and finishing up in Seattle.

Our road manager in those days was a bloke called Rick

Hilliard. He died in 1986, of a heart attack. I remember not being surprised when that news hit—between the A-type personality and the cocaine and the nonstop hard drinking, I was just amazed he'd lasted that long. Rick got on very well with Cilla—they were relentless, both of them, doing the heavy push thing. Ambitious, you know? Focused, with the difference that Rick wanted Blacklight to be the number one band in the world; he wanted to pass the Stones and Queen and Peter Frampton. Cilla didn't give a shit about what happened to Blacklight; she wanted to be married to the number one rocker in the world. So Rick was relentless for the band, and Cilla was relentless for me.

We'd just played a killer gig at the Hollywood Bowl, and were relaxing into two days off, when Rick got a phone call from the promoter. Hurricane Felina, category four and very early in the season for this sort of thing, had just ripped through the Caribbean. It looked bad, a lot of people estimated killed in an unexpected storm surge that hit a bunch of heavily populated coastlines. The promoter had put together an emergency gig, a benefit concert up in San Francisco the following night, a kind of all-star jam session fund-raiser. Blacklight would headline the event, along with some of the local heavyweights. Did we want to do it?

Of course, that was a no-brainer. We'd have done it no matter what; disaster relief is a good reason to lend whatever talents you've got, and we all felt strongly about that. Mac was already involved heavily in things like the Rock Against Racism movement in the U.K., appearing on BBC and Capital Radio, and working with Amnesty International, long before it was fashionable. And even if we'd been inclined to moan about working on an off day, Rick wasn't about to let Blacklight get known as the band who refused to play a fund-raiser.

So, we agreed to fly up to San Francisco in the morning—it

was only an hour flight—and do the show, as a kind of "An Evening with Blacklight and Friends" thing. Besides, we were booked to play the Cow Palace anyway, next stop on the West Coast tour. This just meant getting up there a day early.

I remember Cilla, sitting in front of the hotel mirror that last night in L.A., redoing her makeup. She always did that before bed, the only woman I've ever known who did. It fascinated me about her, that even after five years of marriage, she refused to let me see her without makeup. She left off the lipstick and lash goop, because she said it smeared anyway. But she always wore the rest of the stuff, especially to bed. She always did her hair short, as well; a spiky blond cut that she could run her hands through and get looking the way she wanted. That was unusual, back then—longer hair was very in. It made her easy to spot, even in the dark backstage area. It was a signature, the short spiky hair, like the perfect makeup I never saw her without, and the little black lace gloves she always wore.

"I'm glad we're doing the benefit gig." I loved that *we*: she saw us as a single thing, one person—what was good for me was good for her and the other way round. She'd always been that way, from the night she got my manager to introduce us. She had a lot of energy, and she was always willing to use it for me. For a couple of years after we got married, I don't think there'd been a single photo taken of me that didn't include her. She was very pleased about being Mrs. JP Kinkaid, and she let the world know about it, every chance she got. "It's fabulous publicity for you."

"Whatever." I was stretched out on the bed with my legs crossed at the ankles, watching her. I had a bottle of Jim Beam handy, next to the bed—in those days, I always did and, besides, Cilla was never without a bottle of her own close by. She'd introduced me to a few things, bourbon among them. "I don't give a toss about the publicity, Cilla. It's not like Blacklight is some sort of club circuit band, you know? But if it makes you happy . . ."

"What makes me happy is seeing you where you ought to be—at the top of the heap. You're the best in the fucking world, and I want the world to admit it." She kept her eyes on the mirror, dusting her jawline with powder. "Pour me some of that, JP, will you? And do we have any blow?"

"Yeah, leather case, in the bathroom. I'll get it." I headed into the loo, and came back with a vial, a razor blade, and a hand mirror. "Cut me a line, will you? Not too much—I want some sleep tonight."

The coke—right. I'm not one of those "just say no" people, not for the reasons everyone jumped on that parade float, anyway. I mean, yeah, the stuff's rotten for you, it'll kill you, but so will fast food and beer, and I still see ads for both of them on the telly.

And I don't get the former users, either, the ones who pretend they didn't dig it at the time, going all *mea culpa* on camera. That's bullshit, and it really narks me, that they won't admit it. I always want to shout at the telly, *Oh, please, mate, give me a break, of course you fucking dug it, that's why you paid out all that dosh for the blow.* So did I. For one thing, it added something to the sex, although, knowing what I know now, that was probably more true for Cilla than for me.

So coke was my thing for a good long time there, coke and hard liquor. The coke was a lot easier for me to let go of, when I understood I had to let go of it, and let go of the heroin; I don't think, now, that I liked either of those nearly so much as I thought I did.

Alcohol, though, that was different. That was a lot harder to kick. I didn't know, the night before the Hurricane Felina show, that by the end of that year I was going to have two brand-new habits. One of them would have killed me, sticking with it. The other, well, that could have killed me, losing it.

We sat on the bed, passing the mirror back and forth. Cilla

had her custom "straw," a slim silver tube she preferred using; it was monogrammed, and I never asked her how she got it through airports. I just sweated with fear she'd get nicked for it every time, and she never did.

It's strange, you know? I remember that night so well, back and forth with the mirror, Cilla getting turned on, licking and nibbling the fine white powder from my upper lip, her own lips moving down my chest, me kissing her, her tongue acrid and somehow spicy with the sour taste of the bourbon and the coke, her breath getting short and mine getting shorter, hands all over each other, both of us remembering to be careful about not wasting any of the blow, putting the mirror back in the bathroom, and I remember the crash, her cursing. . . .

"What's up?"

"I broke the fucking mirror." She was in the loo, swearing. "Shit!"

"Seven years bad luck." I don't know why I remember saying it so clearly, but I do; I remember my own voice, impatient and annoyed. "It's just a bloody mirror. I'll buy you another one. Now get your knickers off, and get in here."

The sex was short, sharp, powerful, at least for me. I remember the feel of my own blood, moving around at both ends, fired and fuelled by the coke. I don't remember if I slept.

This was my first tour with Blacklight, and I'd never seen the Cow Palace before. The band had played here twice, so it was nothing new to them, but European venues aren't generally designed for rodeo shows, and the place had me blinking. But the promoter was world-class, best there was, and he had it together for us, stage, full PA, the lot, everything top of the line.

Benefit gigs were also new to me, so I hadn't thought about how many non-music-related personnel would be hanging about, especially at a Bay Area show. The main crew seemed to be the people from the Mission Bells Clinic. Everyone knew about the Clinic—they'd been around for years, and the street people in San Francisco would have had nothing at all in the way of care if the place hadn't existed. Tonight they were out in force, with about twenty volunteers, circulating through the place, changing where they were stationed.

The show was a beauty, just right, and we were glad we'd agreed to let it be recorded and released as part of the fund-raising effort. I hadn't known just how laid-back San Francisco crowds could get, but after the first few minutes, the smell of pot smoke hit me between the eyes and I'd got it, sussed out the calm vibe and basically embraced it. It was really different from any place I'd hung out before, a whole new thing, and I already had the feeling I wanted to come back, hang out for a bit, see what the place was about.

Not Cilla. She headed into the bathroom with Rick Hilliard and came out wiping her nostrils with the back of her hand, looking energised. Being mellow was not on her list of desirable achievements. She'd hated San Francisco from the beginning.

During the last song before the break, I caught an incident out of the corner of my eye. A girl near the front of the house, sitting on her boyfriend's shoulders and puffing continuously on a hash pipe, had apparently had a bit too much to be steady in the saddle. She wavered, slid, and I just caught sight of her crashing to the ground. The crowd around her parted as she hit the hard floor; her boyfriend didn't even seem to notice. He was probably even more stoned than she was.

I glanced toward the wings, trying to catch someone's eye, and the first person I saw was one of the Clinic's volunteers. Luckily, she was watching me—not Mac, even though everyone else in the building was watching Mac. She had her eyes fixed on me. Behind her left shoulder, not more than five feet back, I spotted Cilla's spiky blond do.

I edged closer to the wings. I don't know, now, what I was

planning to do—I think I'd been hoping to catch my wife's eye and get her to do something. But there was this girl, and she had on a staff T-shirt for the Clinic. This was her job.

About her age—I've never been good at guessing women's ages, so I figured her, first look, for twenty, maybe a bit older. This bird was right at home in the wings at a rock show, physically, I mean: skintight black trousers on some long dancer's legs, high cheekbones, and dark red wavy hair, damned near down to her waist.

More than that, she had this vibe, this self-assurance. I don't know how to describe it—the way she stood, what happened a bit later on in the evening, all that? It just spoke to me of someone with nice, easy confidence. Whatever it was, I decided she was older than I'd first thought. No one's that assured during the teen years. When you're a kid, the last thing you've got a stash of is self-confidence.

This is all taking me a lot longer to describe than it did to do. It was all just about four bars of music's worth of time. The girl on the floor was gathering a crowd, none of them Clinic volunteers, from what I could see.

I met the eye of the girl in the wings.

Years later, when she asked me what I'd thought then, I was able to answer her, right off, because the memory stayed fresh and it never faded, and never needed calling up from wherever it is that we keep our memories: *Well, now. Here comes something completely different.*

I was in the shadows now, about a foot away. There was something going on in me, above decks and below, but I didn't have the time or the room to deal with it just then. I jerked my head and the girl was there, leaning forward, not enough to be seen by the audience, enough so that we could connect. The stage lights brushed her face and I got a look at those eyes close up for the first time: deep muddy green, fierce, stuff all the way down in the depths, a kind of confidence, something that my head wanted to label as passion.

"There's a girl taken a bad fall, stage left, front of the house." I spoke into her ear, even as my fingers kept working. "Can you take care of it?"

The girl nodded, her hair swinging. Out of nowhere, there was Cilla, right behind the girl's shoulder. She didn't like me talking to strange women. "What's up, JP?"

The bass suddenly swelled, which meant Luke and I were about to hit the back-and-forth duelling guitars point of the set-closer. I shook my head at Cilla and edged back out into the spotlight. When I glanced down into the audience, I saw the girl who'd fallen, being supported to her feet and competently led off toward the backstage door, by a pair of long legs and a mass of dark auburn hair.

Blacklight's set ended, and we headed backstage. Most of the friends and family were already in the dressing room, hitting the nosh and the goodies. On my way in, I saw a cot had been set up. The girl who had fallen was lying on it, holding a compress to her head, looking dazed and confused. Miss Something Different was right there, murmuring sensible, soothing things. She had a beautiful voice, dark and deep. There was music in there, and I wondered if she was a singer.

". . . you'll be fine. No, it's cool, he knows where you are; you can go back out once one of the staff doctors makes sure you don't have a concussion or anything. The doctor should be here in about a minute. Just hang out for a couple of minutes, okay? Here, sit up—you should have some more water."

I saw one of the Clinic medics heading over, and I tapped Miss Something Different on the shoulder. She didn't look up. All her attention was on helping the girl to sit up.

"Just a minute, please." She gave the girl her water, and stood and turned. "Sorry, I . . ."

Her voice broke off. We stood and looked at each other.

A few years later, when we had that conversation that I mentioned, the whole "what was your first impression of me" conversation, I asked her the same question. Tit for tat, yeah? Her answer made me really happy, because it was just what I thought I saw there.

I told her I'd thought, *here comes something completely different*. And she told me, "I felt something move in my stomach and I think it might have been my soul."

I lost my voice for a moment. Whatever it was that sparked between us, it was heavy and deep and I knew, even through the coke and the music and everything else, that this was something that was going to matter, and cause me trouble, and make me happy. It was just all there, somehow.

Of course, I wasn't exactly falling over myself wanting to believe it; you don't, you know? Kismet or karma or whatever the hell that stuff is? No one wants to believe their world's about to get shaken up. But I knew it. So did she. I saw it right then, and I never forgot it.

"I'm John." See, that was a sure sign, me introducing myself that way. To everyone else—to my own wife—I was JP. But I wasn't ever going to be JP to this girl, whoever she was and wherever she'd dropped into my world from. "John Kinkaid."

"I know." She wasn't smiling; she was staring at my face, so intently that I got nervous. "Believe me, I know. I'm Bree Godwin. I'm glad you saw that girl fall down. She'll be okay—they're going to check her for concussion."

"Do you—are you with the Clinic full-time?" What a fucking bloody stupid conversation. I sounded like a schoolboy. And what was I doing, with my wife backstage? I'd never cheated on Cilla, never even thought about it. What in hell was I thinking? "I mean, if I wanted to get in touch with you again, could I do it by ringing up the Clinic?"

"I'm not with them full-time—I just volunteer there, evenings and during shows." She smiled, a quick smile that faded fast. "But calling the Clinic would definitely find me. My mother's a surgeon—she's on the board."

And then she sealed it, what was already vibrating like a live wire between us. She did something extraordinary. She leaned forward suddenly, reaching out with both hands, and I realised that, even in sensible flat shoes that let her rescue stoners from bad falls, she was taller than I was.

"I can't resist this," she said suddenly. "I'm sorry."

She took my face between her hands and kissed me, full on the mouth, lips slightly parted, tongue tip to tongue tip, warm and strong. She tasted of strawberries.

Something different something different something bloody different.

"You should go backstage." She'd stopped smiling again; her hands had dropped to her sides. "They'll be waiting for you."

"Why are you staring at me like that?" I couldn't take my eyes off her, and I could still taste her. I was dizzy. What had just happened to me, for God's sake? "Is there something wrong with my face?"

"Yes." Her eyes suddenly dropped. "You have white powder on your upper lip."

Then she was gone, and I was left standing there, being gently edged aside by the Clinic doctor, staring after her.

CHAPTER TWO

Most of our friends are musicians. That's the way it works, I've found, especially in a small city like San Francisco—you end up playing with the local musicians, and the local musicians become good friends.

It's not surprising, really. They just *get* it, you know? They get what it's like, what it's all about. You don't have to explain anything to them, and they don't ask stupid questions or go fannish all over you. They've been there, they've done it, they get it. They're players, pros.

Here in the Bay Area, the music scene has always been one of those things, where people wander in and out of each others' recording sessions and in and out of each others' houses as well. They hang out at gigs for late-night jams, they hook each other up with other players, and projects, and information. They warn each other when shit that affects all of them is about to hit the fan. It's a very specific sort of family, but family is what it is.

And Bree, who stays as far away from the Blacklight end of my world as she decently can, loves having our local friends over. I asked her about that once, why she was so easy about entertaining people in the industry. She'd never once gone on tour with Blacklight for fun; she'd done one tour in twenty-five years, and that was because I was sick as a dog, and needed her there. I damned near had to beg her. But when I asked her why having rockers in her living room was okay while going into dressing rooms wasn't, she said something about home court. Not a clue what she meant, but I don't argue about it.

We had some friends over that Saturday, two mates of mine, with their wives. Bree had cooked masses of food, and there was the usual spread out on the big mahogany sideboard in our dining room. No one ever turns down an invite to our place, not with Bree's cooking as part of the deal.

The friends were both longtime members of an established Bay Area band. I'd actually first got to know and play with Kris Corcoran and Tony Mancuso during that Hurricane Felina benefit, back in 1979; I'd contributed some studio guitar work on two CDs for their band, the Bombardiers. They'd started out playing in the same band, but both of them got restless during the seventies; I used to think it was the psychedelics that kept them band-hopping, because they're killer musicians. Tony, in particular, is a shit-hot keyboard player. But they stopped the acid a good long time back, and they're still flighty, so maybe it's just what they are. And these days, they're both back with the Bombardiers anyway, so it's all good.

We hung out for a while, eating, catching up on each other's projects. You'd have thought that just coming off a European tour with Blacklight, I'd have had the most news, but not this time. We talked mostly about Anton Hall, the Bombardiers' lead singer, who had died while Blacklight was playing Rotterdam, from a destroyed liver, thanks to nearly forty years of drinking Southern Comfort like it was water, and a recently diagnosed case of hepatitis C. Bree went off into the kitchen with the other women; I heard bits of their conversation over our industry talk in the next room. Tony had a new song he was trying to work out, and we decided to head into my basement studio, to get some serious playing done.

I stuck my head in through the kitchen door, to tell Bree. She and the other women were clustered round our big table, and I could see right off that I'd interrupted something.

"We're off downstairs, love." There was that shuttered look on Bree's face again. I wondered just what in hell they'd been talking about. "Hello, Sandra. Katia, your old man's kidnapping me to get a bit of work in on his new thing. I'll bring him back in one piece, I promise."

"Cool." Katia was looking at Bree, not at me. Something was definitely happening. All three of them had that look women get when they're talking about something that matters to them: secretive, alert, conspiratorial. Sandra looked smooth, a bit edgy. Bree was carefully blank. "Just don't break him," Katia told me.

"Right." I hesitated a moment. "Everything all right, then, love?"

"Fine. Everything's fine. You go play." It was unnerving, that look on Bree's face, unsettling. I really hate it, and rightly so, because even though it hadn't happened often, it's never meant anything good for me. Last time I'd seen her look quite like that, she'd been responding to an announcement that had ended up leading to seven of the messiest, most miserable months of my life.

And now, here was that look again: bleak, remote, shut down. What in hell had they been talking about in here?

Downstairs in the studio, some light got shed on that little question. We set down some tracks for Tony's idea, a hot boogie number with the kind of old Delta-style blues he fancies playing: hot and tricky, a lot of driving changes in the piano, very Meade "Lux" Lewis, maybe a bit of Sunnyland Slim. Kris did a nice bass line, and I kicked in with some Delta-style finger picking, a kind of Big Bill Broonzy feel to it, and then laid down some slide work. It's always a trip, playing with people I don't tour and record with. It keeps me fresh, feeds the old session player I started out as and, really, I still am.

We'd just finished up the third set of variations when Kris, completely casual, dropped the bomb. "What's this about some sleaze doing a history of Blacklight?"

I'd been playing one of my acoustic guitars, a gorgeous vintage National, for the bottleneck stuff. I'd just been about to set it on its stand, and I damned near dropped it. I turned and stared at him.

"Where did you hear about that?" If the word was already out about Perry Dillon, we might be in deep shit; rehearsals for the American tour were due to start in New York in about three weeks. With the tour itself kicking off at Madison Square Garden a week after that, this sort of distraction was just about the last thing we needed. It would add a whole new set of problems and tensions, and that wasn't even touching the personal issues for me. If Katia and Sandra had walked in already knowing, Bree might already have something disastrous in her head.

"From your Web site. Where else?"

"What!" All of a sudden, my heart was jumping. "What in hell—do you mean Blacklight's Web site?"

"Yeah, Blacklight's." Kris and Tony looked at each other, then back at me. "JP, didn't you know about it? It's not an official announcement—it's in Nial Laybourne's daily blog. Some shit about Perry Dillon, titles, some of the stuff the guy's already done. I don't want to get into your business, man, but I don't know what you guys were doing, giving your set designer the okay to put that crap out on the Internet."

"I don't know either, mate. I'm as gobsmacked as you are."

Twice, I thought. That was twice Ian had done something that concerned the entire band, and not bothered clueing me in. "But I'm damned well going to find out."

"Good idea." Tony ran his hands along the keyboard, a dancy little ripple. I play some piano, very basic stuff, and I keep a very nice old Bechstein upright in the studio. Tony loves it. He's tried to buy it off me too many times to count; the standing joke is that the only reason he hasn't stolen it outright is because it's too big to nick without me noticing. "So, have you met this Dillon dude yet, JP?"

"Yeah." I suddenly wanted everyone to go home, and let me go upstairs, check Bree's computer, see if Nial had actually done what Kris said he'd done. If he had, Carla was going to find a message in her voice mail first thing in the morning.

After that, what I wanted was to have the confrontation with my old lady that I knew was coming. There's a lot of history, a lot of stuff to do with the two women I've loved in my life, that no one knew about but us. I had a strong feeling that we needed to keep it that way. "I went down to L.A. right after I got back from London. I did a one-hour sitdown interview with him."

"Wow." Kris was coiling cables and putting his bass away. "That was fast. Sounds like your management is on top of that, even if they don't have enough sense not to wash the dirty laundry on the World Wide Web. What's Dillon like?"

"He's a fucking reptile. Sleazy prying little shit. I'd like to break his neck, personally." I heard my own voice and nearly jumped, myself—I didn't know I could sound that mean. Kris and Tony were both staring at me. "Sorry. He—it wasn't a pleasant way to spend an hour. And if someone's paid him a lot of money, it's going to get even less pleasant as we go along. I was first up—luck of the draw, me living in the States. I don't even want to think about what's going to happen when he sits down with Mac. If you have any secrets, Mac's just the bloke to spill them. He hasn't got two inhibitions to rub together to make fire with. It's not deliberate; he's got one of the kindest hearts on the planet, but he just doesn't think."

They exchanged a look. "Well," Kris said, "You'll be in New York in a couple of weeks. Just have Dillon barred from the hotels and from the shows. Fuck him, anyway."

"That's right." Tony was nodding. "No law says you guys have to make it easy for him. You don't owe him shit."

I took a look around, making sure mics and amps and mixers were all powered down. "True," I said, and killed the lights. "I just wish I thought there was any chance of getting Bree to come with me on this one."

Later, when everyone had gone and I'd helped Bree do the washing up, she suggested one of our rare evening walks.

I may not be the most observant man alive, but I'm not entirely dim, either. I can do basic sums. If I took that whispering back in the kitchen earlier, and added in the look on her face, and now the desire for a conversation on neutral territory, it all added up to a Big Announcement.

"Right. Stay in the neighbourhood, or were you thinking down at the beach?" Our part of town, Pacific Heights, is called that for a reason. "I honestly don't think my legs are up to the local thirty-degree angles tonight, love. Let's do the beach, all right?"

Immediately, she went into protective mode. "Oh, John, I'm sorry! Why didn't you tell me you were relapsing? I could have kicked everyone out earlier—"

"Bree, belt up, will you? I'm fine." I stood up, doing what I could to hide the shakes in both legs. "It's mostly just the jet lag catching up. A walk will do me good—just, not up one of the local alps, all right? Let's head for flat ground."

She drove us out to Ocean Beach. It was a good night for it, no fog in sight—the Marin headlands looked so close, you felt you could count the trees on Mount Tamalpais, across the water. The tide was mostly out, just beginning the evening push back landward, and we had a lot of beach to walk on. It was early enough for the usual hordes of beer-soaked teenagers to be elsewhere. By full dark, they'd be out in force, lighting driftwood fires and generally being pains in the arse, but for now, it was the two of us, and soft wavelets moving up onto the edge of the shore, and the stars sparking to life overhead.

We didn't talk for a while, just walked. It's that kind of silence you get only after years of knowing each other; young couples think they always have to be talking, saying something, as if their togetherness was all about words, and had to be announced to the world, to each other.

After a few minutes of walking, I reached for her hand and pulled her to a stop.

"Right." In this light, you couldn't see where her hair was coming in grey; she could have been twenty or seventy, no way to tell. "Bree, look. I know something's up. Why don't you just tell me, yeah? Save the grief? Come on, love. Dish."

"Damn, you're good." She grinned at me suddenly, and a lot of the apprehension I'd been feeling vaporised, gone, off and away. "You know me too damned well, you know that?"

"What, you wanted to be Woman of Mystery? Sorry about that—if you did, you shouldn't have slept with me all these years." I grinned back at her; I could do that now, no strain. Whatever it was, it wasn't bad news. "Seriously, Bree, I'm not completely dim. It was pretty obvious you had something on your mind. Spit it out, love. What's going on?"

"I want to do this tour with you. That's what."

I stood there and gaped at her. She looked back at me, her head tilted to one side. It was dark enough, now, that I couldn't read her eyes.

"You do? Really?" What in hell was all the big mystery, then? "That's fantastic! What, the entire tour? Rehearsals as well? I know you're not a fan of New York, but if you really mean it, I'll let Carla know first thing in the morning. Of course, after she hears my message about Nial's damned blog, she may not want to listen for a week or two."

"I don't know." There it was, that guarded look again. There was something she still wasn't telling me, and no way I was going to dig it out of her right now. But I was willing to bet that, whatever it was, she was trying to protect me from something. She can be so damned exasperating. . . . "I mean, I don't know about the entire tour yet. But yes on the New York end of it. Rehearsals, too, I guess. You don't mind?"

"You trying to be funny?" I reached out and pulled her into my arms; a gay couple, walking their dog along the beach, smiled at us and nodded, and kept going. "I've been trying to get you out on the road with me forever. The only reason I stopped trying was because you hate it so much, and now I'm supposed to mind? Why would I?"

She didn't answer that, and she didn't need to, not really. Somewhere in her head, there was always going to be those three times I had left, responded to the pleading of the woman I'd actually married all those years ago.

It's tricky, our history. See, I have this idea that if you make a promise, a vow, you do your best to honour it. You can't always do that—life's got a way of shoving you off the path—but you're supposed to try. Thing about Bree is, she feels the same way. She didn't try to stop me going, when Cilla'd said she needed me—not after that first time when I'd left Bree sitting in our bedroom, saying *"Please, John, don't go, don't do this to me, don't do this to us."*

I'd done, then, what I felt I had to do. It was the last thing in the world I wanted to do, but I'd done it: gone back to London, to Cilla, to my wife, who was sick and frightened and alone and who needed me there while the doctors tested to find out what was wrong. . . .

"Call Carla."

Bree's voice jerked me back to the present. She stayed where she was physically, within the circle of my arm, but she'd distanced herself a bit from me emotionally, and I knew my face had given away that I'd been remembering one of the bad times. "I'm coming for New York, at least. We'll see how it goes from there. But for rehearsals and opening night, definitely. I'll need flights. Call Carla in the morning."

"Good evening, New York!"

Opening night, full house, and New York fans aren't shy little wallflowers about making their feelings known. The crowd was half off its collective nut out there. The show had been due to start at eight; it was now seven minutes past, and for every second of those extra seven minutes, the foot-stamping and chanting had got louder and more emphatic.

There was something really primal about it: *"BlackLIGHT! BlackLIGHT!"* Catcalls, as well, same things we heard everywhere. Here in the States, we got fewer polite euphemisms than we did in other countries; out in the balcony, all the way at the back of the house, someone had draped a huge banner that read FUCK ME, MAC!

"Ladies and gentlemen, boys and girls . . ."

A few feet away from me, Ian was scanning the house, doing the routine head stuff that road managers do. Ian's a chunky bloke, but right now, he looked skinny and stressed. Not surprising, what with Nial's cock-up.

It turned out that since Ian had talked about the Dillon thing in the dressing room, Nial hadn't understood that we wanted it kept under our control. So he'd blogged it, and all hell had broken loose, because when you put something out on the Internet, that's what happens. Carla got back to me, about what Nial had thought he was doing, and why the band's management had left it right where it was. Carla's reasoning was infuriating, but it was also sound: Once it hit the Internet, taking it down would have got more attention than just leaving it.

And, of course, just the name Perry Dillon was enough to send the rags who make their living printing that sort of trash into a digging frenzy. Everyone was being hassled, and everyone was thoroughly pissed off and edgy about it; Stu had found a tabloid reporter muscling up to his wife, Cynthia, after our third day of rehearsal, and got into a shoving match with the bloke, and there'd been cops involved. Not the ideal way to start a tour, you know?

I glanced behind me, around me. Discreetly in the wings, Dom, dressed for action in Lycra and leather and knee-high Doc Marten head-stomper boots, stayed just about a hand's reach from Mac. I knew she'd stay where she was until he took the stage. After that, she'd be moving.

"... *this is what you've all been waiting for* ..."

The noise was deafening, and we hadn't played a note yet. I looked around for Bree. She'd slipped off about half an hour earlier, just for a breather; there were legitimate media people there, and record company executives, and about two hundred people I'd never set eyes on before. There were too many old friends as well. One of the big drawbacks of making yourself as rare as she does is that, when you actually are there, people tend to really notice. Between that and the band tensions, she was really nervous, really edgy.

But here she was, drop-dead gorgeous in a pale green designer thing, standing a few feet off to one side, catching my eye. She wasn't smiling. She never did smile when she had to be here, unless she got genuinely caught up in the music. But I knew she'd be here until we finished. As I think I mentioned, my old lady puts as high a premium on loyalty as I do. I blew her a kiss, and saw the corners of her mouth twitch upward as she bit back the smile.

"*. . . put your hands together and give it up . . .*"

"Man, I love first nights. Fucking amazing energy." Luke was at my other shoulder, watching the lights for the cue to hit the stage. In this light, you couldn't see that his ponytail, which used to be the colour of old gold, had gone grey. Out there under the spotlights, he looked as if he hadn't aged at all—that's one of the benefits of blond hair. The rest of us get to show the grey streaks. One of the coolest things about Luke is that he can relax entirely when he's playing; he never lets anything get in his way onstage. "Bree! I didn't see you there, love. Great dress."

"*. . . Madison Square Garden is proud to present . . .*"

The lighting changed, pale up front, darkness behind. We slipped out onto the stage as Mac hit the spotlight and the crowd went berserk.

"*BLACKLIGHT!*"

Right. Showtime.

I wish, now, that I could remember more about that gig. It should have been one of the greats, and despite everything, there are a lot of people who were there, who swear it was one of the best shows we'd ever done. Pity I'll never know. What happened later that night has buried it, and buried it deep.

I do remember little things, unimportant things. I remember what I was wearing, nice understated black, from my usual designer. Once upon a time, Cilla had picked out every stitch I wore onstage, judging for maximum rock star impact, but that was then and this is now, and I'm up over fifty and these days, even if Cilla had still been there and still trying to dress me, I'd leave the heavy flash to Mac anyway. I only ever really wore the shiny stuff to please my wife.

I remember a security guard, one of our own people hired especially for the American leg of the tour, put there by our security chief, Phil MacDermott. This bloke was out in the audience, just beyond the backstage door. I remember him because he had waist-length dreads, and he was moving to the music, and the dreads kept flapping against him.

I remember that Cal broke the D string on his Alembic bass in the middle of a song. That's quite a feat, breaking a string that thick; it almost never happens. I remember how fast he got the Alembic off his neck and over to Pete, his guitar tech, and how fast he had his Tobias up and back into the groove, not seeming to miss a note. I remember Stu doing an interesting little thing with his kick-drum to mask any lack of bass.

And I remember glancing into the wings somewhere in the middle of the show, feeling that *déjà vu* again, wanting it this time: there were Cyn Corrigan and Barb Wilson, dressed for opening night, dancing away. And there was Ian, but Solange wasn't there. Neither was a girl with long red hair and dancer's legs.

And neither was Bree.

I think that's when the evening started going really wrong for me—I looked into the wings, expecting that flutter of pale green, and Bree was gone. She wasn't there.

An hour, ninety minutes, up near the two-hour mark. The sound mix was about as good as I'd ever heard at the Garden. Whatever line arrays our sound bloke, Ronan Greene, had chosen were spot on, but I couldn't relax and dig it, you know? I kept glancing into the wings, checking out the house, looking for that pale green designer silk, and not finding it.

I caught sight of Dom, patrolling the edges, watching. She was getting around; I saw her all over the place, in the house, in the wings on both sides. Reassuring as that might have been for Mac, it wasn't doing a damned thing for me. I was getting well into edgy. Where in hell was Bree?

And suddenly, there she was, precisely where I'd kept looking and not seeing her, back in the wings, just offstage. She was almost completely in shadow; all I could see was her hair, and one half of her face, and the soft shine of that green dress. She was talking to someone I didn't recognise, a bloke decked out in some kind of uniform—a security guard? One of our people? I couldn't tell.

We were into the set-closer now, a hot showstopper from the current album called "Long Day in the Hot, Hot Sun." I had my Deluxe cranked up, taking the long bitchy guitar solo that I'd written for the song. Luke kicked his Strat over to the back pickup, giving a bit of angry backbite to what I was doing on the Deluxe. Halfway through, I looked up and caught sight of the rest of the band, and nearly missed the riff entirely.

Everyone was staring. For a really long second there, I thought they were staring at me. It took me just about another second to realise that something was going on behind me.

Mac was looking shaken, but he was still Mac. This was opening night, it was Madison Square Garden, and those were our fans out there. He snaked the mic stand between his thighs, held it with his knees, and hit the beginning of the final chorus:

". . . if you think you get away without payin' for your fun?
Prepare to spend a long, long day in the hot, hot sun."

I kept playing, and Luke did as well, and Mac hit the crescendo of the ending vocal. The drums and bass were kicking it over the top, and the crowd was screaming.

And finally, the set was over. Mac did what he always does, the appropriate *Thank you, New York City!* The crowd was roaring, stamping, the houselights went down instead of up, which, as anyone who's ever been to a gig knows, means there's an encore coming.

"What the hell? . . ."

Cal was next to me, with Stu behind him. We were offstage now, just in the wings, and the place was insane, full of people that shouldn't need to be here.

Uniforms. There were a dozen uniforms back here in the wings. And they weren't our security people.

Ian was gesturing, his arms flapping like some kind of frantic bird, and the wings were suddenly just too damned crowded. Everyone was clustered tight, surrounded by the uniforms who'd herded them there.

They kept us there on stage, no dressing room break before the encore. Instead, we were handed water and towels by shaken-looking roadies, and then told by the uniforms that there was a problem backstage, in one of the dressing rooms, and would we please stay up here? We didn't want to cause a panic; just do the encore and get the audience safely out of the building. . . .

"Look, wait a damned minute . . ." My heart was beginning to chatter, the murmur reacting to the stress by becoming actual arrhythmia. I didn't realise it then, but all the uniforms, the general weirdness, not knowing where Bree was, had me right up with one foot over the edge into panic and the other on a grease spot. I had no idea what was going on, and no one seemed willing to tell us any details. "I want to know—"

"Someone's dead, backstage." Ian was a very bad colour. "In one of the dressing rooms. Look, mates, get back out there, will

51

you? Do the encore, hurry it up, we need to get the crowd out of here."

"Shit!" I caught sight of a cop talking to Phil MacDermott, who looked horrified. Mac, with Domitra glued to his side, was right in on the conversation. Dom was gesturing, looking furious about something, and I suddenly wondered if maybe the crazy boyfriend who'd been sending Mac death threats had somehow got in, and got loose backstage. If that was it, someone was going to bloody well get sacked over this.

"Let's do it." Mac was stone-faced. "We need to clear the place out, and we need to do it without letting them know there's a problem. Come on. Let's go."

We played the encore. If the crowd noticed anything wrong, they didn't show it; it was all business as usual, arms around each other, bowing. Only difference was Mac not spraying the crowd with champagne—they hadn't let him down to get any and no one had thought to bring any up onstage.

"John—?"

"Bree!" The houselights were up, but we were all still onstage, in the wings, just out of view. The audience was taking its own sweet time clearing out of the Garden. "Bloody hell, where were you? I kept looking for you and I didn't see you. What's going on? Why are there police all over the place?"

"Excuse me." There was a cop at her side, and he'd somehow got between us. "Are you John Kinkaid?"

"Yes. I am." I didn't even glance his way. Bree's face—she looked desolate, lost. Her lips were shaking and her skin had no colour at all, and there was something wrong with her dress. "Bree, what is it? What's happened?"

"I found him." She was whispering, her eyes wide and staring. There was some sort of stain at the front of her dress, a dark reddish smear; for a horrifying moment I thought it was blood, and then I realised it was vomit, partly scrubbed away. "I went into the dressing room and he was just—oh God oh God oh *God*."

She began to shake, one hand going to cover her mouth. I could see her fighting back nausea. I moved toward her, but found myself blocked by the cop.

"Just a minute, Mr. Kinkaid, please—"

"What the hell is all this?" I was suddenly outraged at this bloke, this nameless official, keeping me from my old lady. "What the hell is going on?"

"Perry Dillon." It was Bree, still in that near-whisper, nearly babbling. "They told me it was Perry Dillon. He's in there—he's in the dressing room. He's dead in your dressing room. I was walking by and I looked in and I saw someone on the floor, just sprawled out on his back, and I went in to see if they'd passed out and he was there, and he was all blue, his face I mean, his throat was all wrong, crushed, oh Jesus, John, it was so horrible. . . ."

She began to sway, to sag. I moved, and this time the cop stayed out of my way, and I had hold of her and was smoothing her hair, and feeling the tears of reaction against my face.

CHAPTER THREE

We didn't get back to the hotel until nearly six in the morning, and we did it—all of us—under police warnings not to leave NYC until given clearance.

That was ridiculous, of course. There was a massive sold-out tour to do, tickets, arenas booked and paid for. You can't just dump a tour that easily. But at the moment, the tour was the least of my worries. I wasn't even thinking about it—that was management's job, and Ian Hendry was on the phone, waking up Carla in Los Angeles, within minutes of finishing up his conversation with New York's finest. Right now, I had other things on my mind.

About the cops, and being questioned, I don't know what I'd been expecting. I don't read thrillers, or watch that stuff on telly very often—I had a vague sort of idea that they'd take us all into separate rooms, not let us talk to each other, try to trip us up.

But it was fairly obvious, early on, that no one in the band was under suspicion for the actual crime. The only reason I could think of for that is that someone, the police doctor or whoever, had been able to say when Perry Dillon had got his Adam's apple smashed with something heavy and blunt, and that it had happened while we were onstage. Since Blacklight doesn't break during the show itself, we were in the clear. You can't be onstage, trading licks with your bass player in front of a capacity crowd, and bashing someone in the neck in your own dressing room at the same time, you know?

Bree, though, she was coming in for extra attention. Not only hadn't she been onstage—she'd actually found the body.

I was surprised that they'd let me stay with Bree while they were asking her questions. The cop in charge was a bloke called Lt. Patrick Ormand, and my first impression was that he seemed professional, and chilly with it. When he took the two of us aside and told Bree he'd like her to answer a few questions, I announced that I wanted to be there as well.

"Sure, that's okay with me, if Ms. Godwin would be more comfortable that way." Bree nodded, but she looked stiff, almost unwilling, and I started to get that heartbeat again. There was something in her face, in the way she was holding herself, that made me wonder if she really didn't want me along.

Ormand led us off toward an unoccupied dressing room and tossed a casual question over his shoulder. "Are you Ms. Godwin's husband, Mr. Kinkaid?"

I was looking at Ormand, not at Bree, but I could almost feel her going pale. For a moment, I felt—I don't know, guilty, culpable. I wondered how often she'd been asked that question and had the colour fade out of her face just that way over the answer, during the years we'd been together.

"I'm her life partner," I told him. My voice was a bit louder than it needed to be. "We've lived together for twenty-five years. Will that do you? I want to be there."

"Like I said, I don't see why not."

Another cop was already in the dressing room, taking notes or something. We grabbed some of the bottled water from the cooler in the corner. I had a moment of wondering whether the cops had stumbled across anything in the way of narcotics, but that was unlikely, really; no one in the band indulges anymore. The nearest thing to recreational drugs they'd be likely to find backstage at a Blacklight show is a tank or two of nitrous oxide, courtesy of the venue's own staff. Last I heard, laughing gas is legal, and if it's not, it's not my problem. I don't partake, myself.

Ormand's questions started out innocuously enough. He led her through what she'd been doing before the show, the people she'd seen and spoken to during the early part of the evening, anything in the way of any kind of incident that might prove noteworthy. He seemed to be more interested in getting a broad picture of what backstage had been like, the atmosphere and placement of people, than he was specifically in Bree. I relaxed a bit, enough to realise that not everyone has the bone-deep familiarity with it that someone like me has, and I decided to save us a bit of time.

"Hang on a minute." I lifted one hand. "You know, I'm not sure you really get the level of madness involved here. Hard to scope, if you aren't familiar with it. You do understand that there were probably two hundred people backstage before we went on, right?"

"Are you kidding?" Ormand stared at me. "Two *hundred*?"

"Easily." I glanced at Bree. She was still rigid, her hands locked together in her lap, her eyes cast down. That was unsettling—Bree talks with her hands, and if she had them forcibly shut down, then she was afraid of saying something she wanted to keep quiet. "Probably more, actually—our road manager, Ian Hendry, would know for sure. This was the opening night of our tour: full press coverage, suits from our American record label, catering staff, family, friends, and then all the plus-ones. So, yeah—easily two hundred people. Might be closer to three hundred. Ask Ian."

"Plus-ones?" Ormand looked from me to Bree, and back again. I wondered if I'd imagined a tiny noise from Bree. What in hell? "What are those, Mr. Kinkaid?"

"Guests of guests." I hadn't imagined it; beside me, Bree was actually holding her breath. "You put someone on the guest list, it allows them in free, and allows them in backstage."

"So, anyone on the guest list for backstage at one of your shows gets—what? Free run of the place?"

"No." I flexed my wrists; they were aching. "There's more than one kind of access at a show. There's an all-access list, that allows the guest access to everywhere the band goes, even the stage—those are laminated and hung on cords. Not too many of them given out. They're mostly family and road crew—here, Bree's wearing hers, have a look."

"I see." He peered at Bree's badge. She wasn't pale right now; she was chalky. "Go on, Mr. Kinkaid, please."

"Then there's the comp list, which lets guests into the show for free, but doesn't get them backstage access—those are the people in the first three rows, mostly press and media, and some record company people. The list at the back door, though, that's the most extensive—that's the real guest list. It goes down to the back door with whoever's guarding the door that night, right about when the band takes a dinner break. That happens after the sound check, a few hours before the gig. And it gets added to, sometimes even when the band's already gone on-stage. Latecomers, you know?"

"Got it." Ormand looked interested. "About plus-ones? . . ."

"Right. Normally, unless there's a specific reason not to do it that way, management adds a plus-one to the guest's name, so that he or she can bring their significant other, or their kid, or maybe just a friend. Someone to keep them company. So, if you were on the backstage guest list, it would be your name, Patrick Ormand, plus one."

"Okay. Let me see if I understand this. What you're saying is, all the people backstage, theoretically at least, were either on the guest list, or came as plus-ones of someone who was? Guests of guests?"

"Right." I heard my own voice thin out. "But theoretically, that's the word, all right. Because there's no way Perry Dillon should have been able to get backstage. He'd been officially barred from any access to the band, hotels, shows, rehearsals, the lot. He was writing an unauthorised history of Blacklight. Even though we'd agreed to talk to him—I spent an hour with him, a few weeks ago, at our office in Los Angeles, but I don't know if anyone else in the band's spoken with him yet—we'd let his agent know that he would be forbidden access at least until the tour was done next month. And I want to know how he got in, because when I find out, there's going to be hell to pay."

"I think I can answer that for you." Ormand shuffled through the pile of papers on the table next to him. He pulled out a clipboard, and I recognised the official sheets of the back door list. There's one at every show, two versions—management's original typed list, and the stage door list, the one with the last-minute add-ons, written in late. The one Ormand was passing over to me was the door list—I could see a dozen or so names, different handwriting, some scrawled, some carefully printed out.

"Would you take a look at these, Mr. Kinkaid? You, too, Ms. Godwin." Ormand was watching us. "It's all right—these are photocopies. The originals have been taken to forensics."

I reached out and took the sheets. Bree's hands stayed locked up. She lifted her head and looked, and the fact that she didn't want to was so damned obvious, she might as well have had it tattooed on her forehead.

"Look at the very last page, please." Ormand's voice was completely neutral. "The very last entry."

I looked down, scrolling the list of typewritten names. Some I knew, some I didn't. The last dozen or so entries were the inevitable last-minute invitees, written in by hand.

All the way at the bottom, in careful block letters, were the words PERRY DILLON. There was a plus-one attached. Both Dillon's name and the plus-one had small pencilled checkmarks next to them.

Perry Dillon had been given a pass. So had his guest, whoever it was.

Silence, and it went on too long. I know I was gawking at the sheet; Bree, next to me, was completely still, not moving, barely breathing.

I handed the pages back to Ormand. He took them and put them back where he'd found them.

"I don't suppose you recognise that handwriting? Either of you?" His voice wasn't neutral anymore—it had an edge to it now, and his eyes had stopped being neutral and were cold and considering. *Hunter,* I thought, *something pacing you behind the hedges, sniffing around, looking for something injured or sick or old, wanting blood to lick.*

"No, I don't." I was glad it was the truth. Lying to that chilly voice, to those flat eyes, would have been tricky, and I don't like lying anyway. "That's not handwriting—it's block lettering. Either way, I've never seen it before."

He was waiting. I turned my head, trying to catch Bree's eye, willing her to say something that would put the neutrality back in Ormand's eyes and get us the hell out of there. "Bree? What about you, love?"

"No." Her voice was rusty, and she cleared her throat. "Sorry. I just can't get the picture of him lying on the floor out of my head. No. Sorry. I don't recognise it either."

She was terrified half out of her mind. Ormand had no way of knowing that—he didn't know Bree. But I did, and I could see it, sense it, smell it on her skin. She was scared to death. Every word was an effort.

"That's a shame. It would have saved us some digging." He turned away from me and focused on Bree. There was something in the way he was looking at her that made me want to physically step between them, make him focus on me instead. "Speaking of digging, we've been busy tonight. I spent some time on the phone with my colleagues in Northern California. Just checking on people, getting some background. Basic background stuff." The smile widened. "Just like they do on all the TV cop shows."

It was my turn to stiffen up. Bree was milk white.

"The guys in NorCal dug up some interesting stuff, off my initial request—a nice bonus to the information about members of your band. Seems you have a record, Ms. Godwin—a juvenile record, but it's a nasty one, isn't it? Busted at seventeen for being in the company of an adult, on enclosed premises, with hard narcotics and drug paraphernalia?"

Here it was, a crucial bit of the past we'd kept quiet so long. I stayed silent, aiming thoughts at Bree: *Don't say anything, not a damned word, he's after blood. . . .*

"It could have been worse, I guess." Ormand glanced from me to Bree. "That record, I mean. The guy I talked to told me he worked SFPD narcotics, back in the seventies. Makes me wonder who the guy was, the one you supplied stuff to. Without your mother's intervention, her taking the blame, that clinic she worked for could have lost its license, and you could have done some serious time. . . ."

I stood up. For a moment, I was back in Carla's office and this wasn't a cop; it was Perry Dillon getting too close, smelling the same blood Ormand was smelling. Déjà vu.

I locked stares with Ormand. I was furious, shaken, and I

wasn't asking myself just who I was furious with, not right then. The bastard had known, when he asked me about my relationship with Bree, that we weren't married; he'd already checked us out.

And I'd fallen for it. He'd known about her bust. I'd bet money he knew about me being deported as well. *A nice bonus to the information about members of your band.*

"So, what, we're talking about cop shows? Right. This is where I tell you that our lawyer will be in touch with you in the morning. Bree's not talking to you lot without a lawyer. She's not answering one damned question, and neither am I. Unless you have a warrant, I don't think you can detain either of us. Do you have a warrant, Lieutenant Ormand?"

He shook his head, smiling, easy, not even bothering to answer the question. "You two go back to your hotel. It's been a long night. Get some sleep, if you can. We'll be in touch with you later. Thanks for the information about the guest list—very helpful. Oh, and Ms. Godwin, some friendly advice: I'd make sure you told your lawyer everything, if I were you."

The view from our hotel on West Fifty-ninth Street was amazing: Central Park, with the first sun of the day touching the grass and the trees, slanting off windows on Fifth Avenue to the east and Broadway to the west. Stunning view. I hadn't so much as glanced out.

The hotel was already under siege. There were reporters out on the street, reporters in the lobby, photographers swarming like a plague of locusts. Luckily, Phil MacDermott is a pro. He had his shit together enough to coordinate our security crew with the hotel. We were able to get into the place, into the lift, up to our suite, without any of the press getting closer than twenty feet. Good job, too, because the mood I was in, I'd have gladly got into a punch-up with any of them.

We did the ride up in silence. Bree hadn't said a word since we'd left Ormand's office—she seemed to have just closed down completely. I'd got her by the arm, maybe a bit harder than necessary, but I was shaken up and scared and she seemed so damned remote and far away from me, somehow. I needed something, some way, to bring us back into the sort of connection, the contact, I'd come to depend on.

"Talk to me, Bree." I sat her down on the end of the bed and just stood there, waiting. "What the fuck is going on?"

"What do you want me to say, John? That I didn't kill Perry Dillon in your dressing room?" She sat on the end of the bed, rubbing her arm. She seemed to find the carpet at her feet fascinating; she wasn't meeting my eyes. "Okay. I didn't."

"Bloody hell!" I was planted in front of her. Just by sitting, she'd given me the advantage, since this way I was taller than she was, and besides, this way the only way she could get round me was by putting herself off balance. The simple fact, that I felt I needed some sort of physical advantage over my old lady, was enough to clue me in to just how angry I was, and how spooked.

"You know damned well what I want you to say, and it's got nothing to do with Perry Dillon, alive or dead." There was something here, something I didn't know about. Even knowing as little as I do about how a murder investigation works, I wasn't dim enough to think keeping secrets from each other would fly. "Cut the bullshit, Bree. I know about your drug bust, God knows I ought to, but I want the full truth. I can't protect either of us without it. All you've ever told me was that you got busted for supplying me with stuff, and that you'd got probation. We've never talked about it—okay, right, that's as much my doing as yours. As of right now, that's done. We're having this out. What did Ormand mean by that, about your mum taking the blame?"

Maybe it was what I'd said about protecting us—I don't know. But out of nowhere, she broke.

I wish I could say I'd never seen it happen before, but that

62

wouldn't be true; Cilla was another strong woman and I watched her break, shatter like a factory-made wineglass, after the heroin and the bourbon and her own need for me to be someone I wasn't and didn't want to be had ganged up on her and dragged her down.

For Cilla, the breakdown had been slow, gradual. Now here was Bree, breaking down, sobbing, the dam cracked and maybe not fixable. It scared the shit out of me, but I'd asked for this, and I had no choice. I needed to know.

"Talk to me." I stayed on my feet. It wasn't easy; my right leg was twitching and jerking in a way that hadn't happened in years. Myokymia, it's called, when muscles start contracting under the skin, and it hurts like hell. The burn ran up my leg into my hip. I fed on it, wanting to hold on to the anger. For the moment, the disease was my ally.

But this was Bree, and even at this moment, she knew me. "Not unless you sit down," she managed. "You have to sit."

I sat. Bree began to speak, letting it out, telling a story I'd been right in the middle of, and about which I remembered almost nothing except the before and the after.

Not long after the Hurricane Felina benefit, Cilla and I discovered heroin, and she went back to London without me.

Blacklight had wrapped the tour in Seattle, and done what I would discover was the standard post-tour splintering of personnel. See, a touring band, you're stuck with your bandmates for company 24–7—dressing rooms, hotels, planes, tour buses—until it ends. When it does end, people pack up, tell each other they'll meet next year to do a new record, and head off in different directions as fast as they can. I'd got used to sessions, where you're there for a couple of hours, maybe a couple of days, and then you're gone.

This time, everyone else had left, but Cilla and I were still in Seattle. The last gig had been about a week earlier, and we'd actually been heading out the backstage door at the Seattle Center Coliseum when we saw a little party going on in one of the dressing rooms and stopped to see who was hanging out, and what was being passed around.

It looked like coke, white powder laid out on a mirror, people snorting straight lines through a rolled-up hundred. I didn't know any of the people, but they were backstage, so they were safe. They were quite pleased to see us and they offered the mirror. We accepted a few toots. No one told us it wasn't straight coke.

It wasn't. It was cocaine cut fifty–fifty with heroin: snowballs, they called it.

The rush was immediate, ice cold, red hot, an incredible flash buzz, a high like nothing else I've ever come across. We were in from the first rush, and it didn't take two days before we were trying for a faster, deeper high, the needle instead of the blow.

People think that heroin kills the sex drive. Apparently, we didn't get that memo; the sex went from good to amazing. If I'd noticed that Cilla no longer had any interest in sex without snowball or straight coke, I wasn't admitting that to myself.

We got piggish with it, unfortunately, a major binge with the good-size stash we'd got hold of. For a few days, it was amazing: nonstop lines and fantastic sex, with very little time to come down before we ran it back and began again. Knowing what I do now about the stuff, we're lucky we both didn't keel over and die.

The problem was that, in Seattle, even looking for someone to hook us up was dodgy. We didn't really know anyone up there, and I didn't trust dealing with street buyers. Cilla was nagging at me to book us home to London; we knew everyone in London, she said, we could get what we needed, and besides, she was bored with America and she wanted to go home now. In her head, it was all nice and simple.

But it wasn't that simple, not for me. I had a weird reluctance to leave the West Coast, and anyway, Tony Mancuso, the keyboard player for the Bombardiers, had rung me up at the Seattle hotel, asking if I wanted to come down and lay down some guitar work for their new album. The idea was appealing, and I told Cilla I was up for doing it.

To say she hadn't taken it well—right. She fucking flipped out. We had a huge screaming fight, not the first one we'd ever had, but this time, instead of falling into bed and shagging to make up, she crammed her clothes into her suitcases and told me that I had no ambition, what was I doing wasting time with some hippies in San Francisco, I was a member of one of the greatest rock and roll bands in the world and I had no business wasting my time with nobodies. I said a few things myself, about being a musician and not a fucking status symbol, and that if she wanted a gold record with a willy attached, she'd married the wrong bloke. When we'd both got to the point of throwing things, she stormed out, slamming the door behind her. I found out she'd got a cab to the airport and gone straight back to London, but that was later. Just then, I was so narked, I could have happily never seen her again.

It's amazing, looking back, that I didn't connect her behaviour—or my own, for that matter—with heroin withdrawal. I'd got twitchy with coke, and this was different enough to have rung a few bells in my head. And with coke, I'd kept it to a small constant stream—there wasn't ever any reason for me to not have it. Coke was handy in those days, and when you're a rocker, everyone wants to give you something.

But I didn't know anything about heroin. I just knew I was feeling edgy and temperamental. I thought maybe I was missing playing.

And it's weird, but true, that I didn't have the slightest desire to ring Cilla in London, make sure she was okay, try to make up. I wonder, now, how much of us as a couple I'd already written off when that hotel room door slammed behind her.

So I called Tony back in San Francisco and told him yeah, love to do a few sessions, and I was on my way. Then I booked a hotel room and got a flight down.

We stayed in the studio for three days, working. I got to be damned good friends with the Bombardiers, and we made some stellar music. I think playing both helped and made it worse. It helped because no matter how sick I am, I can always play, and concentrate on it, but at the same time, being into the music was masking the fact that I was getting sicker, getting worse, getting crazier.

So I got edgier and more twitchy, but the subject of coke never came up, much less heroin; these guys weren't into that at all. There was plenty of pot, and that calmed me down, but I wasn't eating and I wasn't sleeping.

By the time I got back to the hotel on that third night, I'd hit the point that I know now is basic withdrawal. And it hit me hard—my head was slipping, thoughts and realities going in and out, impossible to deal with. My skin was cold and clammy, I was twitching and shaking, and it felt as if things I couldn't see were crawling on me. I needed help. I needed something, anyway.

Trouble was, I had no connections in San Francisco, except the people I'd been working with, and I wasn't about to ask them. Even as fucked up as I was, I knew that wouldn't fly.

So I lay down and tried to relax, tried to ease up, but all that happened was the memory of that fight with Cilla. It kept cycling around, her slamming out and leaving me there with no one to turn to.

And then, out of nowhere, I remembered a girl falling off her boyfriend's shoulders because she was stoned, and the volunteers from the Mission Bells Clinic.

That's where my own memory ends. The rest came from Bree, what she'd told me at the time, over the years, and that morning in the New York hotel, with a murder hanging over us.

Bree was working the help lines at the Clinic that night. What she'd told me backstage at the Felina benefit was true. She often volunteered—Bree was one of the regulars, had been since she was thirteen. Her mother, Miranda Godwin, was on the board; she was also one of the city's leading advocates for drug programs, someone who gave her time, someone who helped people who couldn't afford American health care. She'd been one of the original movers in getting the Clinic licensed for community outreach, specifically to connect with the local junkies, treat them, help them cope.

The night I rang, Bree was two weeks past her seventeenth birthday. I didn't know that then, of course, but truth is, I wouldn't have cared, or thought to ask. I was in no shape to ask or care about anything except what was happening to me. Yeah, I know. Self-absorbed, much?

So it was pure bad luck that when a babbling incoherent English guitar player with the horrors rang the Clinic's help line that night, Dr. Godwin's daughter had taken that particular call. And it was even worse luck, for Dr. Godwin anyway, that the guitar player in question had, a few weeks earlier, had an encounter with Bree, that each of them had recognised something in the other, that Bree had reached out and kissed the guitar player, and tasted the cocaine on his upper lip.

Bree took the call that night. Twenty-six years down the line, with the press in the lobby of our fancy hotel and the New York homicide people digging into what Bree knew and I didn't, she told me the full story, unable to meet my eyes.

"You were crying." She wasn't even trying to control her voice. "I knew it was you, I recognised your voice, and I remembered that you'd asked about calling me at the Clinic. I never thought you would, I mean, why would you? I was just a kid and you had women climbing over each other to get next to you, but there you were, calling. It was you, but you were crying and you said there were bugs crawling on your arms and you hadn't had any snowball for three days and you said your wife had run off and left you, abandoned you. And you remembered my name—you called me by it. You said, 'Bree, I'm dying.'"

I didn't say anything—there was nothing to say. This was new to me, all of it. I didn't remember one moment of this. But the truth was there in her voice, in her face, in the tears that were dripping off her face onto the lap of the pricey green dress, already ruined when she'd vomited at the sight of Perry Dillon on that dressing room floor.

"I asked you where you were. I didn't know what snowballs were—I was going to find my mother and ask her. She worked with drugs all the time, she'd know. You said, the Saturn Hotel, and you were sobbing and saying things that didn't go together. I told you to hold on, I would come and bring you help."

I had no words. How was it possible that she had said nothing of this to me, not once, not in all our time together? And how was it possible that I'd forgotten it to begin with? The shaking little voice, so unlike Bree's, went on.

"I hung up, and I was totally freaked. I was going to call an ambulance—that was my first thought. But the drugs were illegal and I didn't know what they'd do to you. And then I thought, I'll ask Mom, she'll help him, but my mother wasn't there that night. I went into her office—she usually left the key with me when she was on call, because she trusted me not to screw it up. I told myself I only wanted to look up snowballs in her reference list. I did, but I read about it and it described withdrawal, and it sounded so horrible, John. And you'd been crying on the phone, and you said you were dying. I couldn't stand it."

"Bree?" I finally got my voice back, and I got up off the bed. I couldn't sit any longer—my entire body was demanding movement, some release of whatever was building up inside me. "What are you telling me? What did you do?"

She stared at me. "What do you think I did? I broke into the locked storage and I got something that looked right. And yes, I was an idiot, and yes, you could have died from it. Don't you think I know that? I've lived with it, all these years. I was seventeen years old. You don't have to tell me, okay? I'd seen junkies, what not having their stuff did to them. My mother fought the city for years, for the right to treat these people."

"You broke into your mother's supplies—Bree, for God's sake!"

"No, John, not for God's sake." She was getting angry. "For your sake, and for mine. God had nothing to do with it. If Mom had been there, I could have asked her, but she wasn't there, and I was frantic. I grabbed a glassine envelope—it was marked something like 'eighty/twenty c/h,' and I figured that was coke and heroin and that was the ratio. I figured you'd know if that was the right amount, because I sure as hell didn't know. I just took it. And then I took some money out of the petty cash drawer and I got a cab and I went over to the Saturn Hotel."

Nothing. I remembered nothing. My first clear memory of what she was telling would have been about three days later, when I woke up in hospital in San Francisco, and was told that I was lucky not to have died from what I'd snorted, and that my supplier was in some very hot water. I hadn't been in any shape to argue, or to ask them anything at all. I was in detox, for one thing, and they'd booted me out of the country as soon as I could travel, and getting back in again, that took some doing. I knew it had to be Bree, and they confirmed it, but that's all they told me. And at that point, once they let me know no charges were being filed against me, I was too relieved and too sick to argue about it.

"I had my Clinic T-shirt on, and the guy at the desk sent me upstairs and let me in. They didn't ask me any questions; they must have had junkies up there all the time." She saw me flinch, and closed her eyes for a moment. "You were—I can't describe it.

But you were lying there and you were the wrong colour and you were covered in sweat and you were panting. I sat down on the bed next to you. I was thinking please, don't die, just don't die. And you opened your eyes and looked at me, and you smiled—oh, man, you looked so tired, so weak. It just about broke me. And I put my face close to yours and you said, 'you came.' And then you pulled me down to you, on the bed."

"Christ," I whispered. "Bree—did I do anything? Hurt you? Try to hurt you?"

"You mean rape?" She shook her head. "No. You were in no condition to hurt anyone—you barely had the strength to close your fingers. And you being you, I doubt that would ever have crossed your mind anyway. But you kissed me. Your breath . . ." Over the years, I saw her remember and saw her shudder. "I showed you the envelope I'd taken from my mother's office, and I started to say something, ask you if it was right. But I didn't get the chance—you took it away from me and dumped the whole pile out on the nightstand, and pulled a razor blade out of the drawer. You started to chop it up, very fast, very fine, but your hands were shaking and you cut yourself. There was blood mixed in with a lot of the powder."

"Did I offer you any?" My voice was shaking. "Was I at least a nice little gent? Did I offer the schoolgirl come to save me from myself a little taste?"

"John . . ."

"*Did I?*"

"No." Her voice had dropped. "You just looked at the cut and the blood for a second or two, and you laughed. You pulled this thing out of your pocket, a little skinny metal tube, and you sucked the pile of powder up, all of it, except the part that was sticky and bloody, about a quarter of it, maybe a third. My mother told me later that probably saved you from dying—that you didn't do all of it."

I'd never owned a silver tube. It was Cilla's, not mine. In her pissy push to leave me in Seattle, she'd left the tube behind and I'd brought it with me. The girl I was about to fall in love with had brought me a couple of grams of basically pure, uncut smack and coke, probably medicinal quality. I'd snorted it using my wife's equipment. If I appreciated irony, at all, this would be at the top of the fucking pile, you know?

"You OD'd." She was looking back into the past now, open-eyed and in horror. I could see it all there, on her face, what she hadn't said, trying to protect me, all these years. "I freaked. I thought I'd killed you. I didn't know what to do. It looked as if your heart had stopped, and you stopped breathing. Your chest wasn't moving at all. If you'd died . . ."

She stopped, and swallowed. If she was waiting for me to say something, she was in for a long wait. I had no words.

"I did chest compression, basic CPR stuff they taught everyone at the Clinic." Her voice had gone thin. "You jerked a little, and I saw you start breathing again. I called the Clinic and they called 911 and there were paramedics and then there were police and they sent you off in the ambulance, but they wouldn't let me go with you. You were alone, unconscious for a couple of days. Nobody would tell me anything. They took me downtown instead."

She stopped. Her breath was coming in short painful spasms. I stood back away, out of touching distance. Right that moment, there was too much going on in me, and none of it was pretty.

All those years, all those secrets. I knew what that theft of hers should have meant, even to a minor. Yet, so far as I knew, she hadn't ever been to jail; when I'd got back the following spring, for the rest of the tour, she was free and clear and the subject never even came up. And when I'd come back to San Francisco to stay, and we came together, she was already enrolled at the culinary academy.

I'd had enough of secrets. I'd had enough of being protected, lies, walls built to keep the world from harming me.

"Bree. I asked you once." I heard myself and nearly jumped—that couldn't be me talking that way, surely, not to Bree, anyway. "Don't make me ask you again. What did Ormand mean, about your mother? What was he talking about?"

"She took the blame for me—protecting her child. She told the police she'd been careless with the packet, not locking it away—that anyone could have walked off with it. Said it was her fault. They had to know that was bullshit. But they couldn't prove it, and that meant they couldn't prove the stuff you had was the stuff from the Clinic, and they couldn't prove I'd stolen it. I got nailed for being underage with someone on enclosed premises who was in possession of dangerous narcotics and illegal drug paraphernalia—six months' probation."

"And Miranda? What did they do to her?"

"You want the truth?" The green eyes locked on me. "Fine. I told her everything, about the kiss at the benefit, that you'd called me for help. I didn't know you were just calling the Clinic, John. I thought you wanted me, particularly me. You *asked* for me—you knew my name. So I told her what I'd done."

"And she took the blame."

"Of course she did. She knew I'd be screwed if they could prove it against me. There was no way in hell she was going to stand by and let them lock me up."

"What happened to her?" I had my hands jammed into my pockets, curled into fists. "I want the truth, Bree."

"They had a hearing. The Clinic got to keep its license, but she was suspended from practice for six months and kicked off the board." She lifted her head and glared at me. "You wanted to know, you got it. There. Happy now? Goddamnit, John, why the hell couldn't you just let it rest?"

"Let it rest?" I saw her face change, registering the difference in anything she'd ever heard from me, felt from me before. "Are you fucking joking?"

"John—"

"Christ." I was shaking my head, and my leg was in flames. "So, you sacrificed your mum to protect me? And she went along with it? Nice and noble. You Godwin women, you're unbelievable, you know that? I understand her wanting to protect you and you letting her do it, but to protect me? Did you ever stop to wonder if I'd want it that way? Maybe give me a say?"

"John, please—"

"All these years, me being so fond of Miranda, she's always so nice to me, and all this time, you two have had this little secret? Protect John from himself and the big bad world? You honestly think I'd have let that happen, if I'd been given a choice? It never seems to occur to you to check with me before you build a fortress around me, does it?"

I wasn't stopping to ask myself where the rage was coming from or if it was fair. Not now. I wasn't stopping to censor myself. I've never hit a woman in my life, but from the look on her face, the words could easily have been fists.

"I'm going," I told her. "I can't be here."

She didn't answer me. She didn't need to. It was there, echoing in the fancy hotel suite, words she'd said to me once before, and only once: *Please, John, don't go, don't do this to me.*

I walked out into the New York morning, closing the door behind me.

CHAPTER FOUR

Central Park, at seven in the morning, can be a good place to separate from the world. Even with cabs and joggers and people walking their dogs, it's possible to find an empty bench and just sit there, all by yourself. There's a sort of emptiness to it, and emptiness was what I needed right then.

My head was light, and my legs were wobbly. I walked east, heading toward the Fifth Avenue side, and found an unoccupied bench not far from the Children's Zoo.

I was still royally pissed off, but I was also in that state of weird clarity you get when you're coming down from an adrenaline rush. Between the stress of first night, the lack of sleep for twenty-four hours, and the adrenaline rush backing off, the rage that had kept me on my feet was fading out and my legs had begun to seriously hurt.

I sat down, wishing I'd stopped at one of the corner carts

and got myself a hot coffee. It was going to be a warm day, but for now, there was dew on the grass and a bit on the bench as well. I could feel it through the backs of my trousers. The air smelled fresh, and clean, and breathable.

Bree's confession, if that's what it had been, had got under my skin in a way I couldn't really define. If I couldn't define it, I wasn't going to be able to cope with it, and coping with it had suddenly become my top priority.

Things were going to get ugly. The question of who had put Perry Dillon on the guest list and why, what he'd been doing in that dressing room, and how he'd fetched up sprawled out dead on the floor with his throat bashed, all those things were going to hit the papers, the news, and our lives. There wasn't going to be any escape, not from any of it. It had started thanks to that damned post of Nial's, but what had happened last night was going to send it sky-high. All that filthy laundry was going to be hung out for the world to see. Whether she knew it or not, Bree could kiss her obsessive desire for invisibility good-bye.

My hands were stabbing at me, and I realised I'd walked out of the hotel and left my morning meds behind. I closed my eyes for a moment, trying to remember if I'd taken any last night, after the gig. Immediately, there was a picture: Bree, sitting on the edge of the bed, biting back words, refusing to beg me.

She'd begged me once, not to go, and I'd gone anyway. Now I'd done it again, but this time, she hadn't begged. Come to think of it, she'd never once argued with me not to do anything, not after that first failure. She'd let me go, every time.

I shook my head, trying to clear it, forcing my mind back to the question of meds. I couldn't remember taking them last night; I hadn't taken any this morning.

I could feel the sun on my eyelids, too bright, too warm.

Sleep, I thought, *that's what I want, sleep*, where I can go all the way down and not have to cope with anything at all for a few hours, just easy deep breaths, sleep. . . .

"JP?"

The voice was musical, English with a Caribbean undertone. I opened my eyes.

Domitra Calley, in black sweats and custom running shoes, was standing on the path, looking down at me.

"Hey, Dom." I was out of energy entirely. Speaking wasn't a problem, but if I'd wanted to play the gent and rise for the lady, I was out of luck; it wasn't going to happen. I was pretty sure now that I hadn't taken any of my meds last night, or this morning, either. Standing just wasn't on the agenda. "Out for a jog, are you?"

She ignored that. One of the things that makes her so terrifying is how analytical she can be. She didn't waste her time asking or answering stupid questions, and that one had an obvious answer.

"Why are you sleeping on a park bench?"

"Because Bree told me something she should have told me twenty years ago, and I flipped my shit, lost my temper, needed to get out of the room for a bit." I looked up at her. "Would you mind sitting, Dom? If we're going to talk, that is? Because I haven't slept since the night before last and my head feels too heavy to look up at you. Of course, if we're not going to talk, carry on. I don't want to mess up your routine."

"Nah, no problem. I can pick up the run again." She sat, and I turned slightly sideways to look at her. A few more people were out now, hurrying toward their jobs, nannies heading for the playground with their kids, professional dog-walkers. It was going be a busy Saturday in Central Park.

It's a testament to just how solid Dom's professional face is that no one—not a single gossip columnist—had ever so much as hinted that Dom and Mac might have something going beyond their rock star–bodyguard relationship. Because Dom is beautiful—she's long and elegant and perfectly muscled and fierce and her skin is the precise colour you get when you stir that first bit of cream into very dark roast coffee. Her hair is bleached blond-white, and kept cropped close to a superbly defined skull. She's got cheekbones and attitude and the chops to fold most people in half and shove them into a body bag before they know what hit them. Mac pays her a fortune, and she's worth every penny.

"So, anyway." She stretched her legs out, twisting each one, listening for the snap and pop of joints resetting. "I spent half the night talking to the police, getting some backchannel news on what happened, answering questions. Mostly answering questions, though. And listening. I heard stuff."

All of a sudden, I was a bit more awake. "Can you share, please? I've got no information at all, and I need some."

"Well, let's see. First off, they can't find anyone who will admit to putting Dillon on the guest list, and they can't find anyone who will admit to actually letting him in. I didn't get that direct from the cops—I got it from some of the security people they'd been questioning. They're going to talk to everyone and anyone who might have had anything to do with the backstage door last night."

"Did they suspect you?" I couldn't think of why they would, except that she was so obviously able.

"Nah. I looked to be a suspect, probably still am, but I didn't get that I was too high up on the hit parade. No motive, and anyway, not my style, using a weapon, especially not what was used on him." She smiled. "I wouldn't need anything that leaves that kind of trace evidence. I've got feet."

"And? . . ."

"How he died, I got that direct. Someone took a guitar

77

stand, one of the old-fashioned metal ones, and bashed him in the throat with it. Crushed the larynx—he died. And the stand was wiped afterwards, or at least, really smeared. What?"

"Shit!" I was completely awake now, and for some reason, the air no longer felt warm. "I'm the only band member who uses metal stands. Everyone else has composite black ones. And they're kept in my dressing room. Dom, is there anything else?"

"Apparently they've impounded his interview tapes, and they were talking about checking his phone calls for the past few months. Oh, and he died very shortly before whoever found him says they found him. Within ten minutes, they said. Close to the end of the show, anyway. Why are you looking so sick?"

"Bree found him." *My guitar stand*, I thought, *my old lady, her enemy.*

"I didn't know that. But it does explain some of the tidbits I overhead at the station. They seem to think maybe she killed him. I wondered why." Dom was looking at me, curious, up front. "She must be upset; scared shitless. Hell, in her shoes, I would be, and I don't scare easy. So why are you sitting in Central Park? If that was my sweetie who found a dead guy and was suspected of bashing him, I'd be making myself useful, not scarce. This state has the death penalty, dude."

"Well . . ." I suddenly needed to talk, tell my side of it, let someone besides Bree hear me. I told Dom the entire story, the benefit, what Bree had told me. I think I was even more spaced than I knew, because I even told her about Bree, that first time Cilla had begged me to come home, and how Bree had pleaded with me to stay, and how I'd gone. . . .

"Wow." Dom had her head tilted. You could almost see the gears working. "You know, I don't know Bree, hardly at all, so let me see if I get it. What you're saying is, you and your wife split, you fell in love with a girl who was barely seventeen, she stole drugs and got herself a police record and got her mother fired from her job to protect you, and she never told you about it. And now you demanded she tell you, she did, and you're pissed off enough over it to slam on out and leave her alone, even though she's maybe number one on the suspect list for a murder. And you have the feeling she isn't telling you everything even now, and also that you're tired of being protected for your own good without being consulted, and you don't want any more secrets. Is that right?"

"Right. But you make it sound—I don't know . . ."

"I'm not making it sound like anything at all. I'm just saying what I think I hear. But right now, if I understood what you've been laying out for me? I'd have to say you're either a dimwit or a dick."

My jaw dropped. She shook her head at me.

"Maybe you can't see it because you're too close to it. Maybe you care too much. See, for me? I don't give a shit, so I can see it just fine. Try it this way, dude. Bree doesn't care about protecting herself—you get everything you want from her, and you always have. She's all about protecting you, giving you what she thinks you need, giving you what you say you need. Yeah? I get that right?"

I said nothing. My sleep-deprived brain was putting things together, and I was squirming inwardly. Dom was right, of course she was right. Her voice, even and merciless, kept on.

"So why is she scared about some stupid drug story from a hundred years ago or whatever coming out now? She wouldn't be scared for herself, not from what you're telling me about her. If she's scared of something happening, she's scared for you. And by the way, as a woman, I have a question of my own. Maybe you won't like to hear it, though."

The path was filling up. Somewhere on Fifth Avenue,

church bells struck eight times. I swallowed, hard. "Go on. Tit for tat. Ask away."

"Cool, because I want to know. You've been with Bree all this time, and you tell me you went back to your crazy fucked-up junkie wife three times. So what I want to know is, how come you've still *got* a crazy fucked-up junkie wife anyway, if you love Bree so much? What's that bullshit about? Fuck protecting you, man. If I was Bree, I'd whip your ass and leave you crying all alone."

"Now wait just a bloody minute, Dom—"

"No, man, you told me to spill it out. You said you were tired of people protecting you. Okay, cool—then deal with it. Shit, you're with the band, I'll protect your body if you're near Mac, but I don't owe your ego any strokes. I'm not your mama or your old lady—no free titty from me. You know what's wrong with you, JP? You're so spoiled, you want your cake and your frosting and tequila on the side with a straw, and Bree lets you have it all, the big dope. Why don't you just pick one or the other, and be with her? You love Bree, how come you don't just divorce Cilla?"

"Because I can't!" She'd been truthful, all right. Too truthful. "Easy to tell you've never done it. There's huge sums of money involved, and lawyers, and press. Bree never asked me to divorce Cilla, Dom. But of course I've considered it. I did bring up divorce once, and Cilla freaked. She said she'd commit suicide if I did that. I can't carry that kind of weight."

"Honey, from what you've been telling me, you don't want to carry *any* weight. All you want is to be protected. Wait, I forgot, you also want the right to bitch about being protected. Man, that's some damned fine passive-aggressive, you know?" Dom got up, and rested one leg on the bench, stretching and bending. "So Cilla threatened to off herself if you signed papers. I bet you told Bree that, huh?"

"Of course I told Bree." *Shit, shit, shit.* If I'd thought my words to Bree earlier were like fists, I was being served some of my own sauce back again. "Bloody hell, Dom, wouldn't you have?"

"Me? Well, yeah, if I was looking for a way to make sure Bree never asked me to actually get off my sorry ass and do it. If I wanted a way off the hook, and to keep both women attached to me at the same time, sure." She stretched the second leg, brought both feet down on the path, and began jogging in place. "Like I said: cake, frosting, and tequila with a straw. You're a nice guy, JP. Very sweet. But what I told you before? It's true—you've been spoiled rotten. You really could stand to have your ass kicked. And you're not very self-aware. I need to get back soon; there's press all over the place at the hotel, sniffing around and looking to get next to Mac. Anyway, I need to get my cardio up—see you later."

Then she was gone, running north and deeper into the park.

The walk from that park bench back to the hotel seemed to take half a lifetime.

My head was doing cartwheels by this time, but not nearly so much as my ego was, in the worst possible way. Domitra had laid the hammer down, without any personal stake or any reason to care, and she'd hit so hard, she'd left bruises. If she'd been wrong, it wouldn't have mattered. But everything she'd said had stung, and the only way it could sting was if I believed her.

She must be upset; scared shitless.

I'd walked out. I'd left Bree alone.

I hoisted myself off the bench. It took a scary few minutes of sinking back, trying again, sinking back—lather, rinse, repeat. Every time I stood up, my right leg began to tremble.

This was something new, something my neurologist had

warned me might happen eventually. Ataxia, it's called, when the muscles in your legs suddenly stop communicating with each other, the myelin-deprived nerves stop coordinating the signals between muscles and brain, and you get unsteady on your pins.

I'm used to the occasional relapse, bad days when even putting my feet on the ground takes pretty much everything I've got, but this was the first time I'd ever tried to stand up and had my entire leg, instep to groin, decide that it wasn't attached and wanted to go another direction entirely. And it couldn't be happening at a worse time.

You're pissed off enough over it to slam on out and leave her alone, even though she's maybe number one on the suspect list for a murder.

I managed it eventually, after a few tries that left me sweating. I began the walk back to the hotel, shambling really, stopping every few minutes to rest. All the time, I was mentally giving my right leg a stern talking-to: *Right, you'll point forward and go in the same direction as the left leg, don't you get stroppy with me, you'll do as you're told.*

Halfway back, it occurred to me that I had my cell phone with me. Leaning against a building, trying to block out the noise that never seems to ease up in Manhattan, I listened to it ringing: one ring, two, three, and then her voice mail message. *"You've reached Bree Godwin at Noshing but the Best Catering. I'm sorry I'm not available to take your call. Please leave a message and a number at the tone."*

"Damn it! Bree? Damn. Could you pick up? It's me. Look, love, listen, I'm sorry. I acted like a complete idiot. I'm on my way back to the hotel—if you get this, don't go out, all right? Wait for me."

Beep, click. I disconnected, thought about it, and rang the hotel directly, asking to be put through to our suite.

Cake, frosting, and tequila with a straw. Spoiled rotten.

One ring, two rings, three rings. Nothing. After eight rings, there was a tiny click and the same person who'd tried to connect me came back to tell me that the guest in 814 wasn't responding, and did I want to leave a message?

I rang off. My hands were sweating.

Maybe she was sleeping. After all, she'd been awake for just as long as I'd been, she'd been just as stressed, and she'd found Perry Dillon's murdered body in my dressing room. Not to mention that confession I'd forced out of her. Not to mention me walking out and leaving her there. . . .

This state has the death penalty, dude.

I broke into a sort of trot, dragged the shaking leg after me. This time I didn't stop until I got through the hotel's front doors.

If I'd thought there were a lot of press people in the lobby earlier, I'd been naive. The lobby was jammed with them, wall to wall, elbow to elbow. It was a madhouse.

Our staff was still down there, a different collection of faces; Phil MacDermott, wise bloke, must be staggering them in shifts. This time, the media people recognised me, and a bunch of voices started yelling my name, throwing out questions.

I ignored them all. Up in the lift to the eighth floor. The band had two full floors booked, twenty individual luxury suites. I had no clue whether we needed the lot, but booking the floor allowed us some control over our own privacy levels. At the moment, control of any kind felt like a gift from God.

My hands had joined my leg in their refusal to cooperate. First try with the electronic key, I dropped the damned thing; second try, I couldn't get a clean swipe. Finally, third try, the red light over the lock turned green. I pushed the door open and let myself in.

The suite was empty. She wasn't there.

The first thing I did was take my morning meds, with an extra bit of painkiller as a chaser. Then I put in a call to room service, for a pot of tea and some toast. I wasn't ready to take on the possibilities of why Bree wasn't here, not yet, but there was one thing I ought to get over with, one way or the other. I took a deep breath and slid back the mirrored doors to the walk-in closet, where she'd hung her clothes for the tour.

I think I'd subconsciously been flashing back to Cilla leaving me in Seattle. But this time, the wardrobe was full. The green dress Bree'd been wearing was crumpled up on the floor of the closet. Her suitcases were at the back, where she'd stored them. Her shoes looked to all be there as well, at least her dressy ones. She loves high heels, does Bree, and buys a lot of them, especially since I've managed to get her to believe over the years that I actually get turned on by being five-foot-eight to her Amazon six-foot-plus in full heels. I didn't know how many she'd brought along, but there were four pairs of pricey shoes in there, including a pair of pale blue Jimmy Choos that were her current favourites.

My heart rate settled a bit. Whatever she was doing and wherever she was doing it, she hadn't just packed up and left, and she hadn't gone home without telling me. But where in hell was she, then?

Dom had called me spoiled, and maybe I was, but when it comes to hotel services, at least, I'm damned if I'll apologise for it. Room service sent someone up with my breakfast five minutes after I'd rung them. Breakfast turned out to have been a good idea—the tea kicked me back to basic functionality, without speeding me up too much.

The second thing I did was to open the paper that had been

left outside our door, and see what the press was saying about the whole mess.

The headline, in bold black type, jumped out at me:

MURDER AT THE GARDEN.

Controversial Biographer Murdered at Rock Concert

Legendary British rock band Blacklight's opening show at Madison Square Garden last night ended with an encore of sudden death. The body of celebrity biographer Perry Dillon, 44, was found in a dressing room after the show was over, by a member of the band's entourage. Dillon, often in the news, had recently announced that his next project would be a history of the band and its members. . . .

Oh, bloody hell. If the *New York Times* was announcing the biography angle on the front page, the less well-mannered mainstream press were going to go nuts, joining the tabloid sleazes who were already digging in the dirt. They'd be doing half Ormand's work for him.

A representative for Blacklight issued a statement this morning, saying in effect that Dillon's presence backstage at the Garden last night remains a source of concern, since he had been officially barred from any contact with the band or any of its members during their American tour. . . . Lt. Patrick Ormand, heading up the investigation, said that evidence is being gathered and examined, and that several areas of information are already being explored. . . .

It was front page, of course. There was no way something this juicy would be anywhere else. The story, bare bones, had been given a full quarter of the page. I had the feeling that just getting into and out of the hotel was going to need the kind of planning you'd expect for a military campaign.

I folded the paper and tried to get my brain to function. At some point, I was going to have to crash. Tomorrow night, we were supposed to be playing a sold-out Boston gig, and right now, I had no idea whether we were even going to be allowed to leave Manhattan. I would need to talk to Ian.

As I was finishing my toast, the room phone rang. I grabbed for it so quickly, I nearly knocked the tray off the table.

"Mr. Kinkaid? This is Lieutenant Ormand. I was wondering if we could get together later today—we have a few things we need to ask you about. Or do I need to go through your lawyer? I don't seem to have a name or number."

"I haven't rung him yet." My shoulders had slumped. *Not Bree.* "And I don't mind answering any questions you've got, but it's going to have to be later in the day. I'm in the middle of a full-scale exacerbation and I haven't slept since the night before last. Right now, I can barely walk and I'll be useless until I rest. Why don't you ring me back around two this afternoon? You have my cell number, yeah? I gave it to you last night, at the Garden."

"Yes, I have it. That'll be fine. What do you mean by an exacerbation, Mr. Kinkaid? An exacerbation of what?"

"I've got multiple sclerosis, the less crippling kind. Relapsing-remitting, it's called. And right now, it's front and centre and I need to sleep. Sorry, Lieutenant, I'm off. I'll talk with you later."

"Oh, I'm sorry—I didn't know about that. Mr. Kinkaid? I don't know whether or not your lawyer is also Ms. Godwin's legal representative. Either way, we'd like to speak to Ms. Godwin today, too."

"Right." Ormand had just answered one question, without me having to ask it. Wherever she was, it wasn't with the police. "She's not here at the moment. Look, I have to sleep. I'll talk to you later, all right?"

I rang off. Sleep was suddenly very far down on my list of priorities.

She wasn't with the police, unless Ormand was being tricky for no good reason I could think of. She hadn't left for good, since all her clothes were still here.

What if she has left for good? What if she's just dumped her clothes and panicked and run?

"No." I heard myself say it out loud. I felt a chilly sweat break out around my hairline. "She didn't. She wouldn't. This is Bree we're talking about, damn it."

Suppose she has run. Does that mean she killed Perry Dillon?

"Oh, rubbish. She wouldn't kill anyone, not for anything."

She would, for you. It's just what Dom said: Bree doesn't care about protecting herself. She's all about protecting you. If she thought Perry Dillon was a threat to you, she wouldn't stop to think twice.

I was into the full-scale shakes now, the kind I last remembered having during the bad days of quitting drinking, days when Bree'd held my head in her lap while I had the horrors, making her promise me she wouldn't walk away, promise she'd always be there.

I curled up on the bed, shivering. With my cell phone on the pillow next to my head, I closed my eyes and waited for sleep.

CHAPTER FIVE

I slept until just before one, and woke up alone.

There were no messages for me, not with the hotel staff, not in my voice mail. At twenty past one, having spent a few surreal minutes on the phone with the high-powered criminal attorney referred to me by Blacklight's American legal representatives, I'd tried Bree's cell phone again, hearing my own voice getting more urgent with every word, more worried, a bit louder.

I set the phone down on the bathroom vanity and headed into the shower. There's that old saw, about the phone ringing when you're in the bath or the toast always dropping with the messy bit facing down, you know? Sod's Law. This had to be the first time in my life I'd ever hoped it was true.

Ormand hadn't called, but I'd told him around two, and it was early yet. The shower had a sort of bar, mounted diagonally, put in for handicapped guests; I held on to it for dear life, letting hot water sluice over me. The legs felt marginally better, but I hadn't got anything like enough sleep to clear the cobwebs out of my skull, and I was very wobbly.

It had been at least four years since I'd had to use a cane to get about—that was before the weekly interferon shot began kicking in and keeping me reasonably ambulatory and functional. I found myself wondering how I was supposed to do fifteen gigs in less than three weeks, if I couldn't stand upright for more than a few minutes at a time.

I let the water run, thoughts looping through my head. Nothing moving about in there was particularly pleasant. What I was really doing, of course, was waiting for the damned cell phone to ring. Fucking Sod's Law, yeah? But it stayed silent.

As I was wrapping a towel around myself, I heard the click of the suite's door. I stuck my head around the door.

"Bree!"

Relief hit me, good and hard. I hadn't understood just how worried I'd been until I saw her. She'd changed into jeans and flat shoes; her hair was coiled up and pinned into a nondescript pile at the back of her skull, her usual way of dealing with what she calls a dirty hair day.

I hitched the towel tighter and got her by the elbows. "Bloody hell, love, I was half out of my mind worried! Are you all right?"

"I'm fine." She moved, very lightly, and my hands fell away, and so did the towel. She stepped back, just out of reach. "I'm supposed to go talk to that cop from last night, in about an hour. He left a message on my cell phone. I suppose I should do something about a lawyer."

Something turned very cold inside me. She wasn't meeting my eyes. She wasn't really seeing me, or talking with me, or even to me. I can't explain it—she was elsewhere, or maybe I was. She seemed to have somehow got herself removed from me. I reached down and grabbed the towel, and tied it around my waist this time. Speaking normally was tricky.

"Don't worry about the lawyer. That's all lined up; the big firm the band uses set us up with some recs. I've got a name and number for you." I looked into her face, trying to get her to meet my eyes. "He says we should have two different lawyers. Just in case of conflict of interest, or something."

"Cool." Her voice was remote, uninvolved, and her gaze flickered past me. "I should call before I head down there, I guess. Can you write down his name and number for me?"

"I already did—it's on the pad over there." I heard my own voice go up a bit. "On the table on your side of our bed."

"Great. Thanks. I'll call him."

"Bree?"

She ignored me and reached for the phone. I swallowed down any more words; I didn't know what I could say to fix things, and anything I said would be wasted breath anyway, while she was talking to the lawyer. Instead, I got dressed in a hurry. There was something about standing there half-naked that left me feeling more vulnerable than I wanted. And I was already on fairly shaky ground, you know?

When she rang off, she sat down on the bed and sighed. It was a long, tired, complicated noise, and I knew then that she hadn't slept at all. She closed her eyes for a minute, and I watched her from where I was standing, not coming too close. Right that moment, I thought that if I tried to touch her and she pushed me away and stepped back from me again, I'd fall the hell apart.

"Bree—we should talk about this meeting with the police."

"Really?" She opened her eyes and finally, finally, met my eyes. "Why? What's there to talk about?"

I gaped at her. She sounded totally calm, remote really. I don't think I'd ever heard this tone of voice from her—as if nothing could harm her or damage or even touch her, including me. Her face had gone masklike, unreadable. The woman I'd spent all these years with had never looked or felt this way.

"Are you joking?" I stayed where I was, letting the soles of my feet complain. "Right. Inventory. Reality check. Bree, someone let that wanker in. No one's admitting to it—I had a long talk with Domitra this morning; she spent the night with the cops. He was killed in my dressing room. He was killed with one of my guitar stands. He was killed just a few minutes before he was found. And you found him!" My voice had spiralled all the way up. I bit down hard on it. "Do you realise, there's a damned good chance they think you did it? So what in hell do we tell the police, then?"

"I didn't kill Perry Dillon." She sounded almost bored.

"Of course you didn't! Don't you think I know that?"

"No, I don't think you know that."

Those words, in that voice, stopped me cold. Bloody hell, here I was, thinking I knew her, and I didn't know her half so well as she knew me, because she was dead right: I wasn't sure she hadn't killed him. Dom's voice came back to me: *anything to protect you . . .*

"Amazing." She sounded even further away, more detached, than she had before. "No, really. You think I picked up your guitar stand, in your dressing room, and slammed it across that guy's throat and killed him. Amazing. And then I did what, exactly? Came out and danced in the wings to my rock star boy-toy's hot little guitar riffs?" Out of nowhere, her eyes were blazing. "And then told the cops? Was that before or after I'd puked up my dinner?"

"I don't—"

"Bullshit." Maybe she wasn't so far away as I'd thought, because I could see her mouth wanting to shake. "Maybe I don't know or understand you as well as I thought I did—this morning showed me that, thank you very much—but I know when you're full of shit, even if you won't admit it. And you know what? You're full of shit. You think I killed him. Well, fuck you. I didn't kill him. Deal with it."

"Bree, for God's sake—"

"Excuse me. I need to wash my face." She got up and walked past me, toward the bathroom. "I don't feel very well. I haven't eaten and I haven't slept and now I have to put my life in the hands of some asshole lawyer I've never even met, because the one human being on the planet who I should be able to rely on thinks I'm a murderer."

I reached out, unthinking, and grabbed her sleeve. She went rigid.

"Let go of me." Her voice shook. "Don't touch me. Don't look at me. Let go of me."

"No. No, I'm not letting go of you. Look at me." Some instinct had finally kicked in. Dom had been right, about me spoiled and not self-aware, but right here, right now, I'd sussed that this was our happiness and our future at stake.

I'd walked out and caused this mess, just the way I'd walked out before. It was ridiculous—I'd taken the easy way every time. Dom was right about that, as well, and Bree had enabled me, by being noble and long-suffering about it. And here she was, doing it again. Same pattern, every time.

But this time, I'd be damned if I was going to play. There was too much at stake right now. I could see that; if I took the easy road right now, Bree and I were done.

"I told you to look at me. *Look at me!*"

She turned her head slightly. She still wasn't meeting my eyes. I'm not used to handing out orders, but I managed it. I sounded so stern, I scared myself. "All the way round, Bree. I'm not talking to the side of your head. I said, look at me."

She didn't move. I jerked, putting all the strength I had left into it, which wasn't much. It was enough, though, and we were face-to-face, and I finally got our eyes to lock up.

"I know damned well you didn't kill Perry Dillon." The green stare was devastating, but I wasn't about to break first. "I also know that you're hiding something. Bloody hell, Bree, anyone could see it. So yeah, maybe I ballsed things up between us. Maybe Domitra's right, and I'm a dimwit and a dick. Maybe she's right about you being a twit for letting me get away with so much shit. But I know you and I love you and maybe it's my turn to do some protecting around here, and how the fuck am I supposed to be able to do that, if you won't be straight up with me? You're so bloody good at putting those walls up, wanting to keep everyone away from us, you don't ever seem to get that you're keeping me out as well. And I'm tired of it. I'm not having any more of it. I'm a big boy, Bree, you know?"

She stared at me, and I shook her, hard. "Come back, Bree. This is me, remember? It's John. Talk to me. There's nothing you can say I wouldn't believe. And if you don't get that by now, then you're dimmer than I'll ever be."

"A dick and a dimwit?" There was the glimmer of a smile there, and her face had begun to relax. "Domitra really said that? When? Where?"

"This morning, on a bench in the park. She was jogging and saw me dozing there, and stopped for a chat that turned into her ripping me a new one. That, by the way, was after I'd acted like a complete idiot and stormed out of here and left you alone—which, by the way, I am not going to do again. Sorry, love. You're going to have to find another way to enable me. My poor masculine ego won't take the kind of smackdown I got this morning. And by the way, you didn't get off any better than I did. She called you a big dope."

"She called me a what?"

"You heard me." I glanced at the clock. "Look, it's just gone two. If we're supposed to go see lawyers and lieutenants and things, we should get started, yeah?" I hesitated, wondering how to say what I wanted to say. "Look—I'm not going to press you, but if there's anything you think I ought to know—about anything at all—this would be a good time to tell me."

"No. There's really nothing to tell, not now, anyway." I opened my mouth to speak. She added, very quietly, "You said you wouldn't press me. Either you trust me, or you don't, John. If you don't—"

"I trust you. Go get your shower. Your hair's a mess." I kissed her, hard and fast, startling her. "If we're late, they can bloody well wait."

From the moment we sat down at Lieutenant Ormand's desk, I knew they had something.

The two lawyers were waiting for us when we got there. Bree went off into one corner of the room with hers, and I sat down with mine. I don't really know what I'd been expecting, but the bloke—his name was Leo Pasquini—was friendly, professional and completely terrifying, in just the right way. He told me what to expect in the way of questions, told me that saying less was a better idea than saying more if there was any chance that the more in question might lead to complications, and mentioned that he'd be there for the interview with me.

"If I break in and answer for you," he said, "go with me on it, all right? As your counsel, it gives me better control of the situation on your behalf."

"Right." Bree and the second lawyer, a bloke called Jameson, were talking, across the room, in their own corner. Their conversation didn't seem to be so easy or so brief as the one I was having with Pasquini. "Will Bree's lawyer be in for this, as well?"

"Certainly." Pasquini glanced toward them. "His job is a bit different than mine, though. After all, you were onstage at the time of the murder."

He didn't say it, but I heard it in my head anyway: *And Bree hadn't been.* I couldn't remember much about the show itself, but one thing was pretty vivid in my head, and that was the complete absence of Bree until she'd turned up in the wings with a copper at her side and vomit on her dress. I remembered it too damned well, looking for her, seeing Domitra circling, Cyn Corrigan and Barb Wilson dancing, seeing damned near everyone but Bree, wondering where the hell she was. But when during the set had that been? Early? Late? I couldn't remember.

"So you're not under suspicion." He smiled at me, as if he thought I ought to be pleased about it. For a moment, I wanted to take a swing at him. I put that little idea away in a hurry. He couldn't know I was worried half to death about Bree. He couldn't feel about it the way I did, and I wouldn't want him to. But he'd made it really clear that I hadn't been wrong, that Domitra hadn't been wrong: it was Bree they were looking at.

But really, except for circumstantial bits, it wasn't as if they had any reason to think she'd killed anyone. Motive? Yeah, all right, maybe, but enough to take seriously? The bastard had done books on at least ten other unfortunates, real smear jobs, too, and no one had taken him out until now.

What else did police traditionally look for, anyway? Opportunity? She hadn't got any more than two hundred other people backstage that night. The weapon? It seemed to me pretty obvious, that whoever had bashed Dillon had grabbed what was handy. If it had happened in a kitchen, he'd have got bashed with a skillet or something. But this was backstage at a major rock venue, it happened where people kept guitar stands, and the killer would have used one. Why were they looking at Bree?

Ormand came out and got us eventually. I'd been watching him through the window between his office and the waiting room. I'd been getting some interested looks, overt stares from the girl at the desk and more sidelong ones from some of the cops themselves. It seemed a bit weird under those circs, but I suppose even a cop shop isn't going to be immune to the shine of celebrity, even if the shine's a bit elderly and dull.

"Sorry to keep you waiting." Ormand—he looked, I don't know, I can't describe it. Intensity, maybe, and there was a touch of satisfaction there as well. Every nerve ending I had was on red alert.

"No problem, we don't mind waiting."

"Thank you." He got us all seated, crowding into his office. His eyes stayed on Bree, cold, considering. "We had to finish up a few interviews with the Garden staff. And of course, with your band's own security staff. They were very helpful, very forthcoming. Seems there was more than one person handling the backstage door last night."

He stopped, and seemed to be waiting for a response. I raised an eyebrow at my lawyer, and Pasquini nodded. "Well, yeah," I told Ormand. "Whoever's got door for a particular gig has to be there from the dinner break on—I told you that last night. You can't ask someone to stay there from six in the evening until midnight without giving him a rest and a break of his own, you know? Hard on the bladder—anyway, the roadies are union."

"Thanks." He hadn't even glanced at me. He and Bree were locked up. Her face was expressionless, and Jameson was looking puzzled and uneasy. My stomach was doing some seriously iffy things. "The guy on main door duty last night was one of Blacklight's staff, not Garden crew: Jerry Rubenstein. Know him? Apparently, he got to take a couple of breaks during the show."

Ormand smiled suddenly, and everything in me locked down hard. That smile was aimed straight at my old lady. Wolf in a fairy story . . .

"You didn't mention last night that you took over the door for about ten minutes, Ms. Godwin. Even brought him a beer, is that right? According to him, that was just a few minutes before nine thirty, somewhere between nine twenty and half past. He says he was gone about ten minutes, maybe fifteen. Rubenstein also says he doesn't think Perry Dillon's name was on that list before you got there."

Jameson opened his mouth, but she held up a hand.

"Yes, I brought him a beer." Her voice was calm, easy. "I was heading to the bathroom and he caught my eye and I realised he'd probably been there for two hours without a break, so I grabbed a beer, cruised over, and handed it to him. We talked for a couple of minutes, he said he needed to take a leak, I asked him if anyone had come by to spell him yet. He said no, he hadn't even had dinner yet. So I offered to watch the door while he did his thing and grabbed something to eat. He headed off, and I played door dragon for about fifteen minutes. It's easy enough—they knock, you open, they say their name, you find it, end of story. Is any of that criminal?"

"Not the way you tell it, no." He must have been a killer poker player; I couldn't get anything off his voice or his look. "Did you let Perry Dillon in, Ms. Godwin?"

"No." She was telling the truth, at least about that—I could see it. "At least, no one came up and said they were Perry Dillon while I was sitting there. A bunch of people came in right around half past nine. There was a kind of wave of latecomers; I signed in about a dozen people in about two minutes. I didn't know any of them—they said their names or whether they were a plus-one for a named guest, I ticked them off the way Jerry showed me, I gave them their backstage sticker, and that's all."

"What about Perry Dillon's plus-one?" His voice was chilly, smooth, insinuating. "Did you check his plus-one in?"

There was a moment of silence. It went on half a heartbeat too long. *Shit.*

"I don't know." Was that a faint sheen of perspiration around her hairline? I swallowed hard, and waited. "I didn't know any of the people I checked in. I told you that. So I don't know. I may have. I can't be sure."

"You don't know." Blood in the water, oh Christ. He was scenting it, and it was Bree's blood. "This guy was proposing to smear the story of your mother's trouble with her clinic, and your boyfriend getting booted out of the U.S., not to mention his being in a hotel room with an underage girl and your narcotics involvement, all over the book review page of the *New York Times*. And you don't know if one of the people you gave access to said they were Perry Dillon's plus-one? You know, I find that hard to believe."

"That's enough." Blessedly, Jameson finally spoke up, and this time, she let him. "My client has answered your questions, Lieutenant. She's perfectly willing to cooperate with you, but the tone is unacceptable. She hasn't had any sleep for the past thirty-six hours, and her husband's band is at the beginning of a North American tour—"

"He's not my husband," she said, too fast, too loud. "I need some sleep, and some food, too. Is there any reason I can't go do either of those things?"

"Sorry you object to the tone of my questions," Ormand told Jameson. "I have one more question I want to ask Ms. Godwin, if you don't mind. It's a question we're asking everyone, so don't accuse me of bullying your client, okay? Where were you between nine and noon this morning, Ms. Godwin?"

"Out walking. From our hotel—that's on West Fifty-ninth—down Fifth Avenue, all the way to Herald Square, and back again." She stared at him, clearly bewildered. "Why? What happened this morning?"

"Someone broke into Perry Dillon's apartment, over on the East Side." I couldn't tell whether or not he believed her. "Ransacked the place. I don't know what they wanted so bad, but we'd already located the apartment and been there a few hours earlier. Whatever they were looking for, I don't think they found it."

CHAPTER SIX

By the time we got back to the hotel, the story had exploded. We walked into a complete media zoo.

We'd ridden back from the police station in nearly total silence. I wouldn't have talked about it in a taxi anyway, since it was hardly a discussion for any ears but our own. The thing is, I was beginning to realise just how hobbled I was by that promise I'd made, not to press her. I'd given that promise and I was going to stand by it. But I'd given it before I knew where she'd been while I was onstage, wondering why she wasn't there.

And Bree hadn't been straight with me. I'd known she was hiding something, I'd said so, and she'd offered me one choice: to trust her, or not. Right, so I'd said, *Yeah, I trust you*—and now I was stuck. Because if I'd thought she was hiding something before, I damned well knew it now. There was no chance in hell she wouldn't remember someone, even a total stranger, telling her that they were Perry Dillon's plus-one.

I knew it. And so did Lieutenant Ormand, Homicide, of the NYPD.

Bree was absolutely quiet on the ride back. I reached out and got hold of her hand, and held it; she turned and smiled at me then, but she stayed quiet, not a word.

I got the driver to let us out half a block from the hotel. Looking west, I'd spotted some harassed-looking traffic cops outside the hotel, arm-waving and head-shaking, having what looked to be pointed conversations with an assortment of union types. Along the curb on the north side of the street, where the fancy horse-drawn carriages and their drivers usually hang out, I saw a line of satellite uplink trucks from the television news outlets. There were at least a dozen of the damned things.

"Shit!" Bree was behind me, wincing. I heard panic in her voice. "John—"

"Yeah, I know. Looks like the media's got it. Half the country's probably looking at streamers across the bottom of their tellies right now: *Murder at Madison Square Garden!* Damn."

She said nothing. She was too busy staring out at the sea of media. She looked to be on the edge of a complete meltdown. It was time for me to step up.

"Look, love, tell you what—I'll go in first, see if I can draw some attention. You wait a couple of minutes, okay? Then slip in, get upstairs. Maybe no one will notice. Got your room key?"

She nodded, and I kissed her. The hard hug I got surprised me a bit—she didn't seem to want to let go for a moment. When she did, I grinned at her. "Right. Off I go."

In a way, even though I got lucky, the deal in the hotel lobby was a smack to the ego. Yeah, there were a lot of people, journalists, photographers, people with press cred dangling off their necks. There were even a couple of people I suspected were fans; our security people were all over the place as well, and once they noticed the stragglers, they'd be turfed straight out.

But no one paid me any attention at all, and no one was going to notice Bree. The crowd in the lobby was actually spillover, the ones who hadn't been able to cram into the conference room off the hotel's business center. That seemed to be where the action was.

I'm not a tall bloke, so seeing around some of the heads was iffy, and I didn't really want to draw attention by elbowing my way in. But I did manage to get to the door, and got a good look inside.

There was a long podium set up at the back of the room. Ian, Carla, and some bloke I didn't know but who looked very lawyerish were surrounding Mac. Mac had a mic on the table in front of him; the lawyer-looking bloke was going back and forth between looking approving and looking paranoid. If I guessed right, Carla was kicking Mac under the table when he got too close to a wrong answer or a dangerous comment.

I glanced back through the crowd. Bree should have got inside and upstairs by now. I'd forgotten to remind her to order us some food; the tea and little bit of breakfast hadn't gone the distance, and I was feeling light-headed and hungry.

". . . affect the rest of your tour?"

The question had come from someone in the middle of the room, and Mac leaned up toward the mic to answer it. I grinned to myself; microphones and Malcolm Sharpe are the ultimate true pairing, a match made in heaven.

No one who's ever seen Blacklight needs me to tell them about Mac. I mean, what's there to say, really? It's like having to explain Princess Diana or JFK or the Beatles—forces of nature, basically. You'd have to have been sequestered in a monastery for thirty years, or out in deep space, not to be aware of them.

A lot of what makes Mac what he is has something to do with what he is physically—that whole thin wiry muscled ball of nonstop energy thing he's got going—and something to do with how he puts himself out to the world. And the phrase, *put out*, that's appropriate. He's a brilliant showman, but I figured out long ago that the whole job requirement—about a rock frontman having to exude sex—that wasn't work for him at all. Some reviewer once said Mac was sex on a stick, natural, hot without thinking twice about it. I'll take her word for it—it sounds right.

And Mac's charisma is so solid, it's as if he's a small planet of his own. He's the only human being I know who can wear leather and spandex at Sunday brunch and carry it off. He's just got that presence. You'd think he's got a gravitational field around him, pulling people in. I've heard him referred to as a cultural icon. I'm not really sure what the hell a cultural icon is or does, you know? But whatever it is, I'm sure Mac would do it well, do it loud, and enjoy every minute of it. A good frontman is born, not made. There's just no way to fake it.

"The tour's going on as planned." If Mac had been up all night, I thought, it hadn't been because he'd been worrying. He has this way of looking at his immediate surroundings and just assuming that if he pays someone else to do a job for him, it's being done and being done properly, and therefore he doesn't have to worry about it. I haven't got a clue how he's reached his middle fifties and still is able to believe that; you'd think all the evidence of incompetence in the world would have clued him in. But he does believe it and he's never been let down, the jammy sod.

Bree was probably safely upstairs by now, and I decided to settle back and watch. After all, I seemed to be completely invisible; no reason not to take advantage of that, yeah? People were yelling questions, a dozen at once. Mac pointed. "Right—second row—oi, is that Will Thompson from the BBC? Cheers, mate! Right—hey, Marian, how's life at CNN treating you? What? Yeah, that's right, Perry Dillon was doing a bio of the band—I hadn't sat down with him yet, though." Carla whispered frantically in his ear. "See, we'd decided to concentrate on the tour, minimise the distractions. . . ."

I watched him for couple of minutes. This was all standard stuff, but Carla—I'd put money on the idea being Carla's—had turfed it out to Mac to handle, and that was a stroke of genius. I mean, serious brilliance, there.

Mac was explaining to the press corps that the New York City police had told them there was no reason to assume the band itself was in any way involved, that the tour was going on as planned, that Blacklight would be playing Boston tomorrow night. He was basically just reading off a prepared statement, maybe ad-libbing now and then. But somehow? He made it sound as if the woman who'd asked the question was his very best friend, or maybe the love of his life, and that he'd spent all morning considering the question so that he could look deep into her eyes and give her the exact answer. What's more, she was falling for it, every word, the "she" in this instance being the entire assembled media presence. He had them all dropping their metaphorical knickers for him. It was beautiful.

No one had noticed me. I slipped out and away, deciding to take a page from Mac's "not my problem, mate" handbook: if Carla and Ian were handling it, I didn't need to worry.

Upstairs, Bree was on the hotel phone. She had her back to me and didn't turn round when I came in. I caught the tail end of what she was saying ". . . yes, of course, I understand . . ." and then she rang off and turned to me. The look on her face stopped me cold.

"Hey." Her smile brought bumps up along my arms; it was totally fake, totally forced. "I ordered some dinner. They're sending it up. There's Perrier in the fridge—you need your afternoon meds—"

"What happened?" I had her by both arms. "Bree, baby, what's wrong? What is it?"

"They want me to stay in New York." She suddenly let go of the force of will that had been holding her upright, and collapsed against me. "They don't want me to leave. Ormand says he doesn't want me leaving the jurisdiction. He seems to think I killed Perry Dillon."

"Yeah, well, you didn't." It was a statement, not a question, and she knew it. She hadn't killed Perry Dillon—the doubts I'd had seemed laughable, in a sick sort of way. Whatever she was hiding, it wasn't that. Bree was a nurturer; if anyone on the planet had reason to know that, I did. And nurturers don't kill people. "He's out of his mind. He's fucking insane. We'll fight it. Where's your lawyer's number? This is his job. Come to think of it, Ormand had no business talking to you. He's supposed to be talking to your lawyer."

"I don't know what to do." She looked at me, and I saw her eyes were blurry with tears. That was like being kicked right over the heart, because Bree doesn't cry in front of me. Hell, it took finding a dead bloke backstage, and me forcing her to break a quarter-century silence and tell me the truth about the worst night of her life, to get her to do that.

Something seemed to have happened inside Bree, thanks to Perry Dillon. I didn't know what it was; I just knew I didn't like it.

Even worse than the tears was what she'd said, about not knowing what to do. That was a killer. Bree always knew what to do; her always knowing, that was the foundation of what we had together. Even when she got it wrong, she was never without a way to deal—Bree always had a starting point.

Just turned seventeen, she'd coped with me ringing her up,

with my overdose; a few months after that, with Blacklight on the second leg of its American tour and me clean as a whistle as part of being allowed back into the States at all, we'd gone to bed together for the first time, and I'd been gone the next day, leaving her to deal, and by God, she'd dealt. A year later, she'd dealt with me, off the narcotics but still drinking and pissed as a rat's nightmare half the time, dealt with me trying to convince U.S. Immigration that I wasn't a hardened criminal and to let me back in, ringing her twice a day, pissing and moaning all over her about Cilla, telling her that me and my wife didn't love each other anymore. Not twenty yet, and there we went again, me living in San Francisco, living with Bree, having the cold horrors, kicking the alcohol. . . .

"Tell me what to do." She had her arms wrapped tight round herself. "I can't think. I'm scared. I don't know what to do."

I was scared shitless, myself. If she'd been secretive, calm, in charge as usual, any of the things that define Bree for me, I'd have found it easy enough to cope. It was weird, understanding that suddenly: her competence made me competent, and without it, I knew fuck-all about how to deal. All these years, drunk or sober, she'd been my strength. I'd relied on her instinctively from moment one, watching her competence with the girl who'd fallen at the Hurricane Felina benefit. I hadn't known, then, that she was hardly more than a baby, and I'd relied on her ever since.

"Right." I took a long breath and tried to get my head together. "You sit. Do a bit of yoga, breathe deep, yeah? You do that and I'll get my meds, and the food should be here in a bit. We both need to eat before we do anything else."

"Okay." She sat, looking up at me, getting her legs tucked up under her. Good. Right. What else?

"Right." I tried to sound as if I knew what I was talking about, tried to sound calm, on top of it. "We'll eat, and then we'll ring your lawyer. It's his job, dealing with Ormand. We're paying these people a shitload of money. This isn't your worry, love. It's theirs. Let them do their job, yeah?"

"Okay. Yes." She closed her eyes, and I saw a tremor run through her shoulders. "I don't want you to leave me here. I don't want to stay in New York alone. I can't, I just can't. I don't want to deal with the media—if they found out I was here alone, I wouldn't be able to leave this room. Wanting to take my picture, shouting questions at me, following me around—oh, God. John, make it better? Please? Fix it for me?"

That tore at my heart. "I will. I swear. We'll do it right after dinner."

When we climbed into bed that night, we'd got official permission for Bree to make the trip to Boston.

Her lawyer, tracked down at dinner somewhere, had done his job. I'd suspected he might have a few choice things to say about Ormand trying an end run with Bree, and I'd been right. He'd rung back in under an hour, to tell us that Bree was cleared to travel, on the understanding that the law firm had guaranteed her full cooperation and immediate return to New York, if the police legitimately wanted her.

It was a huge load off my mind, but the sense of relief lasted only as long as it took for me to register that we hadn't got Bree clear of anything. And since I'd promised to not press her, and she wasn't volunteering anything in the way of information, there wasn't much to do. It looked to be a long, strange evening, locked up in the suite; neither of us felt like watching a movie— Perry Dillon's murder cast too big and dark a shadow to make light, mindless stuff feasible.

But Bree surprised me. When she'd finished packing for the road, I noticed she'd left out those pale blue high heels.

"Oi." I jerked my head at them. "You're not wearing those out to the airport, are you?"

"Nope." She picked them up and dangled them from one finger by the straps. "I was thinking I'd wear them tonight."

"What do you—? Ah." Her eyes had gone that deep green. Maybe a long evening coming up and maybe a strange one, but it didn't look to be boring, after all. And considering Bree's ability to shut out the world when it comes to the bedroom . . .

I pulled her down to me and got a hand inside her blouse. She arched her back at me and made a noise at the back of her throat. "So," I asked her, "what are you planning to wear them with?"

"You." She tossed the shoes on the bed and reached for the buttons on my shirt. "I don't want anything on me tonight except you and my Jimmy Choos."

I think something got into Bree that night—right, bad pun. But it felt almost as if the situation had given her something, some kind of impetus—I tasted her and she tasted new and different somehow; she was sweet and salty but there was something else there. I think, now, it might have been desperation. Whatever it was, it pulled up something in me, something I'd forgotten I had and have no name for, and we just kept responding to each other. Bloody amazing night.

She fell asleep at about eleven, finally, just made a contented little noise, gave me a blinding smile, and passed out cold. Considering the day she'd had—no sleep, emotional cock-up on my part at the crack of dawn, long walk, confrontation with Ormand, and now, apparently, more orgasms than I could count—it was no surprise. I hoped she wouldn't have bad dreams.

I lay awake for a good long while, listening to muscles talking to each other. If she'd been using sex as a distraction or as comfort, she'd done a brilliant job of it. She'd not only knocked herself out, but she'd also given me the sort of workout I hadn't had in years. Maybe fear had put that jagged edge on the sex?

After a bit, I dozed off as well. But as I slid down into the rest of the night, I found myself remembering the first time we'd come together, so many years ago.

In March 1980, Blacklight hit North America for the second wave of the tour, and this time, I came without Cilla.

It was unnerving, really, how different things felt between us. I think I knew, the minute I got off the plane at Heathrow and realised she wasn't there to meet me, that we were done.

In London, I'd gone straight from the airport into a pricey drug-therapy treatment, in a private clinic—hadn't even stopped at our house in North London first. I don't really want to get into the treatment, just that it was no fun at all; it was tough as hell, and it worked because I wanted it to. I stayed there the full thirty-plus days the treatment took. I was committed to getting off the stuff, and it had nothing to do with morals. The way I saw it, it was dead simple: I owed it to Blacklight to be there when they hit the States for the next part of the tour. Unless I could prove to the people in charge of stamping an entry visa on my passport that I wasn't going to be sucking down cocaine or buying nickel bags of heroin on street corners, I was screwing the band, and that was unacceptable to me.

There was also the little matter of not wanting to die. The two days after I'd come out of the overdose and detox had been spent waiting to be deported back to the U.K. And those two days, they'd been the worst two days of my life up to that point. I was cold turkey, nothing at all, letting the shit flush out of my system; they'd mentioned methadone and I'd turned them down flat. The way I understood it, methadone was just as addictive as the drug it was supposed to wean you away from.

While I was going cold, my brain had time to get itself working again and focus, but all it seemed to want to do was to focus on Bree, who'd apparently shown up at the Saturn Hotel with drugs for me, and who was now in deep shit because of it.

No one would let me talk to her—no one would even tell me what was happening. I had no connection to her, legal or otherwise, and I had no grounds to insist.

So there I was, stuck and shut away. I was in bed, weaker than cheap beer, unable to do anything, and as soon as I could travel, they turfed me out of the U.S. and back to the U.K. That made the choice to get clean a no-brainer, really.

I hadn't been five minutes out the front door of the drug clinic, certified clean and free of heroin, before I found a phone and rang up Mission Bells, long-distance. I asked about Bree, and I ran head-on into a brick wall of bureaucracy and silence. No one would tell me anything, except that she wasn't volunteering at the clinic anymore. I didn't know where she was, or how to find her. And that need, to find her and put it right, was really strong and getting stronger.

When I got back to our London house in Camden Town, Cilla was there. I hadn't heard a word from her since Seattle, and my feelings about her were going through some tricky changes. She'd known full well about the overdose and the bust—the London papers had carried it, and besides, she'd been notified because she was my wife, and they'd thought I might die.

But she hadn't come, and she hadn't rung. She'd acted as if I didn't exist. Bit of a difference from Bree; apparently, all I'd had to do was ring Bree and there she'd been. Cilla, my own wife, had done nothing at all.

I was really gobsmacked by the change in her. Cilla was always more about angles than she was about curves—she's got one of those wiry skinny little bodies, small bones and no extra flesh anywhere. She'd always seemed like this elegant little bundle of kinetic energy. But now, she just looked sick—wasted sick, almost as if she hadn't eaten since the last time I saw her. It was a very weird effect, the skin looking stretched too tight but also as if it wanted to sag free from her bones. She looked ten years older. And she couldn't seem to finish a conversation or even a sentence, for that matter.

We spent a really creepy week barely speaking, but then, we didn't have a lot to say to each other right then, either. I was home, it was my house, but walking through that front door, I just felt completely lost and alien, out of sync. Everything I touched felt different and wrong: the dishes, the furniture, the bed. Especially the bed.

I slept on the sofa after the first few nights, and Cilla never said a word. I felt as if the woman I'd loved enough to marry had been replaced with someone else entirely. It wasn't until I was rummaging around for clean towels on our big pantry shelves and found her works, hidden under a pile of bed linens, that the penny dropped. Next to the works was a scary quantity of what could have been either straight coke or snowball.

Whichever it was, I couldn't stay there. I couldn't be in the house with it. I was out of there and out of London, with enough of my clothes to get by with and all my guitars and without a confrontation, before the sun went down that night.

I felt a complete idiot—I hadn't stopped to think that she might not only still be using, but keeping it in the house as well. Yeah, right, that was all I bloody needed. If I wanted to make absolutely certain that the United States immigration people never let me get off a plane inside their borders again, that would have done it.

I stayed out in the country, down in Kent, at Luke Hedley's place. He and Viv—Solange's mum, but Solange was a few years away, yet—had a guesthouse, and they let me have it without a single question asked, bless them. It was probably the best thing that could have happened to me right then, being buried out in the country, because it meant there were no distractions, no temptations. I just lay back and rested.

I did a lot of thinking during that time, trying to sort it all out. My feelings for Cilla were all twisted up, but they were still there. Never mind the seeming stranger I'd found back in London: the Cilla I'd married was in my blood as well as in my house, and so far as I could tell, she wasn't planning on vacating either location any time soon.

But there was also Bree at the back of all this, and I couldn't get her out of my head, either, not what she'd tried to do for me, not her fierceness, not the feeling I had that she was going to be important in my life. And at the back of my memory, vivid and clear, was her kiss, the soft hot pressure of her lips, the taste of her tongue, her breath like strawberries.

Right, so I'm just what Dom had called me, a selfish sod who wants cake and frosting and the lot, but I couldn't get either of them out of my system or out of my head, either. And I didn't know what to do about any of it.

I still don't know what kind of flaming hoops our record label had to jump through to get me back into the United States. But we opened the tour in Philadelphia—this was in the days when we did huge stadium shows for second-leg tours, the full rig, a crew of well over a hundred people, seven trucks to carry all the gear. I know, by today's standards it doesn't sound like much, but for back then, it was grand-scale stuff.

This time, the West Coast swing was at the midway point in the schedule, with the tour ending in Chicago; we'd skipped some cities in the first round, Minneapolis and Chicago among them. We were playing the San Francisco gig at Candlestick Park, to a capacity crowd of over sixty thousand people.

I'd been thinking pretty steadily about Bree, remembering, wondering. I still didn't have any ideas about how to get hold of her, but the chance fell right out of the sky and into my lap. Looking back at it, I shouldn't have been surprised: fate, serendipity, karma, same as that first meeting had been. That's been our pattern from the start.

The day before the show, I did a short live interview with the local radio station. It was just a promo, really, with a quick Q&A about the tour and the record, but at the end of it, I suddenly heard my own voice, saying to the DJ, "Hang on—would you mind if I sent a message out, before we go to commercial? Bree, if you're listening, your name's on the guest list tomorrow night. Please come, love. I miss you."

I never asked her whether she'd heard the show or was told about it, or whether her mother knew. All that mattered was, she came.

Half an hour before showtime, I looked up and there she was, alone, watching me. No T-shirt this time—she was in vintage velvet, a deep sapphire blue number with about a hundred buttons down the back of it, with her hair loose all around her, and high heels.

Something different something different something bloody different.

I'd just picked up my guitar and was about to slide the strap over my shoulder when I saw her. Right then, I stopped noticing anyone else in the place, a huge crush of people, and for just a moment, a second, they all ran together into a blur of colour and became a backdrop, the better to show her off to me. She'd basically just kicked the world to the kerb, and she'd done it just by standing there.

There was no time to talk—we were due onstage in just about six minutes, the audience was roaring, and the lights were already flickering. I shoved the guitar into a roadie's hands and cut through that crowd, straight at her.

She stood there, watching me, just waiting. And then I was with her and I'd reached out and the rest of the world was gone, invisible, vanished.

"You're here." I touched her cheek. "You came."

"Of course I did." She smiled at me then, an extraordinary smile, like nothing I'd ever seen before, intimacy and surrender and commitment, everything I'd hoped for, everything I didn't know I needed. "You asked me to."

I said something, God knows what, and pulled her into my arms.

I've got no clue how long that kiss went on, but however long it was, it wasn't long enough. I pulled her up the stairs to the stage and parked her in the wings, babbling a bit, and the lights went down—"*Good evening, San Francisco!*"—and the crowd went fucking nuts and we went onstage and I don't think I've ever played a better gig. I was on fire, and so was the guitar—the rest of the band kept giving me these startled looks, and Luke picked up the heat and went with it. We nearly burned the stage up, trading licks. And Bree was there, never leaving the wings, watching me, waiting for me.

I don't remember any discussion afterwards; I mean, there wasn't anything to discuss, not really. It was inevitable, her spending the night with me, beyond question. I sussed that climbing into a limo with the rest of the band was completely unsuitable, so I grabbed Rick Hilliard and told him to get me a taxi. We went back to the hotel, just Bree and me, and she sat next to me, not touching me. But I thought I could feel her trembling.

And upstairs in my room at the Miyako, there was still no conversation needed. I didn't realise at first how nervous she was; Christ, at that point in time, I thought she was twenty at least, experienced, an adult. But she wasn't passive, not even then. There was a feeling coming from her, that this was all going to be a splendid new adventure, that I was splendid and new and inevitable in her world.

She stood still when I got behind her, and let me undo every one of the tiny covered buttons at the back of her dress. As I got to the last one, she laughed suddenly.

"What's so funny, lady?" I was finding it hard to talk. Her skin, under the blue velvet, was perfect and pale. I touched my tongue to her back, and ran it down the length of her spine, and she arched and whimpered, a noise of complete pleasure. She was curved, and soft, and she reminded me of a cat.

"There's a zipper." Her breath was coming in small unsteady hitches. She lifted her left arm. "You didn't have to unbutton it. See? Down the side. A zipper."

"Fuck the zipper."

I pulled the dress down, a single hard yank, and got my hands round the front, finding those curves and making them all my own. She sagged against me, and I turned her around, and I saw those eyes, the colour of the traffic signals that tell you go, go go go and don't stop. And there she was, and then there we were, and well, if she was scared, she didn't show it. It was as close to perfect as I've ever got.

Between Cilla and the drug rehab, I'd been celibate for a good long while. Things could have been over very quickly, you know? And I know now, she had no touchstone, no experience that would have let her know it should have been any other way. But I took my time, and I made a discovery about her that blows me away to this day, all the way to the evening the two of us, a quarter century later, had just spent in a New York hotel, with a murder investigation on our doorstep.

That first time together, right about the time I thought she'd be too sore to walk the next day, I did something that triggered the sort of reaction I'd heard about, but had never seen. It was astonishing. I propped up on one elbow and watched her face for a few minutes, as she rippled up, then down, a kind of continual cascade. Something about it made me think of music, a perfect flow of notes, up the scale, down the scale, up again. . . .

After a bit, she opened her eyes and tried to focus on me. I stared down at her upturned face. I thought I'd better ask if what I thought had just happened, really had just happened.

"That was—Bree, did you just—?"

"Mmmm. Yes. I think so. I guess so." Her legs were visibly spasming, and her eyes were nearly all pupils, as if every organ she had was gulping for air. She craned her neck, pulling her head off the pillow. "Whatever it was you did, to make that happen—please, could you do that again?"

"You got it," I said, and bent to her, hoping I'd do it properly. I couldn't really parse what I was feeling—awed, bemused, a certain amount of gratified masculine ego. I must have hit the bull's-eye, because there was that few minutes of rippling cascading tremors again.

I was floored. I thought for a moment about Cilla, needing a hefty line of cocaine to work up to anything at all.

"Right." I smoothed auburn hair away from Bree's face. "Bloody hell. What's that, then? Nine? Ten?"

"I wasn't counting." Her eyes were cloudy with pleasure. "But I think way more than that. Could you do that again, please? It feels yummy."

"Let's wait a minute, love, all right?" I could feel myself beaming like an idiot. But I couldn't help it.

"Wait?" She stared up at me. "Why?"

"Because men can't do this, and it's brilliant to watch." I let myself down beside her, cupping one breast, feeling the beginning of another of those effortless cascades. "And you're bloody lovely."

CHAPTER SEVEN

"Good evening, Boston!"

We stood in the wings, me and Luke, waiting for the spots to hit the stage. Looking out into a packed house, sweating and shaking, I listened to the signals my body was sending and, for the first time ever, wondered if I was going to get through the show.

Bree was behind me, in a gauzy black number I hadn't seen before. She leaned over and spoke into my left ear.

"I'll be right here for the whole show, John. Not going any-where until the encore. Do you want me to get you anything?"

"The Fleet Center is proud to present . . ."

"No, nothing. Just you. Be here, yeah? No wandering off."

"Okay."

"Ladies and gentlemen . . ."

I shrugged the guitar strap, trying to ease the pain in my neck and shoulders. Everything hurt. My right hand couldn't tell whether the guitar pick was a hot coal or a lump of ice. Both legs were on the edge of the ataxia I'd got on my walk back to the hotel yesterday morning. And my face was numb, along the right side of the jaw, except when it wasn't, and when it wasn't, it felt as if I was being given a series of pokes with one of those electric shock wands the police use to control nutters during riots. Trigeminal neuralgia, the face thing is called. I hadn't had an episode of it for four years. The timing for this little exacerbation was shit. This was the worst I'd ever had.

". . . *Blacklight!*"

Bree knew, of course. It had come on during the short ride up from New York to Logan Airport, slamming into gear out of nowhere, no warning at all, just wham, bam, here you go, mate, deal with it. Bree'd seen the relapse hit. I would have felt even worse about the look of helplessness on her face if my attention hadn't been pretty well devoted to not screaming in pain.

By the time we'd got to the hotel, she'd gone into full protect mode. I heard her talking at the door to our room, first to Ian and then to a very worried Luke: No soundcheck for me—the band could do what they chose, but I was resting all afternoon. Otherwise, Blacklight could play Boston with one guitarist, and that was that. Her voice was flat and fierce and no one argued with her. I was vaguely aware of Ian, telling Carla to get a press release ready about the exacerbation, in case I couldn't go on that night, and of Bree closing the door.

I rested for a few hours, dozing in and out, waiting for the painkillers to kick in. Bree brought me lunch, soup, so that I wouldn't have to chew—the jaw neuralgia gets triggered by chewing. For the last hour, she pulled up a chair and sat next to the bed, not wanting to risk making anything worse by climbing in beside me. Knowing she was there, knowing she would wake me when it was time to get dressed and go, I let go of worrying for a bit, and was able to sleep.

I played the Boston show on total autopilot, I'm sorry to say; the fans deserved better, but my body was playing Judas on me, and I did the best I could that night. I'm not saying I sucked—just that I didn't have nearly enough to give for that show. I spent the entire gig on the stool. That made it possible to cope at all, and it didn't hurt that Mac seemed to have picked up an extra flash of energy from somewhere, and was dazzling the audience with it. Every once in a while, I'd glance into the wings, and there was Bree, every time, letting me see her, keeping her promise.

The show was a bit shorter that night. We closed the set, came offstage for the breather, went back and did the encore, and this time, when we came off, I managed five steps toward the backstage stairs, and then suddenly, I couldn't walk. My legs weren't unsteady; they'd gone entirely, and there were shooting pains up and down my left arm that hadn't been there an hour ago, and I somehow didn't think the pain had anything to do with the weight of the guitars.

"John? John!"

I suddenly understood: this wasn't the multiple sclerosis. I was clammy with sweat, breathing was damned near impossible, and my left arm was on fire, and so was my chest, and there seemed to be a weight on me. . . .

I don't really remember the next bit at all well. I know Bree was on her knees next to me and then she was on her cell phone. I heard the beep as she punched in three digits, heard her saying two words, clear and urgent, *heart attack*. After that, everything's all messed up in my head.

I was picked up—no idea who, but I smelled a particular peppery scent that meant Luke, so I suppose he was one of the blokes doing the heavy lifting—and carried into a dressing room nearest the door. I remember being vaguely aware of sirens, this weird silence backstage, roadies keeping the press out of the dressing rooms while the paramedics got me onto a gurney and got my vital signs stabilised; one of them tried to move Bree out of the way and I heard Mac, of all people, telling the bloke that Bree was my wife and she was going along to hospital with me. I remember vaguely expecting that Bree would correct him about us being married, the way she'd corrected Ormand, but she didn't. She just climbed into the ambulance.

I was too far out of it to notice a crowd outside, but there must have been. I remember hearing Bree's voice, asking the paramedic where we were going, and the bloke saying something about Mass General, and their cardiac care unit. I remember Bree holding my hand; once I opened my eyes and got her in focus, for just a moment, through the drugs they were feeding me through the IV tube. I tried to ask her what the fuck was going on; I don't think I got any words out, but she understood what I wanted anyway. She leaned over and told me I'd had a heart attack of some sort, but that the paramedics said it wasn't severe and that I was going to be fine. She kissed me, and straightened back up as the ambulance bounced over a pothole, and her face became misty and then it was gone, and that's all I remember about that.

The rest of that night—right. It's got a bizarre sort of acid trip quality about it, moments of lucidity, things I couldn't be sure were real until well after the event, a few things that I could verify in the morning. I missed the really nasty bit, where they'd apparently run some sort of tube into my leg and all the way up, looking for blockages. Turned out they didn't find any—the arteries were nice and clear. Then they told me to lie flat for a bit; they were going to keep a watch because they were feeding me some sort of blood thinner. At that point, I closed my eyes and was basically gone for the rest of the night.

The one thing I do remember was the doctor—he was an

Asian bloke, top of the line, clear and smart and he didn't make the mistake of talking down to me, or to Bree either. The gist of it was, I'd had a minor heart attack, which had felt major instead of minor because it had triggered severe arrhythmia. Of course, the heart attack happening in the middle of an MS exacerbation hadn't made anything easier. And I doubted the stress and associated bullshit that came along with the murder investigation had helped, either.

He had questions about my ongoing treatment for the MS, but I waved him at Bree—I was too weak to deal, too spaced, and I wanted to sleep. He said something about patient privacy regulations. I looked at Bree and then back at the doctor.

"She's my wife," I told him. "She knows all the info. I'll sign whatever, but right now, I've got to get a bit of kip. Just ask her, okay? She knows everything about me. She'll give you what you need."

I drifted off again. Last thing I remember about that part of the night was just before I went under, wondering why Bree's eyes were wet.

When I woke up again, I just lay there for a bit, not saying anything, taking a kind of inventory. My chest had stopped yelling, and so had everything else, except for a sort of distant throb in the leg, where they'd put the tubing. Excellent painkillers had been provided, and were still being provided. In fact, I was stoned off my skull on whatever narcotics they were feeding me—I suspected morphine, from the fuzziness of my nerve endings, but it might have been Demerol. Either way, the drugs were brilliant.

Prying my eyelids all the way open seemed a bit more work than I wanted to do just then, so I kept them at half-mast and looked around until I saw Bree, standing near the door. There was sunlight coming through the window, which meant morning at least, but she was still in the long black gauze dress. For the first time, I noticed the buttons, a long line of them up the back. *Baby's back*, I thought lazily, *dressed in black, silver buttons up and down her back, she's walkin' the dog.* . . .

I just lay there, dizzy as a debutante, wondering why she was standing with her back to me, and then a few words cut through the morphine haze, and I realised she was on the phone.

". . . yeah, well, fuck that." She sounded so fierce, I was a bit sorry for whoever she was on the phone with. "I know I gave my word. That was before John had a heart attack, goddamn it! I am not leaving this hospital until John does, and that's the end of it. And I can't believe you're trying to argue about this."

I opened my mouth and closed it again. Lazy, fuzzy—whatever it was, she'd handle it. I knew that tone of voice.

". . . willing to answer anything he wants to know. I'm not ducking anything. But I'm not leaving this room. Jesus Christ! Are you insane? Only a lunatic would expect me to leave John here, and don't even think about telling me to watch my language. You're supposed to be protecting my interests. . . ."

Something was making its way through the drug haze, a kind of uneasiness. There was a real world out there, and someone wanted Bree to leave me here, and she was telling them to sod off. I thought I should probably say something, let her know I had her back, but speech wasn't an option, not quite yet. It was better to listen.

"So get him up here." She sounded completely uncompromising and beyond argument. "We'll pay for a chopper from New York; we can afford it. Talk to Ian Hendry—Blacklight's road manager. There's a helipad on the roof of the hospital. If Ormand wants to ask me about cell phone records, cool, what fucking ever. But if he wants me, he's coming here."

Silence. I heard myself sigh, and her head whipped around.

"Look, John's awake. I have to go. Just do what I said, will you please? We'll fly him up and he can ask me whatever dumb-ass questions he wants, but I am not leaving John. Talk to Ian Hendry. If Ormand wants me, he's coming here. Tell him what I said, will you? And feel free to tell him why I said it."

She clicked the phone off and hurried over. "John! Baby, are you okay? Does anything hurt? Should I call a nurse?"

"I—" Nothing came out, and I suddenly got it, that my throat was completely dry. I turned my head sideways and she followed my look to the water jug. A few careful mouthfuls as she supported my head, and I could talk again, sort of.

"Feeling better." It was a whisper, but it was there, and my voice was coming back slowly. "Mostly. Dry as a damned bone. Very stoned, too. Been a long time."

She grinned. "The amount of Demerol they socked into you, I'm not surprised. They needed your medical history, and that included the coke and the heroin. They probably figured you'd have a high tolerance. You were supposed to lie flat, not move, while they were watching you—the doctor said six hours. It's been close to ten. I think you're okay."

"Feel floaty. Nice, really." I moved my right arm experimentally, and it worked without pain, so I hooked Bree with it and tried to pull her down. Not a bloody chance; the muscle in the arm might just as well have been steamed pudding, it was so limp. "Perfectly good bed."

"Yeah, right, big talker." She eased herself down beside me, the gauzy dress riding up to her knees. She'd kicked off her shoes, at least. "Or are you just trying to give *me* a heart attack? Misery loves company?"

"No." We were face-to-face. "Company—on the phone. You said Ormand was coming here." I saw her face close down. "Why?"

"He wants to ask me more questions, something about cell phone records. My lawyer actually thought I was going to pack an overnight bag and scurry off to Manhattan, leave you here because some dumb-ass New York detective has a hair up his ass. Not fucking likely."

"Not a dumb-ass." Our faces were only inches apart, but for some reason, I couldn't seem to hold eye contact with her. "Bad move—thinking that. Not dumb. Like glass—smooth. Sharp."

"You're probably right." She nestled up next to me, closer, burying her face against my armpit. Her voice was muffled. "It doesn't matter, really. He can ask whatever he wants. He can't prove I killed Perry Dillon, because I didn't. You can't prove someone did something they didn't do."

"Not—pressing." I stroked her hair. Maybe the drugs were beginning to wear off; I didn't feel quite so floaty anymore. "Promised. Just—here if needed. Was press—told? About the heart attack?"

It took her a moment. "Oh, you mean, Blacklight? Yes, Carla got a release out last night; the *Globe*'s got it, front page, a small box to itself. I don't know whether the band's postponing Philly, or playing it without you—I haven't left this room."

"Explains the dress." I grinned at her. "Buttons. Is there—a zipper?"

She kissed me suddenly, a hard strong kiss. For a moment, I had an odd visual, likely courtesy of the Demerol, that she was trying to breathe her own health and strength into me.

"Bree. Ormand—did you say helicopter?"

"Damned right." She sat up. "We can afford it, John. And after all, I'm reneging on the condition that I make myself available to be there if the cops wanted me. I don't want to piss him off. I'll pay for it out of my own funds—I should have enough in my account to cover it—but I am not leaving this hospital as long as you're in it. What's funny?"

"You. Writing a cheque for a—a chauffeur-copter. Is that—someone at the door, I think."

It was Ian Hendry, looking rather shaken. Bree waved him in.

"Hey, Ian. It's okay—John's awake, just whacked off his gourd on the Demerol. Did my lawyer call you?"

"Um, yeah, he did. He said you wanted a private chopper for that detective in New York—is that right?"

"Yes. Can you handle it? I can write you a cheque—why are you looking at me like that? John, stop laughing, damn it, you'll hurt yourself."

"No worries. Laughing—at you. Bloody lioness." I was feeling a bit stronger, strong enough to sit partly up and get some more water on my own. "Ian—the chopper's doable, yeah? It would help."

"Yeah, no problem—the hospital has a helipad and they're being told it's official business." He was staring at Bree as if he'd never seen her before. In a way, I suppose he hadn't. The woman who'd wanted nothing more than to stay in the shadows of my public life all this time was suddenly front and centre, and there was no way she was going to be able to retreat back into the shadows when this was over, no matter how it played out. I hoped to hell she knew that.

Lieutenant Ormand arrived with true rock and roll flash, in a chartered helicopter that landed him on the rooftop helipad of Mass General Hospital, a few hours later.

I'm not sure what I was expecting. I was worried as hell over it; Bree had said something about cell phone records, and why he wanted to talk to her about her cell phone, I couldn't imagine. And I didn't know whether her demanding he come to her, and sending a chopper for him at enormous expense, was likely to disarm him or just piss him off.

I'd come back a long way from the heart attack already. An hour's worth of tests showed no damage beyond a slight acceleration of the existing murmur, and something the cardio bloke said might be a prolapse, whatever that was. My blood pressure was up, despite all the controlling meds they'd been pumping into me, but some of that had to be stress from the tour itself, and some had to be stress from having my old lady an apparent suspect in the middle of a murder investigation. I mean, bloody hell, of course my pressure was up; I was just surprised the top of my fucking head hadn't blown right off, you know?

I'd asked Bree to get me the local newspaper. The *Boston Globe* is really good, and I wanted to see what they were saying about the progress of the investigation. Unfortunately, I was still too spaced to think about offering up a different reason, and she dug her heels in and refused; I'd just had a heart attack and according to my bossy old lady, reading a newspaper was a damned good way of bringing on another one. If I'd had my wits up and running, I'd have told her I wanted to see what they were saying about the heart attack—that way, I'd have been able to sneak in a look at the murder news. But I was still a bit loopy and was actually honest with her about why I wanted to see it. I never did get a look at the Boston papers.

I hadn't stopped to consider that Bree's lawyer would also insist on being there; he'd come up in the chopper, along with Ormand. If Ormand was impressed, he was making a good job of hiding it; Jameson, on the other hand, was seriously impressed and making a piss-poor job of hiding it.

It's funny, the rock star treatment, and the way some people react to it, you know? After all these years, I take it for granted. It was obviously this bloke's first taste of one of the perks, and he just as obviously dug it.

"Good afternoon, Ms. Godwin." Ormand seemed just as he'd seemed in New York; there was nothing to read on his face or in his voice. He came in, holding a briefcase, with Jameson on one side of him and my heart bloke on the other, and walked straight over to my bedside. "Mr. Kinkaid, sorry to hear about the heart attack. Your doctor basically threatened to have me served up for lunch in the doctor's cafeteria if I upset you. I'll keep it as brief as possible. Are you feeling any better?"

"Oh yeah, much better, ta." I was sitting up and could see myself in the mirror over the dresser. I looked like hell, actually, bags under my eyes, standard issue pajamas, hair messed; but I was in hospital, not onstage in front of fans, and I wasn't worried about impressing anyone. "They're letting me out tomorrow, if all goes well. Good job, too—we've got a gig in Philly Friday night. Sold out the Wachovia Center. I'd like to be back onstage for that." I saw protest forming on Bree's face and shook my head at her. "Don't argue with me, Bree. If the doctor says I can play, I will—I've got an obligation to Blacklight's audience, after all, not to mention an obligation to the rest of the band."

She was silent. I thought I saw a look of approval, very faint, on Ormand's face. Good moment to take advantage of that. "You know, Lieutenant, I hope you don't hold Bree's refusal to leave me to the hospital's tender mercies against her. We had no intention of being obstructive at all—the chopper probably seems a bit high-handed, but . . ."

Ormand grinned at me suddenly. It was a real grin, and suddenly, just for a moment, I found myself liking him. "You want the truth? It was a blast. I used to work drug traffic for DEA, down in Miami—that's where I'm from originally—and we'd have chopper detail sometimes. Up above South Beach, counting the coke dealers' Porsches, watching them scurry all over the city like expensive cockroaches. I miss it. Some days, I could kick myself for moving up north and switching to homicide."

"Miami?" Bree sounded almost cordial. "Blacklight's playing there after Philly. Too bad the questions couldn't have waited a couple of days; you could have had a trip home."

"Ah, yes. Questions." I saw the sudden impassivity on Bree's face, the alertness on her lawyer's face, heard the subtle change in Ormand's tone, and I braced myself.

"So, you told my lawyer you wanted to ask me about my cell phone." Bree's voice was even and unrevealing. "Is that right? I was half out of my mind over John when the call came in, so if I misunderstood, that's why."

"You didn't misunderstand." Ormand glanced around the room and pulled up a chair. "May I? Thank you."

He set the briefcase on the bed beside me, beside Bree. "As part of the continuing investigation, we're been pursuing a few avenues in Perry Dillon's personal life. A very busy and very well-travelled guy, Dillon was. He had apartments in three cities, that we've been able to locate so far. There may be more. If there are, we'll find them."

He pulled a stack of printouts out of the briefcase, and held them. His eyes, dirty-ice hunter's eyes now, were aimed straight at Bree. I had stopped liking him and started remembering the threat he might represent. "But of course," he said, smooth, sharp, "you knew that, Ms. Godwin."

"Um—nope." Her voice was calm, firm. Whatever he thought he had, he had it wrong. I could see it; he was off base. "I didn't know anything of the kind. I don't know which cities he hung out in. Why would you think I did?"

"Because he called you." He was smiling now, and I was silent, my chest thumping, and Jameson had stiffened visibly. "Twice, in fact. Once from his London apartment, once from a cell phone number we traced to him. One call to your house phone, one call to your cell phone. Why was Perry Dillon calling you, Ms. Godwin?"

The silence was frozen. We looked at Bree, all of us. And all I saw on her face was bewilderment.

"I don't understand." It was the truth. Whatever she'd been

127

expecting, it wasn't this—she had no clue what Ormand was talking about. "I've never exchanged one word with Perry Dillon. Perry Dillon called *me*? When, for God's sake? What cell phone number? What are you talking about?"

Ormand's eyes had narrowed. He was concentrating on her; the look was designed to peel away layers, see what was beneath. But there was nothing to peel. She was telling the truth. It was time I spoke up.

"You don't know Bree, Lieutenant." My heart was making a lot of noise; I could hear it in my own ears, thumping off rhythm like an incompetent drummer. But my own voice sounded calm, peaceful, a bit puzzled. It was amazing, that difference between how I felt and how I sounded. "But I do. And you aren't dim. Look at her. Have you really got any doubt she's telling you the truth?"

"Is that your cell phone number?" Ormand shot the question at her and pointed toward the top sheet. "The two calls highlighted in yellow. Look at them, please. The top one was made from the landline in his London flat, about a month ago—that was to your house phone. One, from his cell phone, the morning of the murder, was to your cell phone. Still say you've never spoken with him?"

"I have never spoken with Perry Dillon." Something had happened to Bree's face, to her eyes, to her voice. She was telling the truth, but something was off, something was wrong. Some big dark dangerous tarnished penny had dropped; something had just come together in her head. I could see it. I didn't know if Jameson could see it, or Ormand. I hoped not.

"Would you be willing to take a lie detector test, Ms. Godwin?" There was no sign of friendliness left in Ormand's face. Jameson opened his mouth, but Bree, looking straight at Ormand, shook her head at him.

"Yes," she told Ormand. "I would. But not if I have to leave

John. I wasn't going to do the entire tour, not before this all happened. But he had a heart attack and he's going to insist on finishing the tour, and I know him, Lieutenant. I won't be able to talk him out of it."

She swivelled her head toward me, her hair swinging. Her voice was odd—resigned, but with something behind it. Anger? Exasperation? Bitterness? "Will I, John? Because you've got that whole loyalty thing going on. Loyal to your fans, for instance, even if it kills you. And where you go, there I go. Assuming I'm allowed to, that is."

She swung her head back around toward Ormand. "Am I allowed to, Lieutenant?"

"Are you asking me if you're under arrest? Being detained?"

"If she isn't, I certainly am." Jameson sounded angry. "My client has just offered to take a lie detector test. She has also stated that she is not going to leave Mr. Kinkaid. I believe Mr. Kinkaid's doctor has stated that, if he continues improving at his present rate, he'll be discharged tomorrow. If you want a lie detector test, set it up before then. And tell me right now, are you detaining my client?"

"Not yet, no." Ormand got to his feet. He looked from me to Bree and shook his head. It was as if he was wondering what species we were, or something. "I'll have a statement prepared, for you to sign—have your lawyer look it over first. And I'll have that lie detector test set up for tomorrow morning."

CHAPTER EIGHT

All things considered, heart attack and everything else, I shouldn't have had any time to pick a fight with Bree. Somehow, though, I managed it.

Bree, with Jameson in tow, had gone off to read and sign a sworn statement, about whether or not she'd ever had any conversations with Perry Dillon. I found out later that the statement was admissible evidence in court; there was also a lie detector test, which probably wasn't.

It was her going off without me that led to me picking a fight. I tried to make her wait for me, but I wasn't let out of hospital in time for it. The doctor had told me he'd be down for a final look at ten the next morning, but he didn't show until noon, and I couldn't shake the suspicion that he and Bree had put their heads together and decided hanging out down at the local lockup was something poor old John, with his dodgy heart, had to be protected from.

So there I was, bloody stuck, sitting in bed and fuming. I wanted to get dressed, get out of hospital, be there for Bree, but Bree was gone a couple of hours and by the time the doctor finally showed up and cleared me to go, Bree was back, and my temper was right at the edge of completely shredding.

She didn't seem too worried by the experience, which did surprise me. She said Jameson was damned good at his job; he'd read over the statement, crossed out a few bits that smelled tricky to him, and told Ormand to have it retyped. He looked that one over, approved it, Bree read it over and signed it. When I asked her about the lie detector test, she shrugged.

"They weren't giving me the results," she told me. She was doing a sweep of the hospital room, making sure we hadn't left any personal belongings. "But since they told me I was free to go to Philadelphia, I'm assuming I passed whatever arcane little standard they use for deciding whether I can control my heart rate, or however they figure this stuff out. Actually, I learned a long time ago how to mess up a lie detector test. It's all about the heart rate—if it stays consistent, either up or down, they can't read it. So you either get agitated from the second they plug you in, or you go totally Yoda over it. I went with agitated. I'm betting the results were inconclusive."

"Cool."

She pulled a sock from under the bed and dumped it into the open overnight bag. "I did enjoy pointing out to Ormand that if he was trying to saddle me with covering up that bust when I was seventeen as a motive, he was in for a long, hard ride. Who in their right mind tries to hide something by committing a noisy, high-profile murder? Kind of defeats the object of the exercise, doesn't it?"

"Good point."

"By the way, he said they're going over all of Perry Dillon's interview tapes next." She gave her head a quick toss, and I heard vertebrae in her neck cracking back where they belonged. "I wonder how they do lie detector tests on people like yogis or gurus? I mean, how would you test a Zen master for that kind of thing? They'd ask, did you rob that liquor store, and he'd smile and say something like, 'I am at one with the liquor store, *namaste*,' wouldn't he?"

"Buggered if I know." I was watching her, feeling myself wanting to pick a fight. That mess-up, the doctor showing up late, so I wouldn't be subjected to the rigors of supporting my woman? A bit too convenient. "So is Ormand still on about you making yourself available whenever he decides he wants you? Spreading them for the coppers?"

The words came out with far more bite than I thought they would. She stopped what she was doing and lifted her head to stare at me.

"Wow," she said. "Pissy, much? What the fuck was that in the name of? 'Available when he decides he wants me'? The man is a homicide detective, John. He's not my supersecret boytoy, or anything. I'm his prime suspect, not his love slave." She turned her head away. "And I only spread them for one person. Unlike some people, I find one lover is plenty. More than enough damned work. Are you about ready?"

After that, we didn't say another unnecessary word to each other for the rest of the afternoon; we met the band at the plane, Bree watched me get settled in, and then closed her eyes and pretended to sleep for the short flight to Philadelphia.

The weird thing is, no one seemed to notice. It was as if she could go invisible at will, you know? Just sort of press a button in the cosmos or somewhere, and hey, presto, no one could see her. It was really uncanny.

That's what got me started thinking. See, the Bree I know is a lot of things. She's fierce and too protective of my privacy and my health, she's completely sensual and has a blistering sexuality when that's what's going on, but the one thing she isn't, is the kind of woman who'd want to be invisible by nature.

But there was that whole cosmic button-press thing. I hadn't thought much about it before, but I was now, and I realised, it wasn't natural to her—she'd learned to do it. And I couldn't shake the feeling that, whatever had happened in my dressing room at Madison Square Garden, it had something to do with that facet of Bree.

Domitra had been spot on. Bree wouldn't give a damn about the story of her bust coming out, and she wouldn't be worried about protecting her mum, either. Dr. Miranda Godwin was very well able to look after herself.

Bree would worry only if it affected me. I had no secrets about that incident—it was public record. The only thing that might not be immediately available was the information that I'd been consorting with a seventeen-year-old girl in a hotel room. But I hadn't known her age then. Besides, it was almost thirty years ago now. That motive didn't exist.

So why had she been horrified by the very idea of the bio? Because she had been, from the first moment. And, now I thought about it, her reaction to my slipup with Perry Dillon didn't add up either. Just one day after she'd refused to come to Los Angeles with me because she didn't want to be anywhere near the interview, she'd done a complete turnabout and shrugged off my screwup, as if it didn't matter.

About a month ago.

What had Ormand said? Something about two calls, one to our home phone and one to Bree's cell phone. That first call—what had Ormand said? About a month ago . . .

We hadn't got any calls at all while I was there. We barely use our house phone for anything anymore, anyway; everything's done on the cells, what with all the travel I have to do. Suppose whoever had rung up our house had done it while I was in Los Angeles, staring at Perry Dillon over the conference table in Carla's office? If that was true, one question was answered: Bree had been telling the truth, and it wasn't Perry Dillon who'd rung her up. . . .

All the way in from the airport, checking in at the Ritz-Carlton, I was thinking. I wasn't narked at Bree anymore, although I suspected she was still pretty narked at me. I was deep into it, trying to figure out what the fuck was going on.

Okay. Say someone had rung up Bree at our house. They'd rung from Perry Dillon's apartment—had Ormand said which apartment? I couldn't remember, and it didn't matter. What mattered was that, whoever it was, it hadn't been Perry Dillon, because the little scumbag had been trying to sneak information out of me in Carla's L.A. office. He'd succeeded, too.

That call to Bree's cell phone, the day we'd played the Garden. Ormand had said that one was from a different phone—from Dillon's cell. And later on that night, Dillon—who'd been told, through his representation, that he was officially being barred from all shows on the tour—had been pencilled in for a restricted-access backstage pass.

And he'd been given a plus-one.

And that plus-one had been there, backstage.

And Bree had been there, helpful and competent, bringing the backstage door guard a beer, asking if he'd had his dinner break, offering to take over. He might not have known who she was, but that badge around her neck—the special one, red and green round the edges, laminated and strung from a gold cord—would have told him he could trust her. The badge said BAND, and we gave them only to family, crew, and management. The door bloke, Jerry Rubenstein, would have trusted her. She was family. She had the badge to prove it.

I was beginning to feel a bit sick. I didn't like where this line of thought seemed headed; it all smelled like some sort of collaboration. But Bree wouldn't collaborate with Perry Dillon. So what the fuck was going on?

"Whoa. Those are new."

I jumped. "Jesus! You nearly gave me another heart attack."

"Sorry. I wasn't trying to be stealthy or anything." Bree had come into the bathroom as I unpacked my meds case, and I'd been so deep in thought, I hadn't heard her. She was peering over my shoulder at the two big bottles of pills with the label of the Mass General Pharmacy on them. "Are those pain meds or what? Please tell me those aren't anything highly addictive? Not Percocet or Vicodin?"

"Much lighter weight, actually." She sounded as if she'd got over her mad. I tried to push the questions away to the back of my skull. "Tylenol Three, with codeine—basic TyCo, in case I get more pain in the leg, where they ran that tube. The other one's clonidine—they want me to keep the blood pressure down for a bit. I convinced them that my routine for the next few weeks was going to be a bit more strenuous than most other cardiac-recovery patients."

"You think?" She grinned at me, a real grin, bona fide Bree; she was definitely over the mad. "I'm glad they loaded you up, actually. I called my mom, while they were doing the angiogram—she gave me some info on what they were likely to look for, and she even named a handful of meds they'd probably prescribe. She was right."

"She usually is. I like your mum." I did, too. Miranda never got in anyone's way or in anyone's face, but when it came to support for Bree, she was a rock. Hell, considering what I'd found out about my overdose and Bree's bust, she was a hell of a lot more than that.

A lot of people wandered in and out of our room that night, and I got a surprise: Bree didn't seem interested in pressing the magic button that knocked her off the radar. Ian and Carla stuck their heads in to check on me; Ian was taking Carla out for dinner. The whole band came up together, including Mac with Domitra, and Cal and Stu with their wives. Everyone wanted to make sure I was really well enough to play the next night.

Bree was right there, going over restaurant choices with the rest of us, weighing in on who was likely to provide Cal's wife, Barb, who was doing a vegan thing, with something she could eat. Bree was laughing, answering food questions like the expert she is, just being there. If there were tensions among anyone in the immediate band family, I couldn't see them. All I felt was support, and Bree was right there, in the middle of it.

It was amazing. None of them had spent any time with Bree until now, except Luke, when he'd stayed with us in California after my MS diagnosis. But you'd have thought they'd all been at school with her or shared a nanny when they were in nappies together, or something. She was totally integrated and totally there, no awkwardness. I just couldn't sort it out.

Halfway through dinner, Mac turned to me over a mouthful of something I couldn't pronounce and wasn't eating; he likes spicy foods, Algerian cookery and whatnot. Right then, I was all about bland food, doctor's orders.

"So"—he grinned—"you had to upstage me, did you, Johnny? Steal the show? The Heart Attack Kid? Way to get your photo on the front page of the *Globe*, you tricky bugger!"

Bree snorted. Mac nodded at her. "You're lucky," he told me, and he wasn't grinning anymore. "Bree had it down. She knew what was happening, she called 911, she told them what to expect when they got there. We flipped out, the lot of us—Stu and Luke carried you offstage, Cal was bellowing at the roadies to clear everyone out of the way. No one knew what the hell to do—we were running around backstage like a bunch of fucking doomed headless chickens. And there was your old lady, just handling it. If I ever get sick, I want her around."

He suddenly bent all the way forward, got hold of Bree's hand, and kissed it. "Here's to you, lady. You rock."

He was dead serious. Next to him, Domitra lifted her bottled water toward Bree in a silent salute, what I figured was likely a tribute to competence. "Damned right," Cyn said, and Barb give a hip-hip cheer. Bree turned pale—she doesn't blush, she goes right over the other side of white when she's moved or embarrassed.

The conversation moved on, discussing upcoming shows, mundane things, nothing to upset anyone. Ormand would have been bored to sobs, had he been there, listening in.

So we spent the night before the Philadelphia gig in a pleasant atmosphere, all family and friends. But I knew that those questions, the ones I'd started following down those uncomfortable little alleys, weren't done with me yet.

I think it was Bree's casual mention of having rung up her mum, that whole thing about her being there for Bree, that left me awake for most of the night while Bree slept.

I kept seeing that New York hotel room, me doing what Domitra called my dimwit-or-dick act: walking out when I was most needed. Even as I'd been leaving—what had Dom called it, damned fine passive-aggressive?—I'd known that Bree wasn't going to ask me to stay. And I'd known why.

It's not a memory I like to take out and look at. There's nothing pleasant about it. But it's there, and I had the feeling I wasn't going to be able to get to what was at bottom of Bree's recent behaviour unless I looked at it squarely. There was probably me wanting to prove Domitra wrong in there, as well. After all, no man wants a woman to look him over and make that sort of pronouncement about him, especially when the woman in question could cripple him without breaking a sweat.

So I lay in the dark, staring up at the outlines of the ceiling fixtures—but what I was seeing, really, was a day in April 1981, when I'd got a call on the newly installed phone in the Pacific Heights Victorian I'd bought with Bree at my side six weeks earlier, and heard my wife at the other end, ringing from London, sobbing and terrified and about to go into hospital because she'd been bleeding and it wasn't stopping.

"Right." I glanced up at Bree, who was unpacking a carton from one of the department stores downtown—it was our china, dishes we'd picked out together. "Right. Cilla, look, calm down. What do they think it is? Do the doctors have any guess yet?"

Bree had her back to me, so I didn't get to see the effect of Cilla's name. But she went stiff, rigid, for just a moment. I saw her shoulders tighten up. Then she got up and walked out of the room. I couldn't see her face; I didn't know whether it was anger or jealousy or the sensitivity to give me privacy, or what.

Cilla was completely hysterical. I managed to get a coherent story out of her after a few minutes, but when I finally put the phone down, I closed my eyes and let it sink in.

I was fucked, and I knew it. The gist of it was that they thought she might have ovarian cancer. If that was true, she was likely dead within the year—ovarian cancer is scary stuff, and her mother had died of it. So there was the family history, as well. I hated the idea of her being so frightened. No one should ever be that frightened. And she was alone.

I stood in the big cheerful kitchen, which still smelled very faintly of fresh paint, and waited for it to sink all the way in. I can't say that I weighed what I ought to do, or what I was going to do—there wasn't any choice, not really.

Cilla was my wife. That hadn't changed. She was still my legal wife and she was sick, maybe dying. There was no one else there to help her through it, no family. And she'd just thrown a huge bloody spanner into the works, into my life, by begging me to come back to London and be there with her, while the doctors sorted out what was happening.

Truth is, there was nothing on earth I wanted to do less. I also still had the memory, nice and clear, of the last time I'd seen her. That was something I wasn't likely to forget.

We'd faced each other, that last time, in the big front room of our London house, the house she and I had picked out together and bought after I'd officially joined Blacklight. It's a beautiful house, on a quiet street near Camden Town, in North London. The street, Howard Crescent, is a long lovely curve of Nash houses, gorgeous eighteenth-century digs with tall windows and big gardens at the back.

I'd always thought of it as our sanctuary, me and Cilla, just us, me coming home from the studio or the road and there she'd be. But that day I reached into the pantry shelves for a towel and found her works and the heroin she'd chosen over me, that was the day I'd written off 18 Howard Crescent, NW1. I'd written Cilla off as well.

She knew I was going, and she knew where. We'd had two huge rows over it. That did surprise me, because I honestly didn't think she gave a damn, not anymore. I didn't mention Bree, but then, I didn't have to. As soon as she knew I was headed out to San Francisco, that I'd applied for a resident visa, that I was planning on buying a house there, she'd flipped her shit completely, and things got ugly, fast.

What really surprised me, shocked me even more than the things she'd called Bree during those rows, was how much she knew about Bree, about what I was doing. I didn't stop to wonder how or where she'd got all that gen. I was too busy trying to get my shit together, get the guitars packed and sent, deal with the immigration people.

That second fight—Christ, that had been ugly. The first one, we'd both been stoned, her on whatever it was she was shooting or snorting, me on too much whiskey. Looking back, that probably made the second row inevitable; I was at the *yeah, right, well fuck off* stage of mean-drunk, and I stormed out of the house. Putting off the moment, you know?

But that second row, that put me over the top. I was stone sober; she'd been standing there, shouting at me, and I'd finally had it, enough, no more. I remember feeling, okay, this was it, time to deal with it.

So I'd waited for her to run out of insults and grievances, long enough for her to have to get some air into her lungs, and I'd spoken up.

"Okay. Do you want a divorce?"

That shut her up, all right. Problem was, I hadn't been trying to shut her up. I wanted to know: Was it one more thing I ought to be getting together before I left for San Francisco?

But she looked as if I'd shot her. It was unbelievable—all the colour went out of her face. When blondes go chalky—and yeah, Cilla was a natural blonde—they look half-dead.

"Don't." She whispered it. "Don't say that. Don't you dare say that!"

"What?" I stared at her. "Look, you've got the house. I'm setting up an automatic bank deposit every month—you won't have to take a job or anything. But I'm going. What the fuck is the point of staying married?"

"You're not taking that away from me." She wasn't even blinking, and her pupils were pinpoints, as if she'd been suddenly plunged into darkness and her eyes were starved for light. It totally freaked me out. "You can't. You don't dare. I'm your wife. You're not taking that. That little tart in California's not taking that."

"Cilla, what—?"

"You file for divorce, I'll kill myself."

We'd been eye to eye, looking into each other, and my skin was coming up in gooseflesh. Her voice was absolutely flat.

I knew the truth when I heard it, and she'd meant it. For whatever reason, being rightfully identified as Mrs. JP Kinkaid was still as important to her as it had ever been, even if, as a couple, we were done.

Now, all these months and all these miles down the road, I was still married to her, still her husband. I'd promised to be there in sickness and health. Even though I had no qualms at all about not being there for the health bit, there was no way I could justify not doing what she was asking of me.

I went off in search of Bree.

The house was still new to both of us, still furnished only in spots. We'd trailed around after realtors, checking out all sorts of places, and then, there it was: 2828 Clay Street. We'd looked at the high ceilings with the moulded trim, at the broad curving stairs, at the built-in cabinets made from the sort of wood you can't get anymore, at the enormous kitchen with its big bay window and the garden just beyond, green and fresh.

Once we'd finished looking at all that, we'd looked at each other. A huge smile had broken across Bree's face, and I'd felt myself smiling right back. I don't think either of us smiled as wide as the Realtor did, though. He knew he'd just made a huge commission on the easiest sale of his life. We were home.

That had been just about a month before. Now I was going to have to leave, for the one reason that would upset Bree more than anything else. And I didn't have a clue for how long.

I found her upstairs, in our bedroom. I love the master bedroom; it's got two enormous bays overlooking the garden, with window seats, and over the years, our parade of cats has always colonised the cushions and slept there. At that point, the only things in the bedroom were our king-size bed and a rocking chair. She was sitting in the rocking chair, with her hands in her lap, woven together tight. She hadn't turned any lights on, and it was blustery outside, rain streaking the big windows.

I felt my stomach do a sort of slow twist. She looked so bloody young, sitting there; she *was* young, still eighteen for another couple of months. The girl I'd turned to for help, the tough, tender young woman I'd taken to bed not knowing how young she was—the truth was, she was as downy as a baby bird.

This was going to hurt her, maybe beyond fixing. And there was fuck-all I could do to prevent it.

"That was Cilla." I stopped.

She looked up at me. She didn't have the hard control she'd learn later on, after two more afternoons like this one—not yet. Her face—oh, God. Bad stuff there: dread, pain, fear, things that aren't supposed to sit on an eighteen-year-old's face. There was no hope in that look she gave me, none at all.

I breathed deep. My own voice was a bit unsteady. "She's sick."

"What . . ." Her throat sounded swollen, closed. She tried again. "What's wrong with her?"

"Something about nonstop bleeding. The thing is, her mum died from ovarian cancer."

Bree closed her eyes. When she opened them again, I found the word I'd been missing, the one that matched the look on her face, in her eyes: bleak.

"You're going back to London." It was a statement, not a question. She knew; she got it, even that young, that there was nothing else I could do. "To—to be with her. That's what she asked you for. Isn't it?"

I nodded. She blinked, hard.

"Don't." It was a whisper, barely audible. "Don't go. Don't do this. Please?"

"I don't want to. Christ, Bree, don't you know that? But she's my wife. And she's sick."

"She wasn't there for you." Bree was pleading with me now, urgent, reasoning, bargaining. There was nothing to bargain for, but she was too young to know that. There were tears on her cheeks; they shocked me, because I'd already come to understand that Bree had no more taste for cheap tears than she had for meaningless hugs or polite social smiles.

"She never even called to see how you were after you OD'd. She never came to see you after you got back to London. You told me. If she's still your wife, aren't you her husband? Why wasn't she there for you? Why do you have to wreck everything, thinking you owe her? How about her owing you? Isn't it supposed to work both ways, that loyalty thing?"

The words were pouring out of her now, urgent, desperate, and they hurt. I honestly hadn't known, before, that words could bruise this way. It was a nightmare. Any minute, I thought, if I was lucky, I would wake up screaming.

"Loyalty's supposed to work that way, yeah." I heard my own voice, awful, gentle, completely final. I saw her hear it, register it, stop hoping. It wasn't a nightmare; it was life, taking yet another bite out of our arses. "But sometimes it doesn't. And her not living up to her vows, that doesn't excuse me from living up to mine. Does it?"

She tried, one last time. She had to know it was hopeless, but she tried. Pleading, begging, doesn't come naturally to her. But she was begging me now.

"Please, John." She forced the words out. "Don't do this to me. Don't do this to us. We're too—we're so *new*. Please?"

I'd never forgotten that, not one moment of it. That afternoon, in our bedroom on Clay Street, that's my touchstone for the essential unfairness of life on earth. Moments when I think life's handed me the worst it can possibly dish out, that one always trumps whatever's just happened. It was why, on the day I was shown the MRI results, with the brain lesions that proved I had MS, I was the one who had to gather a sobbing hysterical Bree into my arms and comfort her, even though the diagnosis was mine. Nothing I ever had to do was as hard as the back and forth with Bree, that day Cilla rang.

I'd love to think Bree doesn't remember how she begged me not to go. I'd love to think she'd forgot what I said and did. But that's rubbish. I remember exactly what I said, and what I did. So does she. Neither of us is likely to ever forget it.

"Cilla's my wife," I told her. "I put a ring on her finger. I made her a promise. She's sick, she's in pain, she's scared. I'll be back as soon as I can."

It would be nearly seven months before I'd see San Francisco again.

For the first month, there were tests, something about an ovarian polyp that might be cancerous, procedures, biopsies. I loathed every minute of it, and was shocked at the change in her; she'd gone from slender to severely underweight, and she admitted to me—she'd had to admit it to her surgeons—that she had settled into a routine of heavy heroin use, cut with the occasional afternoon of freebasing.

So the surgery had to wait. The doctors were adamant about getting her clean and detoxed, since anything they tried to do in the way of surgery would have been affected by the strain the drug use had put on her heart.

The worst moment came the day I heard a scream from the kitchen. I put down the guitar I'd been playing and went in to see what was happening, and found Cilla collapsed on the floor, writhing in agony in a pool of her own blood. Whatever that thing inside was, it had ruptured. We'd got an ambulance and gone roaring off to the casualty ward, and when they'd bustled her indoors, the woman taking down the information turned to me.

"Pardon me," she'd said. "As Mrs. Kinkaid's husband, we'll need you to fill out these forms." She'd given me a smile, very kind, and added, "Not to worry—we'll look after her for you."

I'd taken the stack of papers and gone off to sit down. It didn't take me two minutes to realise that I couldn't answer anything. They wanted to know about her eating habits, drinking habits, drug habits, sexual habits—I think I knew the answers to three of the forty or fifty questions they had, and even those were guesses. What in God's name was I doing here?

They'd got the thing out—one of the doctors came out and told me they'd removed a "ruptured unidentified mass," and they were sending it off to be biopsied. More questions about Cilla that I couldn't answer.

Up to her room, so that she wouldn't be alone when she woke up. The sense I had, when I finally got to leave the hospital and go back to the house I'd come to hate, was that I was escaping from something, on borrowed time.

I'd rung home—what I felt was home—and instead of Bree, I'd got Miranda. She was chilly with me, remote; Bree was in class, at the culinary academy, and how was my wife doing? I'd broken down into a soggy mess, telling Miranda what was going on, hoping for a word of reassurance about anything at all, begging her to tell Bree that I missed her, that I'd be home as soon as I could. I don't know, to this day, whether she ever passed any of that on to Bree.

The biopsy came back positive. The thing was malignant, but it wasn't standard, not your basic ovarian cancer, whatever the hell that was. It seemed to be completely contained, but they didn't want to take any chances on it metastasising, not with Cilla's family history. An emergency hysterectomy needed to be done, but the doctors seemed to agree that, with Cilla firmly entrenched in heroin use, there was a good possibility the surgery would result in a stroke or something. I wasn't clear on what they were worrying about. I wasn't clear on anything, except that I really wanted a good stiff drink most of the time, because getting through the situation with nothing at all was eating me alive.

They slapped Cilla into drug therapy, a highly experimental and potentially toxic version of it; they needed to get her in for surgery and they needed it to happen soon. She was alone, not allowed visitors; the treatment took another three weeks, and then straight into surgery.

The entire time she was being dragged forcibly off her heroin and coke habit, I was indulging in my own alcohol habit, and I was doing it too hard and too often. It felt like the only way to get through, most days; my mates in Blacklight were there for me, but that was tricky as well, since Cal had just stopped drinking himself. It's not good to hang with someone whose entire concentration is fixed on not drinking, not when the only thing getting you through most days is staying sozzled.

So the solidarity I could have had from my mates, that became just one more fine line I had to walk, not letting them know how much I was drinking. In the end, the only way to deal was to not let them know I was drinking at all.

I did put the bottle down, for a while at least, because I had to. Cilla came out of the surgery in a state of complete despair. I'd never seen anything like it, not before, not since; this was the bleakest deepest clinical depression imaginable. She was listless, lifeless, withdrawn, bordering on fugue state or semicatatonic.

There was no physical reason for it, not that they could find. They didn't know so much about things like serotonin or the effects of hormones on balances, as they do now; they didn't connect the drug withdrawal and the shift in hormones with her reaction either, or if they did, they weren't telling me.

And there was no communicating with her. I could talk to her—they wanted me to do a lot of that, and it was pure hell, because I had nothing to say—and all I'd get back was a long empty stare. It could have been unreadable; it could have been blank. I just knew it made me feel invisible. It didn't seem to do her any good, either.

I was stuck. Cilla wasn't sick enough to stay in hospital; that meant taking her out and taking her home. All this time, dealing with it, trying to get her to eat, making sure she took her meds, taking her to physical therapy sessions, occasionally feeling her eyes on me and turning to find them expressionless and uncaring, I was remembering what I'd said to Bree: *Loyalty's supposed to work that way. But sometimes it doesn't.*

It was another four months before she began to come out of it, four months when I thought I had lost Bree, would lose my mind, would never be able to sleep in a bed I considered my own again. I avoided ringing San Francisco. Looking back now, I could kick myself for that—it probably hurt Bree more than anything else I did, or didn't do. But I remembered how cool and detached Miranda had been, and I was afraid I would lose it completely if I got Bree on the phone and heard that same chilly remote tone in her voice.

After four months, Cilla'd recovered enough to get about on her own, and she was beginning to deal with the world again. I was able to spend time in the studio with Blacklight, rehearsing new material, mostly with Stu and Cal, for what would become our *Partly Possible* album. I got good and close to my bandmates during those months. If they guessed that I was back drinking, they never said so.

In the end, my way out came in a way I'd never expected.

It was just past Guy Fawkes, bonfire night in London—I remember that. Cold, chilly day, that sort of seasonal London rain that goes straight through your clothes, into your joints. I was hungover, aching everywhere, and my back was giving me some problems. A few hours in the studio that day was all I could deal with; luckily, Luke had stuff he wanted to work out with Mac, and the session broke up a good two hours before I'd thought I could head out.

I took a taxi back to Camden Town and let myself into the house, thinking about something hot to eat and cold to drink. I remember feeling chilled to the bone.

I also remember pushing open the swinging doors that led

into the kitchen. The house was perfectly quiet. It was so quiet, I remember wondering if Cilla was even home.

She was home, all right. She was sitting there, at the kitchen table.

"Oh." She looked up at me, no curiosity, not giving a damn one way or another. There was a curl of smoke coming from the crack pipe in her hand. "You're back early."

I was on the phone to Bree within about two minutes. I woke her up; I was so frazzled, I'd completely spaced on the eight-hour time difference. I'd been gone for nearly seven months.

"Bree?" My hands were shaking. So was my voice.

"John." She sounded wide awake within seconds; she's always been very catlike that way, she just wakes up. But she sounded cautious, too. I suppose I hadn't given her much reason to expect that the sound of my voice at the other end of the phone was going to bring much joy into her life. "What?"

"Can you leave the light on for me?" I glanced at the closed door. Cilla hadn't stopped what she was doing long enough to follow me out. The freebasing apparently had all her attention. "Please?"

She was quiet a moment. I'd missed her birthday; the day she turned nineteen, I'd been trying to fill out forms, trying to answer questions for Cilla's doctors, questions I had no way to answer because she'd become a stranger. I wondered how much growing up Bree had done without me. I wondered if she knew what I was asking, if she knew I understood that it was my turn to beg: *Please, can I come home?*

"That light's always on," she told me. "It's always burning. I have no idea how to turn it off."

CHAPTER NINE

The morning after the Philly gig, the hotel phone rang. It was Lieutenant Ormand on the line, and this time, it wasn't Bree he wanted. It was me.

I'm not sure whether he didn't know much about the hours working musicians keep, or whether he was just being an evil bastard. But when I opened one eye and saw the digital alarm clock next to me, I said something loud and rude. It was ten past nine in the morning.

"Gordon *Bennett!*" I'd picked up the phone without even realising it. I was going to raise some serious hell with the hotel management; we had a standing policy with every hotel, part of the booking, that the desk wasn't supposed to put any calls through before ten. "What the *fuck?* . . ."

"Mr. Kinkaid?" Recognising the voice didn't do anything to improve my attitude. "This is Lieutenant Ormand."

"Yeah, I already sussed that, ta. Hang on a minute."

Bree was awake—she swung her legs over the side of the bed and padded off toward the loo. I spent a moment letting Ormand wait and sleepily admired the rear view, since she sleeps nude. I got my own legs over the side, wincing at the usual morning pins and needles, and headed to the door to get the morning paper. They seemed to be offering up *USA Today*.

"You know, we played a show last night." I'd got back into bed, the paper unfolded on the nightstand. "That's two and a half hours of live music, for your information—very hard work. We didn't get to bed until three. I'm just out of hospital, getting over a heart attack. And—oh, right—it's nine o'clock in the bloody morning." I started a yawn, swallowed wrong, nearly choked, and decided a scapegoat was in order. "Are you insane? You'd better have one really good reason for ringing me up this early."

"Sorry." He didn't sound sorry. Bree came back with my pills and a glass of water. "I do have a very good reason. I want to ask you about something, and I didn't know when you were due to leave Philadelphia."

"Not until tomorrow afternoon sometime." I swallowed pills. "The Miami show is Sunday night. What's so important that you couldn't wait for a civilised time of day to wake me up?"

"We've been listening to Perry Dillon's existing tapes for the Blacklight history he was working on." Ormand, for some reason, didn't sound quite so smooth or sharp today. Maybe he'd been up late himself. "There are some things in here I want to go over with you. And I think your lawyer might want to be along for this."

"What, you mean you want me to come to New York?" Bree had gone back into the bathroom; I could hear the shower running. She rarely did that without a cup of coffee first, so her doing the shower straight off was a sure sign she knew something was up, that she might have to throw clothes on and grab a coffee on the way out the front door. "Today, you mean?"

"That would be best, yes." He hesitated. "I really do appreciate your cooperation, Mr. Kinkaid. I know none of this is easy, especially in the middle of your band's tour."

"Right. Well. I'll ring up my lawyer and my publicist and see about booking a flight up. But I need to get back tonight; we've got some press thing in the morning." It was my turn to hesitate. "Look, do I need to drag poor Bree along for this?"

"I don't think so. These are questions you can answer for me better than Ms. Godwin can. I don't think I need her for anything, not at this juncture."

"Okay." Right, I thought, get him off the phone, check the paper while Bree's washing off. "I'll ring you back, let you know when I'm getting there."

USA Today had their bit on the Dillon investigation on page three. It wasn't much, no hard news and no mention at all of Bree by name. I scanned it as quickly as I could:

"... source at NYPD told us that one promising avenue of investigation was Dillon's cell phone records."

Something jumped a bit in me, and then settled down again. Right. It wasn't specific—there was nothing in there to link anything to Bree. A bit farther down, there was a line about Mac's recent brush with the supposedly pregnant girl and her noisy threatening boyfriend. Nothing new, nothing with any substance to it, and nothing at all to give me a clue what Ormand needed from me.

I heard the shower turn off, folded the paper back up, and slid it out of sight. I wasn't up for asking myself why I was hiding my need for information from Bree, not right then.

There wasn't any hiding Ormand's request for my presence from her, though. Needless to say, she threw a fit. As I thought, she'd sussed something was up; she hadn't even got out of the wet towel before demanding to know who'd rung so early. When she heard I was thinking of a quick day trip to Manhattan without her, she went ballistic.

"Without me? You were planning on doing this and leaving me here? Just out of the hospital and it's a murder case and you were just going to scoot on down to Manhattan to party hearty with the law, and leave me here?" She had her hands on her hips, glaring at me. Her feet were bare, planted about two feet apart; the whole stance made her look like a girly prizefighter or something. "Oh, dream the hell *on*, little man."

She only ever uses that phrase—which I bloody hate, and she knows it—when she's serious about digging her heels in. For about a tenth of a second, I debated with myself over whether the argument would be worth the time or the grief. No. No, it wouldn't. Not if she was using "little man." This one was a lost cause before I ever got started. Better to bring her along with me. There were always shoe shops, after all.

"Right. I give." I threw my hands up. "Then make yourself useful, call Carla, and tell her to book you a ticket, as well. And hurry up, because I really don't want to be there longer than a few hours."

She dropped the towel and made a beeline for the closet. I spared a moment to regret the good old days, when naked Bree within ten feet of the bed in the morning meant an entirely different outcome than her rummaging around for her clothes.

"Bree."

She was pulling on a pair of lace knickers. "What?"

"You do realise, love, you aren't coming to see Ormand with me, right? This one's just me and Pasquini. Invite only. You're not on the guest list."

I was braced for an argument, but she just nodded. "No, that's fine. I'll hit Henri Bendel, on Fifth Avenue—I saw an incredible pair of heels in the window, when I walked down that way Saturday morning—" She stopped, biting off the rest of the sentence. "Anyway. I just want to be in New York if that's where you're going to be. I want to be close enough to be useful, if by any sorry chance you happen to need me for anything. Because I'm a flappy old mother hen, and you're one day out of the hospital. That's the way it is. Deal with it."

She pulled on black jeans and zipped them up. Out of nowhere, I suddenly saw Bree as I'd seen her that first time, at the Hurricane Felina benefit. She'd worn black trousers then, as well. We'd come a long way, the pair of us, and now she was standing there, legs just as long as they'd ever been, hair fading to that pinkish grey that auburn hair goes over time, and instead of a T-shirt, she was naked above the waist. And I got to be here. I had a moment of pure gratitude and I wasn't sure why.

Pasquini was waiting for me when I got to Ormand's office. If he was bothered by the short notice of the call, he wasn't showing it. Besides, since I'd been onstage at the time Perry Dillon got bashed, it wasn't as if I was in any danger. His workload wasn't likely to amount to much.

"Afternoon." Ormand had a portable CD player on his desk, with speakers attached. "Mr. Kinkaid, thanks again for being so cooperative."

"No problem." I sat down, Pasquini at my left elbow. "What is it you want me to listen to?"

"Tapes. Segments, excerpts. They all seem to be Dillon himself, recording facts or rumours or gossip so that he could refer back to them. Problem is, he doesn't say, anywhere at all, where he got any of this stuff. Some of it's pretty intense. We've asked the London metropolitan people to take a look for us, at Dillon's flat—see if there's any sign of other CDs, tapes, anything at all that might get us the names of his sources."

I nodded, and he looked from me to Pasquini. "I was hoping

I could play some excerpts and see if anything here could have come from only one source, a source we could identify and go talk to. It would save a lot of digging."

"You mean, if something he recorded was true, but that wasn't public knowledge?" It was a brilliant idea. "Hell, yeah, I can see how narrowing it down might be a huge help." I looked at Pasquini. "Any good reason I shouldn't?"

"No, none at all." My lawyer was nodding his approval.

The first bit of the CD, Perry Dillon's voice drawling out of the little speakers, not only set the tone, it blew my mind.

". . . 1972, Surrey, Malcolm Sharpe caught with underage girl, daughter of the local Tory MP. Completely hushed up, no charges filed—they were having a naked swim together in her father's pool. Alcohol and pot found on the premises, no hard drugs. Girl's first name was Trina, now Lady Coomberleigh. Note, check around with the people who lived in the adjoining houses for confirmation or denial. . . ."

My jaw had gone slack. Where the hell had he got his hands on that little nugget? I'd heard about the incident third-hand, since it happened years before I joined Blacklight, but the girl had grown up and married someone with a shitload of prestige and social clout, and no one had mentioned it for thirty years. I began to see why Ormand wanted to find the source.

". . . 1974, band's road manager, Rick Hilliard, rumored to have put a guy in the hospital after beating him up—story goes that Hilliard was being blackmailed after he was caught in a threesome with two women, both married, large quantities of hard narcotics found.

Guy he hospitalised was dealer. Note to self, source not clear on details, digging needed. . . ."

It was staggering. I began to understand just how deep and how dirty Perry Dillon had gone. Rick Hilliard had always had that kind of rep; I'd been less than thrilled about the fact that Cilla thought he was an okay bloke, that she'd liked hanging out with him, but he was a very efficient road manager and I was new to the band in those days, and I wasn't sure about throwing my weight or band member status around.

". . . 1978, Priscilla Kinkaid popped for shoplifting an amber necklace at Harrods. First offence, no charges filed. The story was never made public; source says husband never knew about the incident. . . ."

"What!"

Ormand hit the pause button. I just sat there, staring. I could feel my heart stuttering, the chambers slapping together, not able to generate anything like a sane rhythm. . . .

"Mr. Kinkaid?"

"Right." They were staring at me, both of them. It took me a moment before I realised I had a hand up to my chest. "Are you asking me if it's true? Because I haven't got a fucking clue. I've never heard the story before." Something, maybe everything that had happened recently, had suddenly come together in the pit of my stomach. I got to my feet. "I need a loo. Where—?"

"Outside, left turn, door at the end." Ormand was standing, pointing. I got up and out.

I brought up the airport breakfast we'd grabbed, and what looked to be everything else I hadn't digested for the past few days as well. Might have been some blood pressure meds mixed in, as well, since I could feel the blood in my head thumping.

I stayed where I was for a bit, and eventually got it together enough to rinse my mouth out, and to get my breathing under some sort of control. Whatever else was on this tape, I couldn't let it kick my legs out from under me this way. I breathed deep for a few minutes, taking my time, getting some self-control back. Fuck it. I was here as a favour to Ormand, and I was paying Pasquini. They could damned well wait for me.

I made my way back to Ormand's office after a bit. He and Pasquini watched me come back in. It occurred to me that they probably felt sorry for me: *Pity the poor dim husband who hadn't known his wife had got nicked for boosting jewelry at Harrods. Wonder what else he doesn't know? . . .*

"Okay." I sat back down. "What do you want to know from me? The incidents he talked about, I can't confirm any of that. I knew about Mac and the MP's brat, but only thirdhand, so that's no good. I hadn't heard the Hilliard story, but it wouldn't surprise me—it was just the sort of thing he used to get up to. He died about twenty years ago, so you can't exactly ask him. Come to think of it, neither could Dillon, yeah? All rumour. All innuendo. Fucking filthy bloody little leech."

My voice shook. I saw something in Ormand's face, and I shook my head at him. "Forget it, Lieutenant. I can admit to hating the bloke seven ways to Sunday. I didn't kill him, and you know it. It's like my old lady said to me, after you'd put in the boot: You can't prove someone did something they didn't do. Oh, and for the record, I have no idea about the shoplifting story, Cilla stealing something from Harrods. Never heard it before. If you ask me, it's probably not true—she could have afforded any jewelry she wanted. 1978, I earned a lot of money that year." *An amber necklace*, I thought. Cilla loved amber; it was her favorite. I wasn't telling them that. "So unless she did it for a lark, or because she was bored or stoned, it's most likely bollocks. You could ask her, but she'd probably lie to you, either that or just stare at you as if you were made of air. Waste of time, if you ask me, but it's your bloody time to waste. What else do you want me to listen to?"

"I'm sorry, Mr. Kinkaid." The bastard really did look sorry. I felt my hands weave together in my lap and clench hard. "One more thing, and this one, I'm afraid, I'm going to request an official comment about. On the record, that is."

He took the CD out and dropped in a second one. He pressed the play button. And then there it was, Perry Dillon's voice one more time, asking a question I'd only partly heard when he'd first asked it.

"You first met Bree Godwin—the schoolgirl who later stole heroin from the clinic she and her mother both worked for, to get you through withdrawal—at a charity event Blacklight did in 1979. Is that right?"

My own voice, distant, faraway, not paying attention, answering. "*Yes, I—*"

I was very glad, at that moment, that Bree was safely out of here. I hoped she was buying the priciest pair of high heels she could find, and I hoped she was putting them on my credit card. I wanted to crawl with shame. How the hell could I have been such a prat?

The pause. The silence. I remembered it, all too clearly. And then my own voice.

"*Out.*" Another pause, the scrape of chairs against Carla's conference room floor. "*Get the hell out of here. Pack your tent and bugger off back to whatever sewer you crawled out of. And if you use one word that deals with my personal life, I'll bloody kill you.*"

"*Good evening, Miami!*"

Some nights, you just know the gig's going to kick ass. You know it early; the crowd picks it up, they feed it back to you, you run with it and turn it into fire and smoke and sex, and you feed it right back to them.

It was in the air, that night at the Miami gig. This was the best kind of electricity, the best kind of knowing it would work—we'd brought some of it with us, from the time we'd got to the venue and begun the sound check.

"... *the American Airlines Center is proud to present* ..."

That crackle, that moment of knowing there's magic in the air and all you've got to do is work it, had happened halfway through the sound check, hours before the gig itself. There was some sort of EQ issue with Cal's bass stack; while the various roadies and tech types fiddled and diddled and tested and asked Calvin anxious questions, I got bored. It's a basic component of sound checks, that's what they're for, but if it isn't your sound being messed about with, it gets tedious.

So, I started arsing with the guitar, just noodling, and out of nowhere, I found myself playing an old song, one the band hadn't done in nearly twenty years. I played a few bars of it, and all of a sudden, there was that smell of magic. That light went on, across the board, you know? You could see it happen: Mac's head jerked, and the rest of the band followed suit.

"Was that from the intro to 'Heart Attack'?" Stu hit a drum roll, the exact roll from the song's original album track, a tricky little 3/4 beat, like a heart. "Shit, I haven't played that since Margaret Thatcher was prime minister. I love that song. Cal? You remember the bass, yeah?"

"Damned right I do." Calvin played it, his neck arched, his ponytail flying. "Fuckin' hell, I love this one. Remember the *Partly Possible* sessions? Why did we stop playing it, anyway?"

"Damned if I know. It's a brilliant song." Luke, who'd been taking a break, draped his Strat around his neck and ran a few licks. "And appropriate, all things considered. JP, mate, can you run the rhythm part? No, not the verse section—I meant the bit you were just doing, just before it does the rollover into the verse? . . ."

Thirty seconds in, and you'd have thought we'd been rehearsing the damned song for a month. No one hit a wrong note; no one missed a beat. Mac came in with the vocal, hot and drawly and very much the voice of a bloke all turned on and ready to go. Every head in the building whipsawed his way, roadies, techs, house staff, and all:

Baby pack your suitcase, don't forget to catch your train
Oh, sweet baby, you know I've had you on the brain
Come on back, now come on back
Daddy's waitin' for you at the sugar shack
Oh pretty mama, you're givin' me a heart attack.

We ran it through once, and everyone in the building began to applaud, completely spontaneous. That sewed it up, all right. We added about six minutes to the show's set list right then and there, and the electricity we'd generated during the sound check lingered all the way through the rest of the sound check and into dinner. Miami was in for a treat.

"*. . . ladies and gentlemen, put your hands together . . .*"

We stood in the wings. The crowd was bouncing, dancing already, and the show hadn't even begun yet. It was going to be bloody sensational.

Bree was right behind me. She'd bought the snakeskin heels and a new dress to go with them, forest green silk, no back to speak of; I couldn't imagine how she was keeping her breasts up, unless the damned thing had a built-in bra or something. The skirt was another eyebrow-raiser; it began right at the small of her back, but there was a single row of tiny covered buttons running about eighteen inches down. They were functional buttons, as well; had I opened those, she'd have shown skin. It didn't look too comfy for sitting, but she didn't seem to mind.

I caught her eye over my shoulder, and she gave me a brilliant smile. I hadn't seen her this relaxed in a long time.

"All right?" I asked her, and she laughed and put her arms around my neck, and kissed me hard, letting her lips trail over my earlobe. She then proceeded to floor me; getting right up behind me, she pressed her entire front side against my back, slipped one hand down between my thighs, cupped, and squeezed.

"Jesus," I managed, and she leaned over and put her lips to my ear.

"Mine," she whispered, and held on for a few seconds longer. She let her fingers stay there a moment, a good solid grip. If the idea was to make it difficult for me to walk, she made a damned good job of it.

I was to remember all of this, over the next little while: that relaxation, that kiss, the green silk with her hair red against it, the little vintage velvet purse over her shoulder.

"Bloody hell." Turned on didn't begin to cover it; thank Christ for loose trousers. "Bree, for fuck's sake!"

"Showtime," she told me. "I'll be right here, as long as the new shoes don't decide to sit me down. Oh, screw it, I can dance barefoot. Do a good gig, baby."

"*. . . give it up . . .*"

"John?"

I paused, just a heartbeat, looked back at her. Even in the dimness, her eyes were bright, vivid green.

"I'm not wearing anything under the dress," she told me, and the stage lights went up.

"*. . . BLACKLIGHT!*"

I remember the Miami show. I've got all sorts of reasons to remember it, but the music? Amazing. Mac was working the kind of energy he used to have. We all felt it; two songs in and I was feeling as if I'd never been ill a day in my life, never had MS, never been taken to Mass General in an ambulance or had a tube run up through an artery in my leg, never had to travel with a special kit designed to hold different medications to keep me out of a wheelchair, keep me functional, keep me alive.

And there was Bree, dancing in the wings. She was as sensual that night as I've ever seen her, and of course, I kept remembering how she'd sent me out onstage, and looking at the outlines of her in that dress, and remembering that she wasn't wearing anything under it, and picturing in detail just what I had in mind for after the show. It got into the music, all that sex—she'd known it would, too. It was her way of feeding the energy, of feeding my energy. Just a little extra kick to the guitar, a little extra kick for the audience. And the audience was kicking back at us. It was beautiful.

We'd played about forty minutes into the show when we hit the point we'd all agreed on. Mac pulled the mic free of its stand; normally, he'll go wireless, but we'd done a last-minute head to head with Nial and Ronan Greene, and the result was a mic with a stand, nice and old-fashioned and thoroughly phallic.

I glanced into the wings, looking for Bree. She was there, but she had her back to me. I could see the pale gleam of that expanse of skin, and one hand, her left, seemed to be held up close to her ear.

"We're gonna to do an oldie for you now," Mac told the crowd. "We weren't planning on it, but it seemed appropriate. We haven't played it since Ronald Reagan was president, so if we screw it up, that's why. It's a little number off our *Partly Possible* album, and it's called 'Heart Attack.'"

The crowd went nuts, of course. They always do, when you take one out that hasn't been played in a good long while. But Mac held a hand up, to quiet them down.

"I want to dedicate this one," he told them. "This one's for our mate, JP Kinkaid, who not only just had a heart attack, but can give you one of your own, the way he plays this tune." He grinned at my dropped jaw. "Cheers, Johnny, you jammy sod. This one's for you. Hit it!"

I played the opening riff, and we thundered into it.

Part of me was probably in shock. I hadn't been expecting that from Mac, not at all. I wasn't glancing anywhere but where I was needed during the tune—we hadn't played it often enough to get it completely right without the risk of messing it up, and that was the last thing I wanted to do, not after that buildup. But I was dying to check out Bree's reaction.

We finished the song and went straight into the next one, and I finally got a chance to swivel round and catch Bree's eye.

She was gone.

It's weird, remembering now, that what I mostly felt was annoyance. I mean, I was actually narked at her, that she'd chosen that moment, of all moments, to slip offstage to the loo or whatever, and missed Mac toasting me to the crowd. I'd love to be able to say that my first thought was worry or even curiosity, but it wouldn't be true. All I thought was, she'd slipped off for a piss and missed my big moment. And I was annoyed with her about it.

Two more songs, three. I glanced over. She hadn't come back. Cyn was there, and Ian, and Carla, looking very hot in a coppery leather thing. But not Bree.

Second to the last song, I edged toward the side of the stage. Luckily, Cyn caught my eye.

"Bree?" I mouthed it at her; the bass was thunder, shaking the building, and the noise was intense. Cyn leaned forward, opened her mouth to reply, and the bass dropped suddenly, and her words echoed in my skull.

". . . phone call," Cyn said. "About an hour ago. She looked upset. Anyway—she left."

CHAPTER TEN

I don't know how I got through the encore. I came offstage at the end of the set, absolute magic out there in the house, the crowd chanting and blissed, and I got offstage and shoved my way straight over to Cyn Corrigan.

"Talk to me, Cyn." I had to lift my voice over the noise backstage, and I probably lifted it a bit too much, because heads from all over the place suddenly turned. "Did you say Bree got a phone call, and left?"

Cyn nodded, looking puzzled. "That's right. She'd kicked her shoes off—great shoes, I want a pair of those—and we were dancing, you were in the middle of that hot guitar call-and-response thing with Luke, near the end of 'Breaking Down the Ladder.' And I guess her phone vibrated—she pulled it out."

That was the song just before we'd done "Heart Attack." I'd seen her with her back to the stage, her hand to one ear.

She'd got a phone call. Someone had rung her up, right in the middle of the show. Ormand? Oh, Christ.

"Then what?" I had begun to shake, my heart rate was spiralling up, and worst of all, my leg—where they'd run the tube in—had begun to throb. All my meds were back at the hotel. I wasn't supposed to need them in the middle of a show. Besides, they were sedatives, both the clonidine and TyCo. You didn't want to load yourself with downers before a gig.

The crowd was chanting the band's name, and Ian was gesturing us toward the stage. I ignored him. I reached out and got hold of Cyn's arm. *"Then what happened?"*

"Are you looking for your old lady?" It was Domitra, at my elbow. "Because Bree went back to the hotel. I went out and helped her find a taxi."

I let go of Cyn. "Oh, Dom, thank Christ. So she was just going back to the hotel?"

"That's what she told the driver. I heard her." Domitra jerked her head toward the stage. "You should go play your encore, dude. She went back to the hotel. You stay offstage too much longer, that crowd's going to get ugly. Makes my job harder."

We did the encore, the arms around each other's shoulders, the deep bow to the audience. Mac sprayed the front few rows with champagne from the dressing room. He told Miami goodnight. And finally, finally, we got offstage and the houselights came up and the gig was over.

I rang the hotel first, limping in place, trying to keep it from going numb on me, trying to rub the sore leg with my free hand at the same time. Had Ms. Godwin come in? Yes, she had.

The surge of relief I felt left me weak. It was all right. She'd gone back to the hotel, that was all. Whatever it was, she was okay, safe at the Four Seasons at Brickell Key. Ormand hadn't called her. He hadn't found something that gave him the reason he wanted to tell her she was under arrest. He hadn't ordered her to go back to New York. She was there, at the hotel. She was fine.

"Could you put me through to our room, please?"

One ring, two. Seven, ten. No answer.

Click. The same receptionist, asking if I wanted to leave a voice message.

"Bree? Bree, baby, it's John. Call me on my cell, as soon as you get this, yeah?"

"Come on, JP, sit down. You look like hell. You're swaying, man. Sit before you topple over."

It was Luke, pushing me into a chair. I sat; I had no choice. My legs weren't holding me.

"Where's Domitra?" She'd seen Bree last. She could let me know how Bree had looked, tell me what she'd said. "Mac? Where the fuck is your bodyguard, man? I need a word."

"Right here." Dom came and perched on the dressing room table. "What do you need?"

"You saw Bree last." I was holding the phone, willing it to vibrate, to make this stop, to kill off this bizarre sense of panic I was feeling. "How did she seem, Dom?"

"Frantic."

The word came out, nice and clear and not loaded with any kind of emotion at all. Dom sounded completely matter-of-fact.

But the dressing room went silent. All the chatter, the murmuring, the mutters, the whispers—all of it shut off. There was just this enormous empty silence. Dom kept her stare, impassive, uninvolved, straight at me.

"Frantic?" *Oh, Bree. Bree, baby, what happened?* "You mean, she was frightened?"

"I didn't say frightened, did I? I said frantic. Frantic, as in upset, in a hurry. But not frightened. She was trying to get her shoes on—damn, those are some hot shoes, yo—and she dropped her purse and picked it up and said, 'Fuck.' I asked her what, and

165

she said she needed to take a cab back to the hotel, she had to go now, right now, and she hadn't brought any money, because why would she bring money to a gig? I said, show's over in an hour, why not wait for the limo? And she said no, she had to go now, it couldn't wait, and could I lend her ten dollars? I said sure, and she was really grateful. She said . . ." Dom's voice, polite and even and uninflected, suddenly stopped.

"What?" Everyone was quiet now; everyone was listening. "What is it?"

"She said it was life and death."

I got to my feet. My chest was on fire, not pain, just panic. "Someone get me a car. I need to get back to the hotel."

Ian, with Carla in tow, brought his own rental round to the stage door. There were fans stretched to the end of the street. I looked out, and I mentally pictured trying to get through them to the car, with one leg tingling courtesy of the MS and the other wailing at me like a banshee at the injection site. . . .

And then, out of nowhere, I had a clear path, the fans sending up yells and cheers. I looked behind me and there was Mac, with Domitra clearing for him, and the fans all turned his way. I caught his eye and mouthed my thanks at him. He nodded at me and began showing off for the fans, drawing all their attention, flirting with the girls closest to him, clearing the path for me to get the hell out of it without having to deal. Domitra was going to find herself busy for the next little while. I made a mental note to find out her shoe size and send her a pair of shoes just like the ones Bree was wearing.

My head was really clear; there's something about genuine panic that'll do that to you, you know? I asked Ian to let me off at the main doors, to find a place nearby to keep the car because I might need him again, and to keep his cell phone ready. I don't think either Ian or Carla had ever heard me sound quite that decisive before.

Into the lobby, into the lift, upstairs to our suite. Fumbling with the electronic key. Green light, a bright flash. I got the door open.

The first thing I saw were the shoes, pale snakeskin heels with the Jimmy Choo signature across the soles, discarded at the foot of the bed. Tossed across the bed itself was the green silk dress she'd had on.

"Bree? Bree!" Bloody useless. She wasn't here. I knew it, I could feel it, I could almost smell the lack of her.

I limped into the bathroom. If she'd packed up her bathroom things, toothbrush and makeup and hair stuff, she'd gone. If it was all still here, whatever she was doing was probably local.

Gone. She'd left a lipstick and forgot her shampoo, on the ledge in the shower, but everything else? Gone.

I was beginning to shake again, and that was no good. I wasn't going to be any use at all if I ended up back in hospital with an exacerbation or another heart attack or something worse. I told myself to calm down, but the pain in my leg was threatening to swamp me, and I had do something. Half a TyCo, I thought—enough to dull things down, but not to knock me out. I reached for my leather meds case and pulled out the bottle of Tylenol 3. It felt wrong, light in my hand, too light.

I twisted the cap off. Even that took me longer than it should have, with my hands unsteady.

I stared at it. The script had been for fifty pills. I'd taken maybe three. Now half the pills were gone.

I reached into the pouch, fumbled around with shaking fingers, and pulled out the clonidine. That script had been for sixty pills, two months' worth, enough to get me through until I got off the road and in to see my own doctor in San Francisco, with a few pills to spare. That bottle was half empty as well.

"Right." I heard myself talking out loud, my own voice echoing around the posh bathroom, and bit down hard. Mustn't go crazy, now. Bad idea. No talking to myself, no jumping to insane conclusions. "Okay. Right."

I went back into our room and opened Bree's end of the closet. If all her luggage was there . . .

It wasn't. Her carryon bag—a nice piece of Louis Vuitton she never flies without—was gone.

I got my cell, and called Ian. "Can you and Carla come up to my room, please? Bree's missing. She's been here, changed clothes, packed a bag—" I stopped, hearing questions, not hearing them. I wasn't going to tell them about the missing drugs, not them, not anyone. Not yet, anyway. "I need to find out where she went, and I think I'm going to need you both."

We wasted a crucial hour, Ian and Carla and me, talking about the best way to find out where she'd gone.

Thinking back, I can't believe how dim we were about it. Ian's a good solid road manager, stellar at his job. Yeah, so, I'd begun this tour pissed off at him, what with not being included in that Perry Dillon news, and him not being on top of Nial's blogging about it. That didn't take away the fact that he'd run every Blacklight tour with total perfection since the day he'd joined the organisation.

We were tired and stressed, and none of us were up to par. We couldn't have been, because there we were, in a luxury hotel, and the easy way to find out what we needed to know was staring us in the face. But we sat there in my suite until a quarter to one in the morning, precious minutes ticking away, Carla calling every airline she had on her list, getting put on hold, asking politely and without emphasis if a Ms. Bree Godwin had taken a flight, getting nowhere.

It was Ian who finally got what we'd been missing. Carla was in the middle of her eighth airline call when he suddenly said something rude and got to his feet.

"Christ, I'm an idiot." He smacked himself in the forehead. "JP, you ought to sack me. Carla, hang up, will you? And shove over, I need the hotel phone."

She moved. Ian grabbed the house phone and punched in a single digit.

"Right, yes, hello—is that the concierge? This is Ian Hendry, with Blacklight. We're trying to locate a member of our party, a Ms. Bree Godwin—"

He broke off, listening to the voice at the other end of the line. With his free hand, he scrabbled in the nightstand drawer for a pen. Carla was on top of that one; she had one of the hotel's courtesy message pads ready.

"Hang on, let me get this down—you booked the flight for her? Right, American to New York—that's JFK? What's the flight number? Right, I've got it—lands at one-oh-three? Thanks. Was there anything else that—?"

He stopped again as the concierge broke in. I was holding my breath.

She'd gone to New York. She'd got a phone call, early on during the show, and she'd borrowed money from Domitra to get back to the hotel. She'd got to the hotel and apparently got hold of the concierge, had him find and book her a flight to JFK. Why? And why had she taken half my pills with her?

It had to be Ormand. Something had come up, he'd found something out, rung her, demanded she return to New York. There was no other reason for her to do what she'd done. There was nothing else that made any sense.

". . . right. Were those traveller's cheques? No, no, just if she used one of the band credit cards, we wouldn't query it—oh, her own card, great, yeah, thanks. Did she leave a number where—? No, right, got it. Cheers."

He rang off. "The concierge says she got here in a cab at just about nine. She ran into the lobby—I'm telling you what he said—and asked specifically for him. He said she asked him to book her on the next nonstop flight to New York he could find that she could reasonably get to from here. He said she handed him her American Express card and asked him to get her a thousand dollars in cash. He says she was in a hurry, but that she didn't seem upset—just rushed, and very on top of it. He got it done, of course. That's what a good concierge is for. They can find you anything, anywhere, anytime."

He stopped, giving me a chance to absorb it.

I understood the concierge's description. She hadn't been upset; she'd been focused. And that meant it couldn't have been Ormand, surely? A demand to return to New York under the threat of imminent arrest would have upset her. And that thousand dollars, what did that have to do with anything? And why had she taken my pills?

I nodded at Ian. "What else?"

"He says she ran for the elevator and came back down a few minutes later, in street clothes, with one piece of luggage. She took the money, the printout with her flight info, peeled off a hundred-dollar bill and handed it to him, said thank you, and ran for her cab." He looked down at his scribbled notes. "American, the ten fifteen flight. Direct nonstop. Lands at Kennedy at three minutes past one."

I glanced at the bedside clock. It had just gone one.

"Ian." My own head had clicked into a higher gear, pain or no pain. "Call Kennedy, yeah? White courtesy. Have them page her when she gets off the plane. Ms. Bree Godwin, please check your voice mail, you have a message. Exactly that, no more, no less. Got it?"

"Yeah. I'm on it."

"Ta." I looked at him. He had his own cell in hand. "The fucking plane is probably going to be on the ground and taxiing toward the gate any second. Hurry, mate."

He nodded. I went into the bathroom, my own cell phone in hand, and hit the autodial. The sound of her voice, even the impersonal voice mail announcement, wrenched at me.

"It's John, love. Look, the concierge gave us your flight information. I haven't got a clue what's going on, and I'm not pressing you. But I need to know you're all right, please. I'm having you paged at the airport, and if you don't get this right away, maybe you'll hear the page." I hesitated a moment. "I love you. Ring me as soon as you can."

For the second time since Perry Dillon took one of my guitar stands across his Adam's apple, I slept alone, with my cell phone on Bree's pillow, next to my head.

I'd asked Ian and Carla to stay quiet about what had happened until I knew more about what was going on. If Bree had heard that white courtesy page, she hadn't answered it. If she'd picked up her messages and got the one from me, she hadn't rung back. Until she did, there was fuck-all I could do.

Physically, I was wrecked. My neurologist told me, early on, that MS doesn't respond well to stress. I'd laughed, and told her that touring once every few years while being driven in limos and sleeping in five-star hotels wouldn't qualify as stress in most people's dictionaries, but that it was trickier than it sounded.

I hadn't forgotten what she'd said about it, though. Seemed she'd been right. Bree has a favourite phrase, usually about the kind of bone-tired weariness of handling a catering gig for seventy people, with a staff of four and cleanup to follow: after a gig like that, she says she feels as if she's been beaten with wet ropes. At the moment, stretched out on the Four Seasons' lovely plush mattress, I knew just what she meant.

I'd taken only half a TyCo, and no more. The leg was making noise at me, but this was a no-brainer. I'd weighed the sedative effect of the full dose against the need to wake if the phone rang, and decided the sedative effect could sod off; I simply couldn't afford the risk.

So the pain had been damped down for a few hours, and now it was back. If I'd wanted something to keep me right at the edge of wakeful, this was just the job.

The night moved along, and I can't remember a slower crawl. I'd doze for a bit, jerk awake, check the clock, check the cell to make sure it was on and I hadn't missed anything, doze a bit, repeat the entire miserable process.

Somewhere during the quiet hours, when the entire world outside the hotel seemed to have gone elsewhere, I had a bad spell, ten or so of the worst minutes of my life. I started out by deciding that she'd left me, then that she was in trouble and couldn't trust me to help, then that she hated me, and finally, that I hated her. I remembered the first time I'd seen her, the first time I'd slept with her, the three times I'd left her to fulfill an obligation I thought I had no right to avoid; I remembered how, after that first time—*Please don't do this to me, to us, we're so new*—she'd never asked me to do anything again, never asked me not to do anything again. I remembered that I'd asked her to leave the light on for me. I remembered what she'd said: *always on, always burning*.

I let those cycle through and didn't even attempt to stop the crying jag that followed. I hadn't cried since I stopped drinking; the last time I'd cried, Bree had just gone twenty and I'd had my head in her lap, using the girl as a confessional, asking her to carry my damned weight one more time. Tonight, of all nights, that memory seemed like a bad joke.

The weepy spell must have had a narcotic effect of its own, because I actually did sleep for a bit after that. I slept and I dreamed that I was in London and it was some sort of holiday, and there were church bells. . . .

Church bells.

I must have been waiting for that phone to ring even in my dreams, because I'd grabbed it off the pillow before the bizarre shaky images of London at Easter faded out.

"John?"

"Hang on. Please, hang on, don't ring off." I rolled over in the dark, punching my shoulder against the nightstand, cursing under my breath. I got the lamp on, finally—felt like it took ages. "Bree? Baby, are you okay?"

"I don't know. I think so. Yes." Weirdly enough, this made sense. "John, look. I don't have a lot of time—I may have to hang up at pretty much any second. I heard the page, at the airport, but I was moving pretty fast, and I couldn't really stop. I just wanted you to know I was all right—to tell you not to worry."

"Not to *worry?* Are you nuts? Bree, who rang you? Where are you? What—?"

"I'm not nuts, and I can't tell you anything, not right now. Not yet." Something was going on with her breathing, and sleepy as I was, I still sussed it: she was trying to keep her voice at a particular volume. "John, listen to me. Please? I know you don't listen to me much, it's usually me listening to you and that's okay, mostly, but right this moment, you have to do this for me—just be quiet and listen. Are you listening?"

It took everything I had, every ounce of self-control, not to flip my shit. The conversation was surreal. Here was my old lady, a suspect in a murder investigation, she'd got a phone call and she wouldn't say from who, she'd run off in the middle of the night, she'd helped herself to half my meds—and what in hell did she mean, I never listened to her?

"Right," I told her. "I'm listening."

"Okay." She took a moment while I waited. Part of me was trying to pinpoint anything, sounds from her end, that might clue me in to what she was doing, where she was. There was nothing, nothing at all. She might as well have been ringing me up from inside a closet.

"I want you to go to Atlanta," she said, at last. "I mean—if I can't come back in time. I don't want you to try and follow me. I want you to go play Atlanta with Blacklight."

I opened my mouth and shut it again. She went on.

"It may not be an issue. This may all resolve itself before then. But I don't think it will. So I want you to do that for me. I don't want you to try and track me down right now—it would be a bad idea, and it wouldn't be fair. And I may only be gone a few days anyway."

"Bree—"

"No, listen to me." Her voice was suddenly ragged around the edges. "I never ask you to do anything for me. I sure as hell never ask you *not* to do anything you really want to do. But I am now. I'm asking you to give the band and the fans and the pro-moters and everyone else their money's worth, and let me just—let me do what I have to do. You promised you wouldn't press me. I'm asking you to keep that promise." There was a shift in her voice, subtle, hard to define. For one moment, I wondered if what I was hearing was amusement. "I know how big you are on keeping promises. I'm big on that myself, that and the whole loyalty thing. And you ought to know that, better than anyone."

"Okay." I kept my voice very quiet, very even. "Can I play this back, make sure I've got the request right? You're not going to tell me anything—you don't want me to follow you or try to find you. I'm betting you're not planning on telling me why you cleaned out half my drug stash. You want me to go to Atlanta, pretend everything's normal, not tell anyone anything, and give the crowd the best show I can give them. And I'm supposed to pretend everything's normal, even though I won't have any idea how long or even if I'm ever going to see you again. Is that it? Have I got it? Have I missed anything?"

She was silent. I gave her a moment, and then went on, keeping my voice steady, calm, not giving in to what really wanted out.

"Right. I can do that. And I will, if that's what you want me to do. I just want to make really sure you know what you're asking of me."

She began to laugh. It hit me like a hard kick to the stomach, because it was sharp, and dark, and right on the edge of hysteria, and Bree doesn't get hysterical.

"Do I know? Do I know what it's like, not knowing if the only person you give a rat's ass about is ever coming back to you? Not knowing how long it'll be before you see them again? Torturing yourself, every minute of every day, with what they're doing, and who they're doing it to?" Her voice was a whip stroke. "No, John, how the hell could I possibly have the faintest idea what that's like?"

"Bree, love, look—"

"Will you do what I'm asking?" Her voice had deadened, flattened out. "Yes or no? It's down to that, John. I've listened to you talk about loyalty for a good long time now. I agree with you. I just want to know if you're willing to put your money where your mouth is. I want some of that famous loyalty. I need it, and it needs to be unconditional. It's now or never, so make up your mind, and tell me, because I have to go: yes or no?"

"Yes."

"I love you." There was something else, a thump, a muffled banging. "I have to go. I'll be back as soon as I can."

"Bree?"

A click and silence. She'd gone.

CHAPTER ELEVEN

I don't remember whether or not I actually got any rest without narcotics being involved, between the echoing silence at the other end of Bree's phone call and the end of the Atlanta show, three days later.

I know I took various meds, monitored my blood pressure, ate, showered, interacted with the band. I remember a furious tirade from Luke—that one's pretty clear in my head, which isn't too surprising, really.

But I don't remember anything else with any clarity. Considering everything that happened, it's probably for the best. You'd have a hard time getting me to believe there was anything there I want to remember, anyway. Even the stuff I do remember, I'd rather forget.

One memory I do have, too damned clear, was the reason for Luke's meltdown. That was in the morning paper, folded neatly outside my room, along with the breakfast I couldn't eat, and the tea I could barely make myself swallow. I wish to hell I could forget about it. It was one of the local rags; the article was on page two, and it wasn't a blurb. Their people had been doing some serious digging.

The piece wasn't about Ormand's progress. It was about Perry Dillon and about us. And as I read, I felt my nerves— already on "stand by to meltdown" status—lock up and lock down. They'd gone down the worst possible path: scrabbling round in the dirt, wondering what Perry Dillon might possibly have got his hands on that could have been worth killing him for.

They'd concentrated on Mac, of course. No surprise there—he's the most flamboyant, the most colourful, the one who gets into the limelight and basically sets up shop and invites the media in for a natter and a few pints. They mentioned the paternity suit, but that was just for starters. They'd found quite a few other things, most of them long ago and far away. There were no motives there, just unverified dirt, the stuff that sells their rags for them.

Mac was fair game. It's not as if he tries to hide this stuff; he doesn't see any reason to bother. If a reporter shoved a mic in Mac's face, Mac would probably just lift an eyebrow and confirm things. He doesn't mind.

But they talked about Luke as well. As I started reading it, I had to set my cup down because I was shaking, splashing hot tea on the back of my hand.

It wasn't a hatchet job, not legally, anyway. One of those being something our lawyers could take them apart for. Hell, if Luke tried to sue them over it, they'd probably stand up there in court and look outraged, pointing out the syrupy tone, claiming it was meant to be sympathetic.

They'd gone back and read up on Viv Hedley's cancer. God, it was ugly: tragic early death of his wife, Luke left a widower with a wild young daughter and a career that was incompatible with good parenting. I mean, that's not how they'd said it, not exactly, but that was how it came off.

It was unbelievable. They made Solange—who's a good kid—sound like some sort of coke-snorting, trick-turning wild child. And nothing could be further away from reality.

Thing is, Solange is the only band baby Blacklight's got. None of the rest of us have ever had any kids, not even accidental ones, and that includes Mac. So we've always all been really protective of her, Chris Fallow's wife, Meg, acting as the mother Solange has been left without before she was old enough to know what she'd lost. Mac is her godfather, and from everything I've seen of them together over the last eighteen years, he's a damned good one. He takes it seriously.

Whoever'd written this piece had made Luke, one of the best fathers alive, sound like an incompetent stoner. There was a bit about Solange having been expelled from her school when she was fifteen, but no mention of why. Fact is, she'd got into a punch-up when she'd found a couple of classmates terrorising a newer student. She'd been raised to put a nice value on loyalty, but I'm betting she'd have got into that slogging match with the school bullies anyway. She's made that way, and she comes by it from both parents.

They'd been careful. There was nothing there that Luke or anyone else could nail them for. The fuckers had gone down a "more to be pitied than censured" road, and in a way, that actually made the entire thing more offensive. The very fact that they had gone digging and were willing to print this stuff left me sick. I hoped to hell Luke was avoiding the papers.

They had a paragraph or two about me as well. Weirdly enough, they'd missed most of the early stuff; they talked about my "early problems with drugs and alcohol," mentioned that I'd been deported once, admitted that I'd got clean and relocated to the States. But there was nothing in there about Bree, not a word. So far as they seemed to think, she didn't exist. They hadn't noticed that I was still legally married, either.

All the way down near the bottom of the article, there was my name, one more time.

> . . . according to an unnamed source, Dillon inter-
> viewed Blacklight guitarist JP Kinkaid in Los Angeles.
> The story remains unconfirmed by Blacklight man-
> agement. Kinkaid has made no comment beyond the
> official press release about the substance of their con-
> versation. . . .

I closed the paper and shut my eyes. Oh, Christ. If they'd got this far, this deep, they weren't likely to stop. At this moment, I didn't know what to hope for right then, except for the power to get my hands on whoever had done that piece and throttle them.

I basically shut down right around then. I remember being hauled off to eat lunch at a Miami restaurant. I remember Luke looking tight-lipped and furious, and Mac talking to him in a low voice. I remember someone making small talk about South Beach. I remember forking food into my mouth, chewing, staying silent. I couldn't tell you what I ordered, what I paid for, what I ate. I don't remember the food having any taste. The conversations floating past me might as well have been dust. I didn't manage to retain any of it.

And then, after the meal, there was a small crowd of press people outside, and one of them got past Ian and was stupid enough to mention the story in the paper to Luke. I heard Solange's name, mispronounced. And of course Luke exploded, lost it completely, and started shouting at the bloke. We got him into the car, but by then I had the shakes.

Not one person at that lunch asked me anything personal or mentioned Bree. And that floored me. I just didn't get it—did no one notice she was gone? I mean, Ian and Carla had been right there with me, last night. They knew, and yet her name wasn't mentioned at all. She'd done her damned invisibility thing again. Or maybe this time I'd done it to her somehow. I wasn't sure of anything anymore.

Later that day, Carla knocked on my door, reminding me that it was Monday, time for my weekly MS shot. Carla looked wasted; if I'd been in any state to think about anything except myself, I'd have realised just how tired and stressed she was. I must have looked like hell myself when she got there—I'd been in bed, staring at the ceiling, just thinking, no sleep at all, and of course, Carla knew Bree had gone.

We were booked to leave for Atlanta on Tuesday night. Already shaky from the complete lack of sleep, I gave myself the weekly shot of interferon.

I've been lucky about this stuff. Something like half the users react with what the manufacturers, in their pamphlets, call "flulike symptoms." That's accurate, if they're talking about the great pandemic of 1917. Or maybe their corporate spin doctors couldn't find a catchy synonym for "the Black Death." One woman I know says she's in bed for two days after every shot. If her husband doesn't remember to feed her painkillers every four hours, the shivering and pains get so bad, she's actually pulled muscles just clenching and tensing.

I'm at the other end of that, in the tiny group of people who usually have no adverse reaction to it at all. I've been using this stuff for about four years, and I think I'd had two reactions in all that time, both really mild.

So of course, circumstance being an ironic bitch, I had a huge physical reaction this time. I got the full spectrum: shakes, aches, the swelling around the bolus that forms when you inject the interferon, the fever. I felt it hit straightaway; there's a sort of nasty heat, moving up and out along the nerve lines, spidering away from the bolus in every direction.

There's nothing you can do about it, either. As soon as it begins, you know you're fucked. All you can do is grit your teeth, go.to bed, and ride it out.

So I spent Monday night shivering in bed. I managed to get Luke on the phone Tuesday morning, tell him what was happening, and asked him to come up. He was there five minutes later—they're good people, my bandmates. Luke came up, and I was babbling, incoherent, feverish. Why he didn't run for his life, I'll never know. Maybe it took his mind off how furious he was about that bloody hatchet job on his daughter.

He got what was needed, straight off. Someone had to pack my stuff, and Bree's as well—I had a fever up over 102 and I wasn't moving any time soon. Luke rang down to Barb Wilson, and she came up and helped.

He was worried about my reaction to the interferon, because he got the concierge to hook us up with a local neurologist on the phone. When I try to remember it now, there's a sort of bizarre quality to it: Saturday morning cartoons, as seen through a really bad nightmare, or maybe corrupted peyote or acid. Luke was asking the doctor questions, the doctor was asking Luke questions, Luke was asking me questions, and I was off my nut, delirious.

Truth is, I didn't care about anything just then, not the pain, not the fever, not anything beyond the feeling that all I wanted right then was Bree. I totally regressed, turned into a five-year-old, wondering the way a kid might wonder if I could make her come home if I just closed my eyes and concentrated on it hard enough.

I thought, *she ought to be here, how could she do this to me, going off and leaving me to cope?* And then another bit of me thought,

fuck, mate, could you be more childish, more selfish, more needy?
What had Dom said, about me being spoiled rotten?

". . . cake," I told Luke, and he looked pretty startled; he
told me, a long time later, that he'd just relayed a question about
what the heart doc had prescribed for the blood pressure. "Cake
and frosting, and tequila with a straw."

Luke got me a TyCo—turned out, after the long round of
questions, that the TyCo was best for the reaction I was having.
It worked, too; the pill knocked me out for a few hours. Thank
God for small blessings in the middle of all that shit.

At some point Tuesday, the interferon reaction began to
ease off, and my head cleared a bit. I found myself thinking
about that conversation with Bree, and the more I thought
about it, the odder it got.

None of it made sense. The reality was simple enough, or at
least, it damned well should have been: She'd got a phone call in
the middle of the show. Whoever it was from, whatever the call
had been about, had sent her off to New York on a late flight.
After that, it got strange.

Bree being Bree, my first reaction was to think, *right,
someone she cared about was in trouble, someone needed her.* Typical crusading, nurturing, save-the-world Bree, yeah? I know
that sounds as if I disapprove, but I don't. Bloody hell, I'm the
last man on earth to disapprove. Without that part of her in
action, I'd have been dead a dozen times over. Or still ad-
dicted to heroin. Or busily drinking myself into a very early
grave.

The picture came into my head suddenly: me and Bree, after I'd asked her to help me quit drinking before it took me out.
It was one more memory I hated pulling out, one I avoided
whenever I could. More responsibility, more of my bullshit
dumped on her shoulders too young, more for her to deal with.

She'd dealt. She always did. She'd done a top-to-bottom

search of the house on Clay Street and she collected eleven hidden bottles. I'd been your classic drunk, little stashes of whiskey and brandy, my two liver-killers of choice at the time, secreted all over the house. She'd emptied every last one of them down the sink in the kitchen. Then she'd methodically smashed the first ten bottles. I watched her do it—hell, I'd asked her to do it.

But then she did something I hadn't asked her to do. She turned to me with the eleventh empty bottle in her hand—Jack Daniel's, I remember it very well. She looked at it, balancing it in her hand, hefting it, feeling the weight. And she looked up at me. I've never forgotten what she said: *"You wanted me to handle it? Cool. We're doing it my way. Listen up: if I find another one of these in the house, ever, I'm going to christen your skull like you were the fucking QE2."*

So yeah, that was my old lady. And that being the case, she hadn't run off and left me alone in Miami, four days the wrong side of a heart attack, without something drastic at the other end of the phone. No amount of me sulking and acting the pissy little shit who had to come first with her was going to alter that, so I'd best try and wrap my head around it, and quickly.

Late Tuesday afternoon, just before we left for the airport, I had a brainstorm. The fever had come down to a manageable level; an idea had parked itself in my head, and the more I looked at it, the more logical it seemed. I looked at the time, counted off three hours, and dialled San Francisco.

"John? Is that you, dear? How's the tour going? Feeling all right?"

Bree's speaking voice, very musical and distinctive—she gets it from her mum. Talking to Miranda is like talking to Bree, only calmer. Miranda's not so fierce as Bree is, but you can't get away with anything, not with Miranda. She sees right through every wall you put up. She knows every trick you've got.

I didn't even consider trying to bullshit her. I just gave her a condensed version of what had gone down Sunday night; the only thing I left out was the bit about the missing drugs.

She listened without saying a word, letting me tell the whole thing. She's a good listener, Miranda is, but there are times it can be a bit daunting, you know?

"Well." She sounded very neutral. "Are you worried about Bree? I wouldn't be, John. In terms of landing on her feet, I didn't have a daughter, I had a kitten. She always comes down the right way up."

"It's not that, Miranda. That's not what's worrying me, not really." I hesitated. "Look—she helped herself to half my painkillers. Also half my blood pressure meds. And don't ask me, am I sure it was Bree. Yeah, I am. They're prescription drugs—"

"Didn't she leave you enough to get by with?"

It was the way she said it, as much as what she said—I knew, right then, that I'd nailed it. If Bree had taken those drugs, it was because she believed she needed them. And she didn't need them for herself. I could read my old lady's thought processes, loud and clear: Someone rang her up, someone was in trouble, something in that selection of drugs might be useful. What would she do? She'd ring her mother, of course, Miranda the world-class surgeon. She'd go straight to the source. She'd figure out what would work best for the situation.

"Right." I heard my own voice sharpen up. "Miranda, look. I'm not worried about running out of pills, and you know it. Bree rang you, obviously. She would. She decided that whatever the situation in New York was, she might need something in the way of meds. So she rang you—I'm guessing it was right around quarter past six on Sunday night, your time. We were onstage right then. So, what? She described what she needed. She told you what was available. Why the hell did she need those drugs,

Miranda? Painkillers, okay, I can see what those are good for, but why would she take the blood pressure meds? What else are they useful for? And by the way, she finally told me the truth about what happened back in 1979—we'd never once discussed it, and I didn't know about your suspension. So would you just bloody talk to me, damn it!"

She was silent for a bit. That's quite a feat, depriving the elegant and articulate Dr. Godwin of speech. I was beginning to lose my temper, though. No sleep, an interferon reaction, Bree gone, leaving for the airport momentarily . . .

"Yes, she called." She broke the silence finally. "She asked me in confidence, John—but I know Bree. I love my daughter, a lot more than I sometimes think you do, but I'm not blind to the fact that she sometimes seems to think she's Joan of Arc. And you know, dear"—her voice was gentle, but it bit, and bit deep—"since you've brought up what happened in 1979? Once upon a time, when she called me to find out what drugs were needed in a life-or-death emergency, I wasn't there for her. So I do try to be, nowadays."

"You're not going to tell me, are you?" Argument wasn't going to get me a damned thing. The bloody Godwin women, there's no getting around them, and I knew it. That didn't stop me giving it one more shot, though.

"Miranda, look. For all you think I don't love her as much as you do, I still love her more than I've ever managed to love anyone or anything else. She's the prime suspect in a murder investigation. It happened in New York. New York has the death penalty. I'd burn the city to the fucking ground if I thought—"

"Oh, for heaven's sake, John! She didn't kill that poor stupid man." Miranda sounded exasperated. "Really, you're as melodramatic as Bree, sometimes. And no, I am not going to tell you anything else about what she asked me. Now go play your tour and try to have a little faith in Bree. I'd have thought she'd earned it by now. Good night."

"Good evening, Atlanta!"

I stood in the wings, Luke close by, Ian and Carla in the shadows behind me, roadies and techs their doing their usual last-second checks on connections, stands, sound levels, lights.

"You all right, JP?"

"Yeah, I'm fine."

That was bullshit, and Luke knew it. I could see the disbelief in his face. He'd been a rock the last couple of days, but there was nothing he could do to fix the truth or even take the edge off it. We'd be onstage in a moment, and the house was packed. He deserved the soothing lie, especially right now. And the fans, loyal buggers, deserved a brilliant show, the best of Blacklight.

"The Phillips Arena is thrilled to present . . ."

Full house, a faceless mass, the usual banners. I remember one, hanging off the top balcony: BLACKLIGHT: BETTER THAN SEX!

I'd rung Bree's cell phone, just before leaving the Ritz-Carlton. There wasn't any chance in hell she'd answer it—I knew that. But I waited for her voice mail announcement, and the beep, and left a message, dead simple: *"It's me, love. No message, really—I just wanted to hear your voice. I'm hoping whatever you're doing is coming close to being done. I miss you."*

There were things bubbling around in my head that wanted looking at. I don't know that I'd have given this stuff a second glance if Perry Dillon hadn't got himself killed in our dressing room—or maybe if Dom hadn't shoved my face up to a mirror last week in Central Park. There'd been no escape from what I'd seen there, none at all.

It would be nice to be able to tell myself that the mirror had been distorted, like those things you get at travelling fairs. But it hadn't been. The reflection had been straight, and true, and as unpleasant as anything I'd ever seen.

Dom had got it right: I was spoiled. First half of my life, I'd been the shining guitar light everyone wanted on their album, the wonder boy. And then there was Cilla, who thought I was the best in the world, always putting me up there, best, best, best, telling the whole world I was golden.

Then Blacklight, and somehow, Bree had happened. And if I'd been spoiled before . . .

"*. . . ladies and gentlemen, give it up . . .*"

Dom had asked why, if I cared so much about Bree, I was still married to Cilla? Since Bree had gone, I'd stopped shying away from the question and faced up to the answer: because I was a lazy fucking sod. I avoided conflict whenever it was possible. I liked having two women who both needed me. And I'd hurt Bree with it for too long, not thinking or dealing with it.

Yeah, Cilla had threatened to do herself in. Yeah, she'd meant it. As my excuse, though, that didn't fly. Dom had been right about that, as well. She'd called it damned fine passive-aggressive. Bloody hell, it was the best passive-aggressive laziness could buy.

If Bree came back to me, there were going to be some changes. I was done coasting, done with the status quo. I'd been damaging her, damaging myself, being unfair to both of us, and to Cilla as well. It wasn't acceptable anymore.

"*. . . BLACKLIGHT!*"

The stage lights went up, the dark and bright trademark lighting lit up, front and back. Mac hit the spotlight and the opening vocal. Luke and I moved into our usual spots, locked up, began the evening's entertainment.

This tour—a relaxed schedule by any standard—had taken

a lot out of me. The MS had got worse; I didn't know if that was permanent or whether the escalation was just a temporary thing, triggered by all the stress of the Dillon situation.

The heart attack, though, I didn't have to wonder about that. There's nothing temporary about having your ticker suddenly decide it wants to cut out on you; it's a one trick pony, that is.

"The lady had issues, she took a little ride. . . ."

For the first time, I was facing the real possibility that I might not be able to carry on as a functional member of Blacklight. Before Bree went missing, the thought would have scared me half to death. Now I could look at it straight on.

They'd kept this tour loose, and with plenty of rest time. The CD had been a solid commercial success—this tour, both legs, could easily have been stadium shows, or twice as many of these indoor arena gigs as they'd set up. We'd earn about $30 million—it could have been twice that.

They'd done it this way to accommodate me. They'd scheduled no shows on Monday or Tuesday nights because they knew I took my interferon shots on Mondays, and they'd had to work with the possibility that what had just happened would happen more often: a reaction to the meds that left me incapacitated.

"She traded in her Harley and she offered up her pride. . . ."

I thought about Luke, flying out to San Francisco after the diagnosis, teaming up with Bree, the pair of them bullying me into accepting that there might be nights where Luke would have to cover the bits I couldn't do with nerve-damaged fingers. I thought about him sitting with me, a full month of it, learning every lick I did in every song, Bree getting over her own desire to be a shadow on the wall of my life, welcoming Luke into her life because he was a vital part of mine.

They were good people, my bandmates. Loyal. They could have said, "Sorry mate, we can't depend on your health." They could have sacked me. They hadn't done it.

Was I being fair to them? I certainly wasn't being fair to my old lady.

"Shadow on her shoulder, she took a little breath. . . ."

If I told them I was out, finished, retiring after this tour, they'd have time to replace me before they headed back into the studio for the next CD. I wasn't going to do that, though, not until I talked it over with Bree. She had the right to weigh in. Just because I'd mentally cast her as sort of the anti-Cilla, wanting the entire world to go away and leave us alone together, that didn't mean she didn't get a vote.

There were eye-openers everywhere: They liked her, my mates. I remembered Mac, with that easy seductive charm so bone-deep, he doesn't waste time playing it, kissing her hand and telling her she rocked. He'd meant it, too. But the real eye-opener for me had been that no one in that room had been surprised at how capable she was. Maybe they knew her better than I thought they did.

"Lady's gone dancin' with the kiss of death!"

I stayed on my feet for most of the Atlanta show. That was a surprise, I think more to the band than it was to me; I played it on autopilot, nothing inspired. Problem was, my brain was so damned busy cycling around that I missed the usual signals from the rest of my body. So I stayed on my feet, moved around, nodded at Luke to let him know it was all right, kept playing.

Two hours, two hours ten. Offstage, into the dressing room; I knocked back some water and ate grapes from the fruit basket backstage. Mac got his bubbly, let the crescendo build up, back onstage, two-song encore, houselights up, bowing, Mac spraying the audience, and another show was in the bag.

Full exhaustion hit on the way back to the hotel. Fact is, I'd been an idiot, standing up all night; just because the brain had been ignoring the warning signals, that didn't mean the signals weren't there. I'd been on my feet for the better part of three hours, and everything suddenly shut down and decided, right, time to hurt like a son of a bitch, you fucking idiot, next time have a lovely sitdown or three, yeah?

Back up to my room, stretching out on the bed, trying to ease it up. I felt something hard under me and swore. It was my cell phone; I'd shoved the damned thing in the back pocket of my street trousers.

I pulled it out. The message light was blinking.

Bree.

I flipped it open, punched in my password, heard the tinny little robot voice: *You have one message, sent today at nine forty-three p.m. To listen to your messages, press star. . . .*

"Mr. Kinkaid? This is Lieutenant Ormand. There have been some developments in the Dillon murder. We've got some new information, and we've heard back from our colleagues in London. I'm afraid I need to ask you to come back to New York, as soon as you can."

CHAPTER TWELVE

I sat on that hotel bed for about ten minutes after I played that message from Ormand. If life was a bad melodrama, some shitty writer would probably say something about my hesitation costing me crucial minutes.

Yeah, well, it didn't. If you've never tried booking a last-minute late-night flight from Atlanta to New York, let me save you some trouble. There aren't any. None. Not one bloody flight after ten at night.

I played Ormand's message twice before I went into that ten-minute shutdown. The words, the tone of voice, the voice at the other end, the demands it was making? Nothing changed: same thing, the second time through. New information, colleagues in London, afraid he needed me in New York. Right.

I got back some control over my heartbeat after a few minutes. That whole workout I'd been giving my brain earlier in the evening, during the show, must have killed off a few million brain cells, because I honestly couldn't think what to do. The last thing I wanted to do was involve the band, but I didn't know what was going to happen once I went to New York.

Ormand was being enigmatic. More information and word from his colleagues in London. What happened if he demanded Bree? There wasn't a chance in hell he'd believe I didn't know where she was. What happened if he wouldn't let me leave, once I got there? We were due to play Dallas on Saturday night.

Shit. What had he found out? Why in hell did he want me there?

I sat there and I tried to think. I made a piss-poor job of it, I'm afraid. The only thing that came through, loud and clear, was the fact that, at some point soon, I was going to have to ring Ormand back.

First things first, though. A flight to New York—Ian? Carla? Get them involved, let them know there might be a legal issue? No, not yet. I rang down to the front desk and got the concierge. It had worked for Bree in Miami, after all.

The Atlanta concierge was as polished and professional as his counterpart in Florida had been. He got the information from me—flight to New York, first class, please, transportation to the airport, as soon as possible. Then he buried me.

"I'm sorry, Mr. Kinkaid—I didn't realise you needed a flight tonight. I'm afraid there aren't any red-eyes—even Delta stops the New York runs at ten, and it's midnight now."

"Oh, bloody hell!"

"I'm sorry, sir." He meant it; he really was sorry. I suppose no one who has the rep—or the job description—of being able to find you anything you want or need at a moment's notice wants to run into something he can't fix. I expect it's a point of pride. "I could book you a charter—but by the time we'd arranged it, it would be morning anyway, and the commercial flights would be available. I'm very sorry."

I took a deep breath. This was the first time in a long time I found myself wanting a few lines of coke, to steady my nerves, with maybe some good single malt as a chaser. Not exactly a shining moment, but I'm being honest.

"Okay," I told him. "What's the first flight out in the morning, then?"

"Half past seven, Mr. Kinkaid. Would you like me to book it for you? And perhaps a limo to the airport?"

I opened my mouth to tell him yes, and closed it again. Something in me had suddenly clicked into gear, and the result was flat rebellion mode.

What in hell was I doing? Panicking, dancing to Ormand's tune without even knowing what this so-called new information was about? Turning my entire life upside down because he wanted to see me, as of now? And this, after I'd made that crack to Bree, about making herself available whenever Ormand wanted her, spreading them for the law?

Sod that. All of a sudden, my nerves seemed to be steadying themselves. A little voice in my head put its two pennies in: *About bloody time.*

"Thanks," I told the concierge. "But not yet. I'll ring you back when I've spoken to New York, yeah? Oh—before you go, can you get me the next edition of the local paper, the minute you can get your hands on it? I'm not certain which paper—"

"That would be the *Journal-Constitution*, Mr. Kinkaid, and certainly, no problem at all. We get ours within an hour of the morning press run; I'll have one put outside your door as soon as it comes in. Would you like *USA Today* as well?"

I waited a minute or two before hitting the callback function. There it was again, uncertainty, knowing I needed to do it, not knowing whether I could deal with what he had to say.

He answered the phone on the second ring. "Ormand."

"Evening, Lieutenant. This is John Kinkaid." I was really pleased with how calm my voice sounded. "You left a message on my cell phone—sorry I'm so late getting back to you, but you called midshow. Sold-out show, packed house. I only just checked my messages. What's all this about, then?"

"Mr. Kinkaid, thanks for getting back to me tonight." He had a focused edge to his voice that reminded me of Bree when she was working. "I'd have understood if you'd waited until morning—I remembered Blacklight had a show tonight after I called. I have a few things I need to play for you."

For one wild moment, I was completely disoriented. Play for me? Did he mean music? I got hold of myself.

"I don't think I follow, Lieutenant. What sort of things?"

"CDs. Digital audio files, recorded on some of the most sophisticated audio spy technology available, uploaded to computer and then downloaded onto CDs. Excuse me a moment. . . ." I heard a muffled noise from the other end of the line; I'd have laid even money that he was sucking down coffee. "One of the first things we did after we found out that Perry Dillon maintained apartments in two cities besides New York was to ask the police in those cities to lock down the premises and take a look around for us. That's standard procedure."

Something was moving at the base of my spine: premonition, I think, knowledge that something nasty was about to come round the corner. I didn't much care for the feeling. "I gather some of your colleagues hit the jackpot, yeah? Struck it lucky?"

"Oh, yes. Yes, indeed." He sounded grim, implacable, indecently pleased. "The London Metro cops came through big-time. They locked down his place within an hour of our request. They've spent the past week taking it apart, inch by inch. They've spoken to his associates, his neighbours, anyone they could find who might have had anything to do with his life over the past few months."

"Very—thorough." *Keep it even*, I thought. Neutral. Not easy, when I could smell bad news coming. And Christ, could I smell bad news. My nerve endings may be messed up from the MS, but they were tingling at me right now: nothing in his voice was going to mean any good for me.

"The police generally are thorough, Mr. Kinkaid. We got the materials today I was hoping for: sound files from Perry Dillon's London computer. We downloaded them onto CDs."

"What sort of sound files?" I think I already knew the answer, what it had to be. Shit, shit, shit.

"Remember that CD I played for you, when you were here with your lawyer, last week? Dillon's self-made tapes, with all the dirt he dictated to himself? Well. The boys in London found the source files. As I say, we're very thorough."

My hands were wet. There was too much satisfaction in Ormand's voice, too much of the hunter who's picked up the scent of something wounded and helpless farther on up the road. "And that has what to do with me, exactly? Not that I don't want to help, I do, but I'm damned if I see . . ."

"He was living with someone." Ormand's voice had got sharp and smooth, the voice I associated with danger, trouble, bad stuff coming down the pike, with him as the messenger. "It seems he'd had a woman there for a while, the same woman—the people in the neighbouring flats have been questioned, and they've all said yes, he had a girlfriend. She was in and out a lot. We've got a very clear description of her. Very quaint language you Brits use, by the way. The cop's exact word was *dolly-bird*."

My throat was tight. "And? . . ."

"And we've listened to some of the stuff the London guys got from Dillon's flat. Unless we're completely off the mark, they're all the same woman. I don't think she knew she was being recorded—they're very disjointed, very rambling. She sounds either drunk or drugged. We think he was wired—spy technology—and didn't tell her."

I had an inkling then, the first real ray of daylight I'd seen, about why he wanted me. If I was right, there wasn't going to be any place to hide from the shitstorm. *No escape from rock and roll* . . .

"So, you want me to come up there and listen to your treasure trove, yeah? Tell you if I recognise the voice?"

"Something like that." Ormand was still sharp, still smooth. "See if you recognise the voice, recognise any of the stuff she's talking about. He's not asking her specific things, although he does do the occasional leading question. And of course, we have a physical description of her."

Light was breaking, hard and fast, and I was struggling like a bloody eel, trying not to give the sleek bastard a single weapon he could use. Control the voice, control it—what had Bree said, about the lie detector test? You could either go agitated or go Zen. Right, Johnny. Try for Zen.

"Right. Well, it's a bit late for me to try for a flight tonight—I'm assuming this can wait until tomorrow? And I'll need to be back here as soon as I'm done up there. We've got Dallas on Sunday night."

"Tomorrow morning is fine. Oh, one more thing, before I let you hang up. Maybe you can help us clear up another mystery. Am I correct in thinking that Blacklight rehearsed for a while in New York before the opening-night show at the Garden?"

"Yeah, for a week." I'd got it under control, I thought, but that question was totally out of the blue. What the hell? . . . "At TriBeCa, the theatre in the complex. You try to rehearse in a setting that reasonably approximates your venue—TriBeCa's a lot smaller, but the Garden wasn't available for three of the seven days we had free for rehearsals. Why?"

"I had a conversation earlier today, with Perry Dillon's agent. Very interesting, and more than a little surprising. He says he got a telephone call the morning of the Garden show, telling him that Dillon would be allowed limited access backstage, after all, and that his name would be on the guest list. A woman, he said—calling from a local number. He says the woman told him to tell Dillon to be there at half past nine, sharp. We're checking the TriBeCa phone log tomorrow, to see what we can find out. Hopefully, we'll have something very soon, at least a reasonably positive ID on the woman who called them. Tell you what—why don't you call me when you're on your way in the morning? I'll have the stuff set up for you."

I said nothing at all. There was nothing to say.

The concierge got me on a flight to New York at half past nine the following morning.

I'd got hold of Ian and Carla as soon as the ticket was booked. There was nothing I wanted to do less than involve the band; I wanted to keep it quiet until I could get more information and maybe even a handle on what was happening or about to happen. I was beginning to understand Bree's desire for invisibility. Right now, stepping back and vanishing into the woodwork sounded like bliss.

But that was wishful thinking, and I knew it. My brain was finally beginning to climb out of whatever little black hole it had been pushed into by Dillon's murder, by the heart attack, by Bree's disappearance. The pictures and possibilities that were offering themselves up weren't pretty. If I was right about the identity of the woman who'd been giving Perry Dillon dirt for Christ only knew how long, keeping it quiet wasn't going to be an option—not now and probably not ever.

The shit was about to hit the fan, and the killer was, it was my shit. And after all my big talk about loyalty, the least I could do was to give my bandmates a shot at minimising how hard and deep we were all buried in it.

I buzzed Ian on the hotel phone, got him on the first try, and then rousted Carla out of bed, and they came upstairs immediately. Any leftover tension between Ian and me, over that business with him not telling me about the biography, was long gone—it hadn't survived the sight of him on the phone to the concierge in the middle of the night, trying to help me find my old lady.

I didn't tell them what I was afraid of, but then, I didn't have to; they aren't dim, either of them. I let them know about the call from Ormand, told them what he'd told me about Dillon's London source, and about the phone call to Dillon's agent, reversing the official decision to bar him from access. When I got to that part, I saw bewilderment and some real trouble on Carla's face.

"JP, wait a minute. Hold on." She stared at me. "That's nuts. I mean, it had to be someone with the band. He said a local number? New York local, you mean?"

"He said local. I assumed he meant local to Manhattan, yeah. But I didn't ask."

"Then I really don't get it. Who the hell? Someone in New York? I wasn't here for the first gig. I'd booked in to come out to Minneapolis, and then Ian got me on a plane right after the murder—and man oh man, I don't even want to think about what's piling up in Los Angeles for me to deal with when I get back. But this doesn't make sense. The staff at TriBeCa has nothing to do with the band. We just rented the theatre rehearsal space from them. So who—?"

There was a very sour spot in the pit of my stomach. What had Ormand said? Something about whoever the woman was, telling Perry's agent to make sure Perry got to the backstage door at nine thirty, sharp? And Bree, my Bree, had been signing guests in at half past nine.

That was the exact time, that crucial fifteen minutes. She'd been there. Bree the invisible had gone completely out of character and made it her business to be there. She'd brought Jerry a beer, been horrified at his lack of a dinner break, nobly sent him off to have a piss and some nosh. . . .

I closed my eyes for a moment, dizzy. A woman with the band, a woman calling from a local phone, a woman setting Perry Dillon up to be backstage where he'd been told he couldn't be.

An accessory before the fact. In a state with the death penalty. Oh, God.

"I don't know." They were watching me. I thought I saw something on Carla's face; it might have been shock or maybe it was just comprehension, the lightbulb going off, her figuring out what it was I was so afraid of. If I was right . . . "Look, I need to fly up in the morning and see Ormand. The concierge booked me an early flight. The thing is, I've got no fucking clue how long it's going to take. I've told him we've got Dallas on Sunday night, but who knows what's going to happen? Depending on what goes down, I could be stuck there. So we need to be prepared. That's why I'm keeping you away from sleep." I hesitated a moment. "I'm sorry about this. I know it's a drag. You've been amazing, both of you, this entire mess."

"Don't be sorry." Ian, maybe the least touchy-feely human being of my acquaintance, reached out and put a hand on my arm for a moment. "I'm glad you told us. I just wish we could make this easier for you, JP. If there's any way, we will."

"Well, yeah—of course we will." Carla sounded almost surprised. "It's what we're here for."

I looked from Ian to Carla, and for a moment, I loved them both. Yeah, Blacklight pays them a lot of money, but the thing is, those two go well beyond what anyone should be expected to have to deal with.

Blacklight, well, we're not divas. We've never been one of

those acts who get themselves banned from hotels by trashing rooms or demanding the concierge set them up with hookers or whatnot. We'd never been the bad boys. Even Mac—flamboyant, publicity-minded, completely-without-inhibitions Mac—was solid. From the time I'd joined the band right up through now, we'd always been just five geezers sitting around with guitars and a drum or two, making music.

So, yeah, Ian and Carla had it fairly easy, mostly. Cushy gigs, you might say, not to mention the glitz and glamour, the limos and first-class travel and brilliant hotels, all the benefits. But this side of it, sitting in my hotel room at half past one in the morning, helping me work out how to avoid or, at least, take some of the impact off a disaster that was none of their fault, and all of mine—we weren't paying them for that. Hell, there wasn't enough money minted to pay them for that. Loyalty, that level, you just can't buy it.

"Can I leave you guys to it?" The night had caught up with me, and I hadn't taken my bedtime meds yet. "I've got a wake-up call set for seven, and I'll need some kip. And you ought to get some, as well. I'll ring up from New York, once I've got more of a handle on what's going on."

I took a taxi straight from JFK to Ormand's office.

There was something weirdly liberating about having left the onus for coping with the band situation on Carla and Ian. It meant I could put all the energy I had—not much, right, but whatever I had left—into dealing with whatever Ormand had ready to dish out.

The concierge had got me both morning papers, and I'd made myself go through them, front to back, making damned sure that I wouldn't miss anything that might be buried.

The *Journal-Constitution* had a small piece, but it was right at the bottom of page one. The header ran POSSIBLE BREAK IN ROCK AND ROLL MURDER? That was followed by:

In a statement issued early this morning, Lt. Patrick Ormand of NYPD announced what he termed a "significant development" in the investigation into the murder of controversial biographer Perry Dillon backstage at Madison Square Garden. When pressed for additional details, Lieutenant Ormand would say only that a close and widespread examination of Perry Dillon's recent life has led them to certain conclusions. . . .

So, I was already sweating when I opened *USA Today*. And there is was, page one, with its very own dark border:

DILLON MURDER ON ICE?

The man heading up the investigation into the backstage homicide of biographer Perry Dillon said this morning that there had been a major break in the case and that an arrest might be expected at any moment. Lt. Patrick Ormand told reporters late last night that he was hoping to have an official announcement shortly. He added that he was expecting to conduct an interview with a woman whose current whereabouts have become "high priority."

Something had locked down hard in my head and heart after reading that. I folded up the paper and set it aside. My hands were sweating and shaking. I'd thought I'd figured out what Ormand had been talking about, but now I wasn't so sure. If he was talking about Bree, if that meant I'd been wrong and Bree's whereabouts were Ormand's high priority, then I was walking into something huge.

Right. He wanted me in New York, did he? Fine. The slippery son of a bitch was going to get me. If the story was even close to accurate, he had no better idea of where Bree was than I did. I was going to New York, and I was going forewarned, forearmed, and ready to muscle up for a bit of protecting of my own.

I'd spent the flight to New York trying to decide whether or not I wanted to ring up Pasquini, tell him to meet me at the station. In the end, I decided against it. Yeah, I know, lawyer, privileged, all that rubbish, but I was still going as much on instinct as I was on actual thinking, and something in me didn't want to do that, not yet. It was the sense of ignorance, of not knowing how much of what I'd come to suspect was really the truth, that was really messing with my head, and my options, too.

So I decided to wait. If I needed him, I could let him know. At the moment, he'd be a hindrance to me and not a help.

For the same reason, I'd turned my cell phone off and decided to leave it that way while I was in Ormand's office. I didn't know where Bree was, and I didn't know what she was up to. I was damned if I'd risk exposing her to Ormand, not until I had enough in my arsenal to protect her. If I'd sussed even a fragment of what had been happening, she was going to need some serious protection. It was my job to provide it.

I walked into Ormand's office alone, with no legal backup and with my link to the outside world turned off. For now, this was going to be the two of us. It might be on his turf, but I had my eyes open. I was as ready as I was going to get.

"Good morning—or is it afternoon?" Ormand surprised me by offering a hand to shake. He sounded friendly. "Don't mind me—I've had a long couple of days. Can I get you something? Coffee?"

"No, thanks, I'm fine. They fed me breakfast on the plane and I hit a Starbucks at JFK." I followed him into his office. There was equipment set up, the same little CD player he'd used to play Dillon's dirt before.

I took a deep breath and sat down. It was time to see what I'd been right about, what I'd been wrong about—time to know.

Showtime.

I suppose there was still a part of me that was in denial. I mean, I could easily have been wrong, in that first blast of intuition I'd been hit with, when Ormand had told me about Dillon's London playmate. God knows, I wanted to be wrong. But wrong or right, the voice coming out of the speakers in that dusty New York police station shouldn't have kicked me in the heart the way it did.

". . . yeah, he never got it. No appreciation. I was out there, pushing him, getting his name out, shaking the big stick, twenty-four fucking seven. He nearly turned down Blacklight. Fucking unbelievable. I mean, Blacklight—huge deal, Malcolm Sharpe, top-five band, up there with the Stones or Pink Floyd or Queen, and all he wanted to do was jack off playing guitar at stupid little sessions with a collection of fucking nobodies. . . ."

I closed my eyes. I couldn't close my ears—this was payback, you know? Karma coming home to hit me where I lived, where I didn't live anymore. But I closed my eyes. I wasn't letting Ormand or anyone else see what that voice, those words, were doing to me.

". . . fucking musicians, stupid as mud—Perry, we have some blow here, right? Where—oh, ta . . . they never notice anything. I mean, did I tell you about when I got nicked by the guard at Harrods? Pretty amber necklace—Rick Hilliard dared me to boost it, and I did, and then I got nicked and Rick had to pay for the necklace. The wanker sniggered all the way back to his place. No sex for him for a week, the shirty bastard. That got him back. And of course JP never knew. Never noticed.

Fucking musicians. Only time he ever noticed anything, and it had to be that little tart in San Francisco. . . ."

How long had it been going on? How long had she been spilling it to Dillon, and for what? As a husband, especially one as definitively estranged as I was, I had no right to ask. It wasn't as if I was there, still bedding her, still taking care of her. But as a member of the band she was helping Perry Dillon smear for money, I had all the right in the world.

". . . [giggle] . . . I remember the second time JP came back to London—fuck, I was so bloody ill, I couldn't stand straight. I rang him and he came, got to give him that. Loyal. But really fucking dim. He had to know what I was up to—that third time, I just wanted to see if I could pull him away from his American bitch. And I could . . . I remember, back in Seattle, that first tour, shit, what was I talking about? . . ."

Somewhere in me, the small boy—you know, the one who'd lain in a hotel bed in Miami and wondered whether concentrating hard enough would bring Bree back to me—was curled up in a ball, sobbing like a bloody baby. She'd mentioned Seattle, that tour, and I remembered how I'd sat on the hotel bed in Los Angeles the night before I met Bree first, watching Cilla, loving how she'd get out and fight for me, glad we were so tight, so close, a team, a couple.

I'd loved this woman once, loved her enough to marry her. So who the hell was this stoned, wasted train wreck, pouring out every bit of personal history and band dirt she could dredge up out of her memory banks?

A voice, male this time. I recognised it—it had slipped in the knife in Carla's L.A. conference room. "So, *she actually stole heroin for him? You were saying earlier, about how her mother took the fall and he got deported? . . . "*

Her voice again. "Bloody hell, Perry, why do you keep asking about that little bitch? Fucking sixteen years old, and she knew every trick in the book. Dear little Bree, that little cunt. He called her up and asked her to score him some snow, did you know that? The brat, she knew what she wanted, all right, and she knew how to get it, and what she wanted was my husband. Yeah, right, you asked—she stole drugs from her mum, and he went cold on it and she got busted and he got booted out of the States for it. Her mum got the sack from her clinic. Little bitch nearly killed him with too much, and the fucking idiot went back to her after that! Can you imagine? Went clean, did anything she wanted. After I'd been there for him, six years, hooked him up, got his name out there, believed in him. . . ."

The venom in her voice was staggering. She said Bree's name, and it sounded like something a cobra might have spit out into the air in Ormand's office.

I heard a click. Ormand had turned the machine off. The silence stretched out—I wasn't breaking it.

"Can you identify this woman for us?" His voice was very gentle, very quiet. No sense of the hunter in there. He was sorry for me. The son of a bitch was pitying me.

I opened my eyes and focused on him.

"Of course I can." My own voice seemed to be coming out of a place I hadn't known existed. It was very calm, dry ice, and bitter. "But you knew that, didn't you? Before you asked me to fly up here and help you? You knew bloody well the woman who'd been feeding Perry Dillon this rubbish was my wife. So why don't we just cut out the game-playing bullshit, yeah?"

"I'm sorry. Yes, I knew—it seemed pretty clear, once I listened to some of these. But I had to ask you." He was watching me steadily. "I'm not exactly enjoying this, either. I'm not in the business of deliberately pile-driving people who are helping in an investigation. Even if I was a sadist—and I'm not—there wouldn't be any benefit to me. I honestly did need you to confirm it. Are you willing to sign a statement? Do you want your lawyer? If you want to call him and get him up here, I'm happy to wait—"

"Yes. No." Reaction was setting in. "I mean yes, I'll sign a statement, once I read it, and no, I don't want my lawyer. Just get the damned statement ready. And keep it simple."

"It's already typed, Mr. Kinkaid. I have it here. If you won't call your lawyer, I suggest reading it carefully."

I read it over. I can't imagine why he thought I needed to read it carefully—it was short, two sentences, nothing tricky, just a statement that I, John Peter Kinkaid, identified the voice of my legal wife, Priscilla Kinkaid, last known place of residence, 18 Howard Crescent, London NW1, England. What the hell had she been doing at Perry Dillon's? I'd given her the London house. . . .

Ah, fuck it. No longer my concern.

I signed the statement. I didn't hesitate—there was a feeling about it, something that was almost relief. This was it, then, after all these years, the thing I should have done years ago, that I'd been too comfortable to bother about.

Comfort—right. That was gone, that comfort zone, gone for good. This two-line statement, this was the divorce decree, no matter what else happened later.

"Here. Take it." I got up, pins and needles in both feet. Bloody MS. "Anything else?"

"I'm afraid so, Mr. Kinkaid. About that telephone call—the one to Perry Dillon's agent." He paused, as if he were hunting for the right words. "We traced the number to a pay phone about two blocks away from the TriBeCa rehearsal space."

I stayed quiet, watching him. He went on carefully. "You know, I could try to lay a trap here, tell you he could identify her voice. But I won't. He doesn't remember much about the woman's voice, except that it was muffled. Pitch, tone, accent—none of that. We may never know."

I waited. It was obvious he wasn't done yet.

"I want to make sure you realise," he told me, "that your wife is now a party to this investigation? We'll be asking the authorities in the United Kingdom to help us locate her, and exploring every possible avenue to find her."

"Right." I thought of Cilla being hunted, caught up in the grind of the state's machinery. Something twisted up inside. But under that, there was relief, a heavy dizzying wash of it, because it confirmed that my second guess, that "high priority whereabouts" thing, had been wrong. It was Cilla, not Bree, that he wanted. "What about it?"

"We may need to ask you to sign releases for us: access to her telephone records, credit card records, anything that will help us find her."

"Me? For Christ's sake, why?" They wanted me to help them hunt her down? The bloke had to be insane. "Lieutenant, look. I've seen Cilla three times in twenty-five years. I haven't exchanged a word with her in at least ten. The word *estranged* could be illustrated in the bloody *OED* with a picture of us. Why the hell are you asking me?"

"Because," Kinkaid told me, "she's now at the top of the list of people we'd like to talk to. And—for whatever reason—you're still legally her husband."

CHAPTER THIRTEEN

When I caught my flight up from Atlanta, I'd thought that I'd be in New York only a few hours. Now, under the circs, there was no way in hell I was leaving yet.

I had a sense of urgency, as if everything was gathering, a huge storm cloud of purest shit, about to blow our way. I was damned if I wanted to be elsewhere when it hit, especially since I still couldn't shake the feeling the bulk of it was going to be aimed straight at Bree.

I made the decision between walking out of Ormand's office and hitting the pavement: I was staying in New York, at least overnight. The problem was, I hadn't even brought a toothbrush with me. I needed a hotel and a change of clothes. I also needed to update Carla and Ian, give them the lowdown on what I'd found out. I didn't want to—the idea made me sick at my stomach. But Cilla had done huge damage—potential damage, anyway—and the damage was to Blacklight, not only to me. Short version: I had no right to keep quiet. This one wasn't blowing away on its own.

I headed for the nearest Starbucks and found a quiet corner upstairs with a hot tea. First order of business was obviously going to be Carla—she could get me a hotel.

This probably makes me out to be a complete berk, but I'd actually forgotten that I turned my cell phone off when I walked into the police station. For half a minute, holding the damned dead thing in my hand, I sat there silently calling myself rude names. Bloody hell—two hours, with no way for anyone to get hold of me.

I got the damned thing on, and of course, there was the message light, blinking away.

For a moment, I didn't want to listen. It sounds insane; I'd done nothing for the past few days but stress about Bree not ringing me, and here I was, turning off my cell. Truth is, after hearing Cilla's voice spewing that filth to Perry Dillon? I was almost afraid of what might be in that message.

I punched in my password, listened to that exasperating, vaguely female robotic voice telling me I had one message, sent about forty-five minutes before. *To listen to your messages, press star . . .*

"John? It's me. I'm still okay—I don't know how much longer I can do this, things are getting kind of weird, but I'm okay, I wanted to tell you—"

A crash of something that sounded distant, faraway background noise, a muffled thump, something that might have been a person crying out, Bree saying something incoherent, and then dead air. Silence.

I sat there, breathing, just forcing the air out of constricted lungs, hearing it whistle out through my nostrils. I knew that if I opened my mouth, I was going to start shouting into the bloody phone. That would have got me booted out or carted off as a nutter, and what I really needed was a bit of the same stuff I'd tried for in Ormand's office—I needed a moment of Zen.

I punched in her cell phone number. No luck—one ring and it dumped me straight into her voice mail announcement. I kept my voice low—it wanted to bounce off the ceiling.

"Bree? Look, I'm sorry I had my phone off. I'm in New York. Ormand rang me up after the show last night, asked me to fly up. Things have been happening, love."

A woman passed by my table, well within earshot, and headed for the stairs. I hesitated. No point, really, in going into too much detail, especially not in a public place. The publicity was probably unavoidable, and even though I'm not Mac, I'm still a member of Blacklight. I wasn't going to risk putting sensitive stuff out there where someone might recognise me.

But I needed to let her know the basics, as soon as possible. I still didn't have a clue what she was up to, but if there was any possibility that fear of Ormand was what was keeping Bree in hiding, the sooner she knew she'd been bumped off the hot seat, the sooner I'd have her back where she belonged.

I took a look around, at the size of my potential listening audience. There were only two other people upstairs, both reasonably distant. I lowered my voice and carried on. "The London police found out who'd been feeding Dillon his dirt, and turns out, it was Cilla. I've just signed a statement identifying her. I hope for her sake she can prove she was in London when Dillon got bashed, but if she can't, I don't fucking care anymore. I'm done, love. She's about to become the focus of Ormand's attention, and I'm not protecting her. It's not my job anymore—that's protecting you, and as of right now, I'm doing just that. Call me when you can, yeah?"

I hung up and rang Carla. I just told her that I was staying in Manhattan for the night and asked her to get me a hotel and then ring me back; I had things to tell her, but that was something that would wait until I was in a room of my own, no listeners, behind a locked door. She told me to stay on the line, was gone about three minutes, and then clicked back in.

"You're at the Omni," she told me. "Madison Avenue at Fifty-second. Check-in is anytime after three, so you're good to go. It's already paid for—Blacklight corporate. You didn't say whether or not you had a flight back to Atlanta booked, and if not, you'll need to let me know; if you're cutting it close, it might make more sense to go straight to Dallas. We'll handle all the luggage. Just keep me posted."

"Right." I had a bad moment, just cringing inside. Damned good people, going out of their way for everyone else in the Blacklight family. They deserved better than Cilla's shit. . . .

"Call me if you need anything else." Some of the sharp Carla edge left her voice, softening it. "JP—is everything all right?"

"No. Unfortunately, everything's seriously wrong. But I'll tell you about it once I'm at the hotel, yeah? All hell is about to break loose, and we're going to need some handle on it before it does. But the stuff I need to pass along to you, middle of a Starbucks is a bad choice of locale. Look, I might not check in for an hour or so—I need to get a change of clothes. I haven't even got a toothbrush or a comb with me." Something struck me. "Carla, by the way, can you put me on hold one more time, and find Domitra? I need to know what size shoe she wears."

"Seven and a half, same as me." Bless the woman, she'd just answered my second question, the one I couldn't have asked her directly. "She let me try on her custom Doc Martens back in Philly. Serious head-stompers, those boots are. Too heavy for me, but they're way cool. Anything else?"

"No. Just keep your own cell handy, yeah? I'll ring you back later."

It makes me happy, looking back on what was essentially a day of complete shit, to remember that two hours of shopping. Speaking just for myself, I don't care one way or the other. I stopped off at Bergdorf Goodman and bought some underwear, some socks, a pair of black trousers, a black silk shirt, a nice leather overnight bag. The local branch of Duane Reade, the chain drugstore, did nicely for emergency toiletries.

Coming out of the drugstore, I had a really bad moment. Up at the register, emptying out the little red carrier basket of toothbrush and hairbrush and dental floss, I found myself next to one of those impulse-geared wire magazine-and-newspaper holders. You know the kind, yeah? Stuffed full of gossip rags and tabloids and those bizarre things Americans seem to like so much, the ones where the current Secretary of State or someone is shown shaking hands with a three-headed alien, usually with something about the world coming to an end as a headline on there somewhere?

These were the usual rubbish, standard. It wasn't until I'd paid and was putting my change away that I realised that I'd been looking at a headline on one of the more lurid rags.

DEAD BIOGRAPHER KEPT SOURCES IN SECRET LOVE NEST

And there he was, that sort of feral fake surfer look, last seen alive by me as he was slipping in the knife during that interview in L.A. Perry Dillon, secretive and dangerous, looking out at the world from the cover of this trashy rag, stone dead.

"Sir? Did you need anything else?"

I jumped about a foot. There was a queue building up behind me, and I hadn't noticed. I'd just been standing there, staring at Perry Dillon and the cheap gossipy headline he was now starring in.

I thought for a moment about what that headline might have behind it. Were there pictures of Cilla, mentions of me?

Had Bree's talent for invisibility failed her entirely, and was she mentioned?

"No." I turned away. There was no way I was going to give in and read the damned thing. "Thanks."

Thank Christ for Jimmy Choo, you know? It was damned near the only thing that could have lightened my day at that point. If the saleswoman was startled at this English geezer walking in and asking for two pairs of the pricey snakeskin high-heeled sandals with the ankle ties, both size seven and a half, here's my credit card, I'll take them with me, oh, and while I'm at it, I'll have that pair of pale yellow heels in size nine and a half, she made a good job hiding it. I walked out with something, however small, that ought to show both women how grateful I was to both of them, although for very different things.

Oh, and this time, I kept my cell phone on. Of course, it stayed silent.

That was one of the strangest evenings I've ever spent. I mean, here I was, alone in New York. Somewhere in this damned city, my old lady was doing something I couldn't even guess at, and she didn't want me to find her. All I could do was sit in my nice hotel and wait.

One of the hardest things I had to deal with was keeping my promise to ring Carla back and give her the rundown on what had happened at Ormand's office. I did it, though—I didn't keep a damned thing back. She went calm stonewall professional at me, which meant she was horrified and not going to show it.

I went out for dinner at a small Italian restaurant and waited while they found me a table in a corner. That's the thing about being one half a couple at home, and part of a band family on the road: I hadn't been out alone for a meal in a good long while. Being treated as if I was either a freak or a pariah who couldn't get a dinner date was really annoying.

I found myself eating a plate of ravioli that, according to

the Zagat rating, was superb, some of the best to be found in midtown. Bree wouldn't have fed this stuff to the cats. I sat there by myself, chewing the fashionably undercooked pasta, and found myself thinking back to what I'd heard Cilla say on those filthy CDs.

I couldn't wrap my mind around any of it. The woman who'd sat there, redoing her face every night before I pinned her to the bed, so that I'd never see her looking less than perfect—was that really the same woman who'd sold us all out to Perry Dillon for a bit of blow, or maybe just a bit of revenge? It floored me, not just the change in her, but my own not noticing. Okay, right, so I'd seen her three times since 1979; this was still beyond my ability to sort out. What in hell had she been doing to fall so deep, to sink so low?

I forced myself to mentally replay what she'd said, and suddenly, the ravioli stopped having any taste at all. She'd been bitter about me, contemptuous, incredulous, angry. All right—I understood that. Cilla was my wife. Those reactions, I could see cause for all of it if I looked at it from her side of the great divide.

But the hatred in her voice when she spoke about Bree, that was something else entirely. That was as ugly as ugly gets. It must have been a forest fire in Cilla's reality, all-consuming, impossible to put out. And I hadn't known. Christ, what else hadn't I known? If that feeling had burned through Cilla, had it burned just as strong in Bree?

I thought about something Cilla had said to Perry Dillon; the third time she'd rung up and said she needed me, she'd done it just to see if she could guilt me away from Bree, just to see if I'd go. I remembered that final trip back to London—a very short stay, that one, less than two weeks, and there had been a day in the middle of it that was carved into my memory, a day that had had nothing to do with Cilla.

My fingers had clenched up, hard and tight around the fork I was holding. I remembered that Bree had busied herself with a major catering project just before I'd gone, throwing herself into cookery, remembered the white, drawn look of desolation on her face, that she'd said nothing at all. I remembered that whatever had been wrong enough with Cilla to prompt her to call me and beg for me to come help, she'd apparently been over it pretty damned quick.

And now, it seemed, there'd been nothing wrong at all. She'd rung me in San Francisco and told me she was sick, that she needed me in London. She'd done it just to see if I'd do it. And I'd gone, leaving Bree again. . . .

"Coffee, sir?"

"No, thanks." I'd eaten the entire plate of pasta, and some bread as well, without even noticing. "Just the bill, please."

And Perry Dillon, dropping questions, recording her without telling her, taking his sleazy little notes—Christ. If there was actually an afterlife, what I was feeling about him at the moment probably had me on Satan's personal guest list, an all-access backstage pass to hell. I just hoped Dillon had one of those as well. There was no way I could regret him getting killed—I was glad the fucker was dead. The only surprise was that no one had bashed him years ago. Good riddance. My only regret was the mess his getting killed had landed us all in.

My cell phone rang on the walk back to the Omni. I ducked into a doorway, trying to block out the traffic noise.

"Hello?"

"Mr. Kinkaid? This is Patrick Ormand. I just wanted to let you know that we probably won't need you to authorise checking Mrs. Kinkaid's credit cards or anything else. We got hold of the customs and immigration people this evening."

Taxis, buses, chattering people . . . there was too much noise, too much going on around me, New York on a warm night not giving me a few seconds of silence. "Right—sorry, I can barely hear you. I'm in midtown and it's noisy. What? . . ."

"We've spoken to the people at Virgin Airlines. Priscilla Kinkaid flew from London Heathrow Airport to JFK two days before your Madison Square Garden show. She filled out the required form, contact information while in the United States. She checked into the Trimball Hotel—it's in SoHo. Not too far from the TriBeCa complex, in fact."

I'd begun to shiver. Ridiculous. The night was warm enough for shirtsleeves. I couldn't be shivering.

"Mr. Kinkaid?"

"Yeah." The shakes moved down through my legs. I put my free hand out, felt the doorjamb of the building I'd sheltered against, and sat down hard. "I'm still here. You said she flew to JFK. And?"

"She remained registered as a guest at the Trimball until Saturday morning. She checked out early Saturday morning, signed out at just after ten, without leaving any forwarding address or additional information. We're trying to get in touch with the clerk on duty when she checked out, to see if she had anyone with her."

Saturday morning. My head was pounding. Saturday, while I was sulking in Central Park and having my head handed to me by my lead singer's bodyguard. Saturday, when I'd gone back to the hotel and Bree'd been gone, and not got back until after one. Saturday, when she claimed she'd been out walking half the length of Manhattan and back again, even though she'd had no sleep. Saturday . . .

"Obviously, Mr. Kinkaid, finding your wife has just become our highest priority." Smooth, sharp. "If you happen to hear from her, please remember, this is a police investigation. Not

216

letting us know would be grounds for possible accessory charges. Don't do anything—heroic. If you—"

"*Heroic?*"

I laughed, about as unpleasant a noise as I'd ever come out with. It shut Ormand off in midsentence, and a couple of passersby stopped to stare at me. Now, that's a feat, getting that sort of reaction in Manhattan at night. Midtown after dark, you need wellies to wade through the weirdness; attracting attention for your own weirdness means you really have to sound as if you're ready for the corn bin.

"Right," I told Ormand. "Okay. Call you. Of course I will. But as for the likelihood of Cilla ringing me, at this point? Here's a friendly bit of advice, mate: Don't hold your breath."

When I got back to the Omni, I got to give yet another concierge a pop at being Superman. My cell phone had given a few warning beeps on the walk back to the hotel, just a friendly little reminder that the battery was getting low. And, of course, my charger was back in my Atlanta hotel room.

Of course, weighed against some of the rock and roll requests concierges have got in the past, my request was probably a walk in the park. The appropriate charger was brought up by one of the concierge's minions within fifteen minutes, coinciding with the arrival of room service and a pot of tea.

When I look back now on the events that led up to me sitting in the Omni Hotel alone on a summer night, I honestly wonder if I'd gone off my nut, a kind of temporary insanity, something that just took me out of my own head and dropped me, nice and safe and secure, right in the middle of nowhere. Bree was gone, I had no idea when or even if she was coming back, what she was doing, and there was some irony in there: no idea whether she was safe, and here I'd finally got the fact that it was my turn to protect her.

I drank tea, sitting in that nice comfortable hotel room with brand-new clothing, a brand-new overnight bag, fifteen hundred dollars' worth of Jimmy Choo dinner sandals in a shopping bag, and my cell phone charging on borrowed equipment, and I decided I'd gone down a rabbit hole somehow, alternate reality. Cilla doing what she'd done, dead bloke in my dressing room, my old lady missing and beyond any help I could hope to give, and here I was, alone at the Omni. Any minute, the Jabberwocky would jump out at me.

Truth is, the situation was driving me bonkers. For the first time in a long time, I was energised, wanting to do something, anything at all. I was literally twitching with the need, tingling, little dark electrical shocks, and this time, those reactions had nothing to do with the MS. And there was fuck-all I could do about anything, other than to sit on my bum and wait for something to happen. The irony there was that I'd just come to realise that sitting on my bum and waiting for something to happen—for about thirty years, now—was the reason we were in this mess.

I put the tea tray outside the door for the staff to take off later and wandered around the room for a bit. I had this weird buzz going; it actually reminded me of the days when I'd done a lot of blow, a sort of strung-out itchy feeling. I thought about watching a movie and decided against it. A movie would take some concentration, and I simply didn't have any. I thought about going out for a late-night walk, but that wasn't really an option—I'd have to do it without the phone, since the bloody thing was going to take an hour at least to charge all the way up. I found myself glaring at the fancy little writing desk holding the phone charger, muttering to myself: "Come on, Bree, fucking ring me, come on, come on . . ."

So—insanity, right, I know, you don't have to tell me—I decided that a hot bath would be the move. There was a weird sort of defiance in there somewhere; basically, if I couldn't do anything useful in the outside world, I'd just do a Bree and kick the outside world to the kerb, and indulge myself.

I locked myself in the bathroom and ran the taps, filling the tub. The ventilation system hummed into life, and I got naked and into the hot water, and decided this had definitely been the right move. If I was going to be helpless and forcibly stuck in this kind of inertia, I could at least try to relax my mind enough to drown out Cilla's slurred venomous voice in my head. Zen, I thought, and hot water moved up around my chin, pure Zen, relax, no worries. . . .

I don't know how long I dozed in there, because I hadn't looked at the time when I climbed in. But I jerked my eyes open when I realised that the water had cooled off, enough to where it was uncomfortable.

The mind relaxation thing had worked, so maybe I wasn't quite so insane as I'd felt. I towelled off, feeling stronger somehow, energised in a better way, more useful. Until the world outside decided it wanted me to come along and play, I was going to hold on to the calm. There wasn't any reason to do anything else, not really.

I wandered out into my room. The city skyline caught my eye out the window; New York is really spectacular at night, if you like tall buildings and electric lights and don't mind having to sit in a skyscraper to see it all. Maybe I ought to watch some telly, after all. . . .

My own reflection held nice and still for a moment against the darkened glass of the windows. There was something there, a light, something moving. I turned back into the room.

The message light on my cell phone was blinking.

Right. Zen. Flip open the cover, enter my password. Listen to the little robot lady, telling me, *You have one message, sent at eleven oh seven. To listen to your message, press star* . . .

I looked at the screen on the cell, taking a moment, taking

in air. The number was international. It had a *11 44* preface. A London number.

My fingers were shaking. I sat down on the edge of the bed and pressed the key for playback.

"JP? Are you there? Look—I'm calling to say I'm sorry. And I hope you don't have one of those fucking thirty-second limits on your voice mail, because this—it's going to go on for a bit."

She sounded tired, beyond tired, exhaustion I couldn't begin to imagine or articulate.

"It wasn't supposed to happen this way. All I wanted was to talk to him, ask him why he wouldn't return my calls. He left me in London, did you know? Didn't tell me where he was going. It was after he left, I found his little stash of spy toys."

She laughed, and I winced. I'd thought my own laughter, on the phone with Ormand, had sounded deranged, but this . . .

"The wanker recorded everything I said to him. Every word, JP. Fed me what I needed, always Dr. Feelgood, right there with a few lines. Really good he was, you know? God, the man was a professional. Fucking reptile."

Where was she calling from? I held the phone to my ear, wanting to shout into it, to tell her to pick up the phone and talk to me, forcing myself to remember that I was listening to a voice, not a woman. What's more, it was a voice that had been and gone. She'd rung half an hour ago—if she was in London, she'd rung just after four in the morning.

"I have to say—Bree helped. Yeah, your little bit of teenage nookie, all grown up—I hate the bitch, I'd love to see her dead, but that won't happen, will it? Pissed-off little saint you've got there. Bloody hell, if I had to put up with her Joan of Arc shit day after day, I'd have throttled her long ago. But she isn't stupid. She's quick, your fucking annoying piece of ass. She knew what to do. Just what to do."

The room suddenly felt very cold. I could hear my own breathing now, shallow and fast, and my heart was slamming at me. *Bree helped? What does that mean?* . . .

"You weren't there when I rang that first time. Fuck, yeah, now there's a big shock, you not being there for me. She was, though. And when I got to New York and rang her again, she knew what to do, setting me up so I could talk to him, straighten it out, tell him I'd deny everything he'd used without my knowledge or permission, let him know I'd sue, have him popped for the drugs back in London. I would have done, too. I didn't care anymore, so long as I could stop him."

I heard myself make a noise, incoherent, God knows what. My hands were suddenly cold.

"I mean, in case you're wondering, I had no clue he was doing a book. I only found that out after he dumped me in London—I got into his computer. The conceited shit thought I was so far gone, he didn't need to lock it down. He even left his cell phone there, and I helped myself to it. No reason to spend my own money, right? Or your money?"

That laugh again, making all the hair on my arms move.

"Anyway. His little mistake. Not his only mistake, either. I found his book proposal, the sample chapters, the letters from his agent, what he was using for his dirt, and it was all me, shit he'd got from me. At least I think it was—I was pretty out of it a lot of the time. So I came over to try and get him to see me, get him to drop it. That's all I wanted to do, JP. I swear it was."

Silence. It went on so long, I wondered if she'd rung off. But then I heard a tiny sigh, chilling me, echoing and regretful down the line and into my phone.

"Backstage at the Garden—God. I was terrified I'd run into you, that you'd know me, even though I'd done my hair dark, and anyway, I've changed a good bit since the last time you bothered to come to London. Bree'd timed it out for me. She said half past nine, and there she was, playing door dragon. It felt really strange, being a plus-one, been a long time. I haven't been near a Blacklight gig since Seattle. A long, long time."

It was something I'd always worried about, Cilla showing up at the backstage door somewhere the band was playing. God only knows how I would have handled it. I'd always been glad it never came up. . . .

"She stamped me in—I mean, how funny is that? My husband's little underage fucktoy, letting your wife into your gig? She sent me off to wait. Perry wasn't there yet. He'd been told half past nine, and of course

222

he wasn't having any of that, now, was he? Of course he had to show up late."

Bree. Oh, Christ. No.

She was in it, up to her neck. She'd known Dillon was coming. She'd let Cilla in backstage. What was that, in a murder charge? Conspiracy?

Ormand was going to have her for lunch. But if Cilla was telling the truth, Bree had been cooperating with her down the line. Why? It didn't make sense. The two women hated each other.

"I didn't mean to flip out. But he laughed at me, JP, you know? Said I could sue all I wanted, the book was going to make so much money, he'd pay any settlement and still have enough to buy himself a dozen stoned little slags like me. I was crying, and he said that, and I flipped the fuck out."

I was shivering, not sure why. I remembered Perry Dillon's voice from Carla's conference room, remembered wondering if the accent was Chicago or not. I could hear him, saying that to Cilla—I could hear his voice.

"I didn't mean for it to happen, JP. I wasn't trying to do anything. I don't even really remember picking up the guitar stand, it's gone all dreamlike. But it was just me and him, and then he was on the floor, all blue."

I hit the pause button. It took me three minutes to get back into the clothes I'd been wearing. I knew, now, where Bree must be, what she must have been doing, why she'd taken those extra pills, the information she must have got from Miranda. When this message had run its length, I wanted to be ready.

Sedatives, opiates. It had been a very long time since I'd been cold on heroin or coke, but if I was stupid enough, I could still bring the horrors of withdrawal up in my memory, fresh as if it had been yesterday.

"Little Saint Bree, yeah, well. God, I hate her. I just fucking hate her. I hate her for everything, but you know what I really want to kill her for, just bash her, watch her brains spatter all over the walls? That she was there for me, and you weren't. Story of my fucking life. She wouldn't help me get out, though, wouldn't help me search Perry's apartment when I asked her, said she wasn't going to be an accessory after the fact. But I'm not dim, even if I am fucked up. I used the rest of my stash and then I got the hell out of my hotel. If you want to know, I'm at a dump called the McKinley Residential Hotel, West 128th Street. Weekly rates, ask no questions. Hell, they let my supplier up, just before I rang you."

My stomach had joined my heart in the slam. I swallowed down bile.

"I've been cold since I got to the McKinley. No shape to read the fucking *New York Times*, I'm afraid. Or *Rolling Stone*. So I didn't know about your heart attack. But I'm glad you had one—your blood pressure pills, those pain pills and shit, that kept me sane. Saint Bree, keeping me from the worst of it. Bitch. Nice to know she hates me as much as I hate her. Anyway."

Something in her voice was changing. Something was coming. A memory came to me of Cilla, a sense memory, of the woman in my arms, in my bed, my wife, me holding her down and laughing down at her, cocaine cold on the tip of her tongue, touching it to my tongue, to my chest, moving down, me laughing, going very still, trusting her . . .

"Even little girly-femme saints have to sleep sometime. I finally got hold of my supplier—he came by with enough good product to hold me for a week. Bree was fathoms deep. She's got a few bruises, I'm afraid. I'm sorry for those. They weren't deliberate, I'd been thrashing around a bit, and she hadn't got any sleep in a couple of days, so she wasn't as strong as she could have been. I did just enough to take the edge off—the rest's still here. Bree never even stirred. I've sent her all the way downtown, to get me Afghan food. Hard to believe she'd be dim enough to fall for that, but maybe she wanted to. She must be bloody sick of me. I know I am."

Tears splashed onto my lap. I knew what she was going to say, before she ever said it. What else was there?

"I'm sorry, JP. Sorry everything went down the way it did. Sorry for you, sorry for myself, maybe even for Perry Dillon, a little bit. Not sorry for Bree, though. She doesn't need any pity from me. Besides, she managed to fuck my entire world, just by existing. But I wanted to ring, you know? Just to say I was sorry."

A pause, this time no longer than a whisper or an indrawn breath.

"Cheers, mate. Bye, now."

225

CHAPTER FOURTEEN

Just to prove I wasn't heroic, I rang Ormand straight away. Of course, what I had to say probably wasn't going down on the plus side of anyone's anti-hero ledger, either.

It took me a bit to track him down. I know, I'm an idiot—all I needed to do was check my own call log, and I'd have found his direct number. After all, he'd rung me from his own desk.

Instead, pulling on shoes, I fumbled my way through the New York City Police Department's telephone tree, wasting a good ten minutes before they got him for me. By the time they finally hooked me up, I was dancing with impatience.

"Ormand."

"Oh, good, there you are. Lieutenant, this is John Kinkaid. I've got a phone message in my voice mail that you need to hear—it's the solution to your case." I took a deep breath. "But

I'm telling you, right now, up front, I want an assurance from you, before I let you hear it."

Of course I was bluffing. My hand had no bloody face cards, and we were in the deepest imaginable pile of shit if he called me on it. I thought of Bree, what she might be looking at, what she was almost certainly going to walk into with a bag full of warm Afghan takeaway, and I heard my own voice, steady and implacable. "You agree to leave Ms. Godwin out of it as much as you legally can. She's done nothing that wasn't from a desire to help, to make things right. That's my condition. Do we have a deal? Because if we don't, I'll hit the erase button and deal with it myself. It's your call."

Silence. For some reason, I pictured him, sitting at his desk and bloody grinning, his light eyes narrowed, enjoying himself. If that mental image was close to accurate, I was going to take pleasure in wiping the grin off his face.

He finally spoke up. "As long as I can hear Ms. Godwin's story from Ms. Godwin herself—without you sitting there trying to guide the conversation—I have no reason to involve her. I can't promise there won't be any legal issues, though, since I don't know the story. But if she neither killed Perry Dillon nor participated in his death, she should be safe enough." His voice went cold suddenly. "And I wouldn't erase that message if I were you, Mr. Kinkaid. This conversation is being recorded, and you've just admitted to being in possession of evidence that might lead to arrest and prosecution on a capital charge. That would make you an accessory."

"Oh, Gordon fucking *Bennett*, mate, try that on the bloody dog, yeah?" I was at the door of my room now, and I was grinning myself, a bit savagely. He'd tried to call my bluff, and he'd failed, because he'd come at me using the wrong weapon. I had the upper hand—without that message, his investigation was dead in the water. "Not good enough. Sorry to be rude, but sod that. It's bollocks and you know it. You've got no proof that I'm not taking the piss out of you—no proof I ever had a voice mail message. And yeah, I know, don't bother saying it—I know you can subpoena the phone records. That won't get you what's actually said, though. I can erase it and you'll never know what it was. Hell, I can sling the bloody phone down a sewer grate or into the river, and you'd have nothing. Now stop playing games, lose the cop-speak, and answer the fucking question. I'm off to see my wife. If you want to be there, you agree to keep Bree out of it and remember, since we're talking about subpoenas and tapes? I can have my lawyers subpoena the tape of this conversation. After all, recording someone, with or without their knowledge, works two ways—shit, Perry Dillon is proof of that, or at least, he ought to be. Ten seconds, Lieutenant: I have a taxi to catch. Yes or no?"

"Goddamn it!" He steadied his voice. "Fine. You win. I'll do my best to keep her out of it. I can't promise any more than that, and if you don't know that, you should. I can't promise anything on behalf of the DA. But I do have control over what the DA gets told in the first place. If that's worth anything, you have that promise."

"Good." I was at the lift, jabbing the button. "Stay by your desk. I'll ring you from the cab with an address in just a few minutes."

"Mr. Kinkaid, wait, don't—"

"Sorry, lift's here. No reception in the lift, yeah? Stay near your phone."

I rang off. Fuck him. This time, he was the one who could sweat.

I stopped at the concierge's desk on my way out. There was a line of taxis directly in front of the hotel, so that wasn't a problem, but I needed an address. Cilla had given me the name of the hotel and the street, but I needed an exact number. I had it inside of thirty seconds. I love competence.

The cab shot off, heading uptown and west, hitting the traffic at Columbus Circle and sitting for a few minutes. My head was incredibly clear, clearer than it had been in longer than I could remember.

I'd committed. I'd made it official, with that phone call to Ormand. I was in this situation now, as deep as Bree, and if what I suspected was about to happen actually went down, the hook I could find myself wriggling on was just as big and sharp and nasty as Bree's hook. If anything went wrong with this, Ormand was going to find a way to lock us both up, so long and deep we'd neither of us ever see daylight again.

So I had to do this right, and I had to be right in what I thought Cilla's call was really in aid of. I kept hearing her voice, circling through my skull: *I'm at a dump called the McKinley Residential Hotel, West 128th Street . . . weekly rates, ask no questions . . . they let my supplier up, just before I rang you . . . he came by with enough good product to hold me for a week . . .*

We were up near the northern end of Central Park, heading up the highway by the river. Hard north, then a bit east, and we were into Spanish Harlem: 105th Street, 110th.

I've sent her all the way downtown, to get me Afghan food . . . hard to believe she'd be dim enough to fall for that, but maybe she wants to . . .

I got my cell out and punched in the redial from my call log. Ormand got it on the first ring.

"Mr. Kinkaid?"

"The McKinley Residential Hotel, West 128th. I'll see you when you get here."

I clicked the phone off before he could say anything and got my cab fare ready. We were minutes away.

Cilla had called the place a dump, but that was unfair. It was a perfectly decent residential hotel, of a kind that's quite common in American cities; residents get a room and some light cooking facilities, and sometimes, for a bit of extra lolly, what they really get is a two-room apartment with a private bath. The carpet was old, but it was clean, and the lobby had a small telly and a couple of comfortable sofas. It wasn't the Four Seasons, but it wasn't a dump, either.

I walked into the lobby, straight up to the bloke behind the desk, and asked for Mrs. Kinkaid.

He barely even glanced at me. "Seven seventeen."

"Right. Do you mind if I sit right here? I'm waiting for someone—they shouldn't be long."

I walked over to one of the two sofas, in full view of the reception desk, and settled down to wait. There was no way I was going up alone, not if what I suspected was right; no way I was taking a chance that Ormand could claim I'd gone up alone.

My nerves were jumping like cold water on hot coals. I kept my eyes on the lobby doors; I was just praying that Bree was still out, still watching a bloke in a turban and an apron load up an insulated Styrofoam container with *mantu* and *qabili pilau* because she hoped the food would tempt Cilla's unpredictable junkie appetite, still all the way downtown or maybe sitting on an uptown subway, with a plastic bag full of fragrant delicacies on her lap. If she wasn't—if she'd got back ahead of us and was already upstairs—we were both fucked, hosed, gone.

Ormand got there five minutes after I did. I saw the blip of the blue light outside; no sirens, just the flashing blue to let the world know it was official business. He hurried into the lobby, in company with two uniforms. When he saw me, he stopped in his tracks.

"Hello, Lieutenant. I got here first, but I just thought I'd wait for you." I locked stares with him. "Down here in the lobby, that is. The nice bloke behind the desk tells me that we want room seven seventeen. Shall we?"

He opened his mouth, probably to tell me where to stuff it.

He looked absolutely furious. I said, very calmly, "She's my wife, Lieutenant. You pointed that out yourself, when you were kind enough to warn me I might need to play copper's nark for you and give you access to her credit card records. It works both ways. If I have the responsibility, I also get the rights. I'm coming up."

Ormand got the pass key from the desk. We rode up the seven flights in absolute silence, me and him and one of the uniforms. He'd left the other copper down in the lobby.

No one said a word. It was just as well, really; I was holding my breath, the entire way up.

At the door to room 717, Ormand turned to me. "Do you want to knock, Mr. Kinkaid? After all, you said it yourself—she's your wife."

"Right." I put my knuckles against the door and rapped, good and hard, once, twice.

Nothing. Silence from inside.

"Try the door, will you?" Ormand was standing a bit behind me, watching me.

"No, I don't think I'll do that. Not that I don't trust you, but I don't see any reason to put my fingerprints all over the doorknob, not under the circs." I stepped back. Behind us and around the corner, I heard a faint chime; the elevator, paged from somewhere else in the hotel, whispered shut and began to hum, making its way elsewhere. *Showtime*, I thought, and felt sweat break out, just along the hairline. "Besides, mate, you've got the badge and the paperwork. Just get on with it, yeah?"

He tried the knob himself. The door was unlocked. And right then, with that unlocked door, I knew I'd been right, and I knew what we were going to find.

The apartment was really not more than a decently sized room with a single bed and a small sofa, a cheap table and two chairs, a small television. There was a fridge; there was a bathroom with the door open, actually quite clean. I wondered if Bree had been the one to scrub it down.

Cilla was there, stretched out on the narrow bed, just as I'd known she would be. She'd passed out without taking the tie-off from just above the crook of her left elbow; odds were, she hadn't felt a thing. Both arms were limp and dangling.

There was a syringe, fallen to the floor next to the bed; there was a small drinking glass on the nightstand, with the dregs of something cloudy and ugly at the bottom. I saw the smear of fresh blood, recently dried, scabbing over on the vein just below the tie-off. And there were a dozen, maybe more than a dozen, glassine packets on the floor, to her right. They were all empty.

Cheers, mate. Bye, now.

I wouldn't have recognised her, not on the first look, or maybe even the second. Her face was puffy and swollen; her hair, that spiky blond bed-head look I remembered so well, was thin and sparse. She'd said, in her good-bye message, that she'd gone dark-haired before the Garden show, trying to disguise herself; the black dye she'd used had begun growing out, and the roots weren't blond; they were white. Her arms were riddled, tracks on both.

A ping, the elevator, stopping on seven. Something caught at me—a faint scent, distant but there.

And suddenly, out of nowhere, I got buried by this huge wave of outrage that Cilla hadn't been given the chance at that last meal. She'd always loved Afghan food, done her best to turn me on to it. You'd think the fates could have given her that much, you know? A last meal? I'd let her down, we'd let each other down. A decent dinner before dying didn't seem like a huge request, but apparently the fucking fates couldn't be bothered to allow it.

Footsteps in the hall. Behind me, a sudden intake of breath, confused noise, the uniform who'd come up with Ormand moving back to the door. I heard her voice—*"oh God no, what happened, I just went out to get her some dinner"*—and I spoke up, hard, sharp, not to be argued with.

Cheers, mate. Bye, now.

"Shut up, Bree." I didn't turn around. "Be quiet, do you hear me? Don't say anything. Not one fucking word."

For the second time since Perry Dillon died, we saw the sun come up over Manhattan through the dirty windows in Ormand's office. This time, the office was a bit more crowded.

Ormand had walked over to Cilla, checked her pulse, held a bit of tissue paper over her lips to see if there was anything in the way of breath. Nothing.

"Forget it," I told Ormand. Despite my own warning to Bree to keep her mouth shut, I couldn't seem to follow my own advice. "She's gone. She rang me a good ninety minutes ago, and I'm betting she's been gone since two minutes after that."

He ignored me. I suddenly got exasperated—I think my nerves were beginning to catch up with my brain, because I was shaky and furious and scared half out of my mind.

"Oh, for fuck's sake, Lieutenant, wake up and smell the heroin," I snapped at him. "She told me her supplier had come by with enough stuff for a week. She did the lot in one shot. Very Macbeth, you know? One fell swoop. Cooked it, did it, gone. Just give it up and get on with it, yeah? Your killer offed herself. Deal with it."

Bree whimpered. I turned finally, and saw her.

She looked terrible, a complete mess. Cilla had said Bree'd got a few bruises, trying to control Cilla's thrashing, but she hadn't mentioned that one bruise, at least, was a livid purple horror that was just beginning to turn a really sickly yellow green over Bree's right cheekbone; there was a spot in the middle that was almost black. She'd pulled her hair back and tied it up, a sure sign she hadn't been able to wash it. The shallows under those big green eyes were dark and deep with lack of sleep, and the green was muddy. She looked beaten, exhausted.

The uniform had one hand on her arm and was holding, hard. I wasn't even sure she'd noticed.

"Oi," I told the cop. "Get your bloody hand off her."

He blinked at me, as if he wasn't sure who I was talking to, and looked at Ormand. So did I.

"Close that door." If I'd thought I'd heard him sound cold before, I'd been mistaken. His voice, right now, was black ice. "Everyone stays right where they are for the moment. Manetta, let go of her and leave her where she is; she's not going anywhere. I want you out in the hall. Call HQ and tell them we have a crime scene. No one comes in here except our people."

Bree made a noise. "Shut up," I told her. "Not a word. Not here, not now. Later."

"Mr. Kinkaid is very wise." He was looking at her, a hyena crouched over a wounded gazelle. My skin was crawling. "You should wait until your lawyer's with you. Don't say anything, Ms. Godwin. Of course, if Mr. Kinkaid was really wise, he'd follow his own advice."

He turned then, to look at me.

We locked up, like a pair of pissy dogs circling each other—facing off for dominance. I held it, held the stare. It's not as if I really had a choice, you know? Cilla was dead and Bree was potentially going to rot in prison for a very long time, if she didn't actually fetch up in the current edition of whatever New York uses in place of the electric chair. So was I, if I didn't play this right. I was committed. I couldn't back down now. I simply couldn't afford to let him win.

He broke first, turning away, looking back at Cilla, dead on the bed. I glanced over at Bree, willing her to stay quiet, to read my mind, to know that I was fighting for her, but she wasn't meeting my eye. Her own eyes were half-closed, looking elsewhere, maybe inside or maybe at memory or maybe, worst thing she could look at, the long road ahead, an investigation, a trial, prison. . . .

I walked over and got her hand, holding it hard. It was about solidarity; she needed to know, I needed to make her understand. I honestly thought Ormand would tell me to back off—somewhere in my own head, I had this confused notion, probably from reading mystery stories years ago, about how the police like to keep suspects separate, to prevent collaboration or something. But I wanted to let Bree know that I was there, I was with her, I was fighting for her, and I wanted to do it before Ormand tried to make me stop.

He didn't, though. He just glanced up at me. "I'd like your cell phone, Mr. Kinkaid. You'll get it back at my office, once we've gone over everything and heard that message, but for now, give it to me." He held out one hand. "You can both call your legal representation from my office, because we're heading there as soon as we finish up here."

I took it out of my pocket with my free hand and handed it over to him. The other hand still had hold of Bree's. She hadn't responded with any returning squeeze of her own, but her head moved slightly, following the cell phone as it left my hand and was tucked safely into Ormand's pocket.

I leaned toward her, stretching to make up that two-inch difference in height, and put my lips to her ear. "You're all right." I breathed it, no more than a breath, tickling her ear with the words, making her hear me. Her shoulders hunched, then rippled. There was something intimate about that whisper, about my lips against her, about those words. It felt almost as if she'd gone away, as far away as Cilla had gone, and I hated it. So I kept whispering, soft as love, hard as sex, just trying to convince myself as well as

Bree. "I'm here. It's okay. They can't hurt you. You're all right now. Stay with me, love."

We stayed in that wretched hotel room, waiting for the police to finish doing their thing, for nearly three hours. The room was hot—no air-conditioning, just a small window fan, and all that did was move warm stale air from one corner of the place to another. After a while, my legs began to shake, and the soles of my feet began to tingle. Between the late hour, the standing, and the heat, I was fading fast.

Ormand must have noticed it. "Do you want to sit down, Mr. Kinkaid? You look a little unsteady."

"Ta. It's just the damned MS giving me the usual late-night fits." I stayed where I was, keeping Bree's hand in mine. She hadn't once given me any sign she was even aware I was holding it, but on the other hand, she hadn't pushed me away, either. "It's long past time for my night meds, and I left them back at the hotel."

At that, Bree finally woke up out of whatever trance denial bullshit fairyland she'd been hiding in since she'd walked through Cilla's door. She swung her head around to look at Ormand.

"He should sit down." Her voice was thin, uninflected; all the music had gone out of it, and all her usual self-assurance with it, just as all the light seemed to have gone out of her eyes. "Is that all right?"

"Of course. That's why I suggested it." Ormand jerked his head toward the sofa. Bree, without another word, led us both across the room. We sat down, side by side. I still had her hand, and I intended to keep it as long as I could.

We sat on that sofa, watching Cilla's body gradually cool. It wasn't deliberate, it was just that the sofa faced the bed, and there was no place else to look. It was beyond bizarre, that wait, the two of us sitting side by side holding hands, as the elevator went up and down and the place started filling up with people: forensics blokes, a medical examiner to pronounce Cilla officially dead and beyond reviving, medical techs, men with a collapsible-stretcher affair, a gurney I think they call it, men with a zippered body bag, lifting Cilla into it. I couldn't make myself watch that bit. I closed my eyes.

The genuinely weird bit is that, the whole time, the smell of Afghan food sat in the still air of the place like a perfume based on saffron or something. I read somewhere once, that smell is the strongest sense, the one that triggers memory the hardest and sharpest. Strange thing for a musician to say, I know—you'd think we'd say it was hearing—but that's true. I haven't been able to cope with the smell of Afghan food since that night.

It was after three when Ormand finally turned to us.

"I'm done here," he remarked. "Let's go."

The car out front, with the removable blue light on top, turned out to be a plain car, not a police cruiser. They put us in the back, with Ormand in the passenger seat up front, and the uniform he'd left in the lobby sitting between us.

Halfway downtown, Bree suddenly spoke up, turning to the cop.

"I need to ask Lieutenant Ormand something," she told him, and the cop nodded. Ormand twisted his head, listening.

"John needs his meds. Neurontin. You can't just miss doses of those—they're antispasmodic. It can cause problems if you don't take them as prescribed. Can we stop at his hotel and get them?" She swallowed hard. "Please?"

"Sure, no problem." There was an unexpected undertone in Ormand's voice—he actually sounded approving, which was a bit surprising. I'd have expected him to hate our bloody guts by now. "Which hotel is it, Ms. Godwin?"

"I don't know." Her voice wavered, and in the darkness of the car, I jerked my head toward her and caught the glint of tears on her face, just before she dashed them away with the back of her hand. "You'll have to ask him. I haven't been there with him."

We woke up our respective lawyers from the police station. Pasquini asked me if I'd been read my rights and I told him no, I hadn't—no one had asked us any questions, or said anything about us being under arrest. I told him about the call from Cilla, gave him a fast rundown of everything that had happened since, and was told to give him ten minutes to get dressed and he'd be on his way, and in the meantime, to stay quiet.

Bree, on another phone at another desk, stayed on the line with Jameson a lot longer than I'd done with Pasquini. But eventually, she rang off. As soon as she did, I was back at her side and got hold of her hand again. This time, she squeezed back. It was faint, barely there, but it was something. We were together again.

Ormand got us settled in his office and sent out for coffee and bagels and orange juice. That's one thing I do like about New York—you can find things at four in the morning, and you usually don't have far to look, either. There was nothing we could do until Pasquini and Jameson showed up, so we sat and ate, me fussing over Bree, making her eat.

There was a moment when I nearly melted down myself—a youngish bloke came in and was introduced as Assistant District Attorney Something or Other. That seemed to me to break the agreement I had with Ormand, but I decided to wait until I had my lawyer there for backup before I did anything at all.

One thing Ormand did do was to call the department's tech people, saying there was going to be an outgoing call made from Ormand's personal line, making sure it was recorded. That struck me as strange; I thought about it for a minute and realised that he was probably talking about recording Cilla's confession on his own phone. It took me a few minutes of sorting out, but

I finally sussed it out: the person making the outgoing call was going to be me. That little notion was really off-putting—no clue why, but it was. It took my appetite completely.

I set my bagel down, half-eaten, and intercepted a worried look from Bree. I looked back at her, shaking my head, and her face smoothed out, went blank, disappeared, faded into some place where I couldn't follow her. I didn't know why she was bothering. Invisibility wasn't going to do her any good at all, not now.

And then Ormand's door opened behind us, and both lawyers were there and were being settled into their own chairs.

"Well, now." Ormand sat back in his own chair. The bastard had complete control, and every possible advantage, and he damned well knew it. "Let's get started."

CHAPTER FIFTEEN

I'm really quite proud of the fact that, in spite of everything that had happened, and in spite of being absolutely shit-scared for Bree, I got the first word in.

"Yeah, let's get started." I looked at Ormand and then at the assistant DA. "First things first, though. We had a deal—it was why I handed you my cell phone. You were going to do everything you could to keep Bree out of this, remember? How about repeating that, so that my lawyer—and Bree's lawyer—can hear you? Also, so that this nice gent over here, from the district attorney's office, knows where we stand? Come on, Lieutenant. Crank up the volume, mate."

He grinned at me. I was expecting the fairy story wolf deal, since he had to be smelling blood and he was brilliant at the whole scary teeth bit. But it was just a grin, a real one, tired but not much else going on there.

"Yes, I did say that. That was the deal." He looked at Jameson and then at Pasquini. "But I'd like to reiterate that I also said I couldn't speak for the district attorney—and this conversation requires the presence of someone representing the DA. What I can do, if it seems like the best course of action after we've heard the entire story, is decide whether any sort of prosecution is of any benefit in this case, and make that recommendation. I should point out that neither the district attorney nor myself gets any gold stars for wasting New York's resources or money."

Suddenly, there were the teeth. "And of course, while I'm pointing things out? The deal is only extended to Ms. Godwin. You aren't covered by it, Mr. Kinkaid."

I was locked up with Ormand again, and I got the feeling we understood each other. "Yeah, I know. The deal's for Bree—I'm not covered. That's fine. Let's get on with it."

Pasquini and Bree both made noise, but I held up a hand. "No, shut up, both of you! I know what I'm bloody doing and I know what matters to me. So yeah, that was the deal. This is for Bree, not for me. Carry on."

"No," she whispered. It was a tiny noise, but it stopped everyone. "No way. I won't allow it."

"You don't get a choice." I kept my voice even and met her stare head-on. "You disappeared for the best part of a week and you told me fuck-all and then, when I finally did get the story, I didn't get it from you, I got it from Cilla. You can just shut your gob, lady."

She stared at me. If she had words, they weren't making it out. I turned back to Ormand.

"Let's get on with it. What do you want me to do?"

"Check your messages." Ormand pushed his desk phone in my direction. "I believe you have something stored in your voice mail that we need to hear?"

I don't know about the rest of you, but when I access my voice mail, the one attached to my cell account, I always do it from the cell itself. There's a special button for that—I press it, there's the robot-lady voice, press star, enter the password. I'd never tried ringing it from a different phone, and I fumbled it a bit—first I couldn't remember the number, because who ever rings up their own cell phone, right? Then I forgot my four-digit password. But I got it in the end.

You'll probably think I'm dim, but it hadn't occurred to me that Ormand would put the entire thing on his speakerphone, for everyone to hear. I honestly thought he'd just meant to record it, have it, as a weapon. But there was a hum and a crackle, and the cheap little speaker came to life and suddenly, there it was, Cilla's voice, the voice of the dead:

"JP? Are you there? Look, I'm calling to say I'm sorry. And I hope you don't have one of those fucking thirty-second limits on your voice mail, because this—it's going to go on for a bit. . . ."

There was nothing, not a damned thing I could do. Knowing what was coming, I reached for Bree's hand, but somehow, I couldn't get hold of it. Her hands were folded tight in her lap, and I couldn't get at them. I couldn't get to her, either. She was hidden beyond high, high walls. She was beyond pale; she looked as dead as Cilla was, with the angry discoloured mess against her cheek, where she'd tried to keep Cilla from hurting herself and taken the hit instead. And part of this was as much my fault as it was Cilla's. What had she said, about Bree being there for her, hating her for it? . . .

Bree was a thousand light-years away, eyes closed, gone off somewhere. I couldn't reach her. I couldn't touch her.

We sat there, listening to the whole thing, Cilla and her

choice comments about Bree, about me, and there it was as well, the bit about Bree fixing the guest list and passing Cilla in backstage. We sat there, and all I could do was wait. I've never felt so completely useless, so thoroughly helpless.

"Cheers, mate. Bye, now."

"Well." Ormand had an odd look on his face. He was ignoring me entirely and focusing on Bree. "Ms. Godwin, I'm going to ask you some questions. Mr. Jameson will let you know if he thinks you ought to answer. All right?"

She opened her eyes then and looked at him, and I saw her face and got a shock. I've seen Bree angry, seen her passionate, remorseful, worried, intent, unhappy, warm, fierce, and careful. I'd never seen her bitter, until now.

I've said it before, I've never hit a woman in my life. But right then, seeing the way Bree's lips twisted up, if I could have brought Cilla back to life for just a moment, I'd have hit her as hard as I knew how. I'm wondering, now, if it was really myself I wanted to hit.

"Questions?"

She laughed, and it was the wrong noise to be coming out of her, all wrong. Something was off, all the way off. Something had broken, and I didn't know what and I didn't know if I could fix it. The DA was staring at her—I felt sick to my stomach.

This was very different from the way she'd broken, telling me the truth about that heroin theft so long ago. That had come with tears, and Bree doesn't cry. This was different, and it was worse, much worse.

"Sure, ask me questions." She stopped laughing, managed to turn off the tap. She looked at me, a direct stare, and there was flame behind it—the green eyes were blazing. "Since John's apparently plea-bargained his ass away for me, I don't have

243

anything to worry about, right? No reason for me to give a damn about what happens next, right? Fine. Whatever. I don't give a shit. Go ahead. Ask anything you want. It's not as if I have anything left to lose anyway—I seem to have lost it all. What do you want to know?"

"Did Mrs. Kinkaid call you to ask for help in derailing Perry Dillon's proposed biography of her husband's band?"

"God, no. Are you nuts? Ask *me* for help? Weren't you listening?" Bree sounded contemptuous, something else I'd never heard from her before. "She hated my guts. I was the—what was that splendid phrase she used?—oh, right, her husband's little fucktoy."

"Bree—"

"I'm talking to Lieutenant Ormand." She never even glanced my way. "No, she didn't call for me. She'd have eaten broken glass before trying that. She called for John. Want some nice juicy irony, Lieutenant? She called on our house phone, in total meltdown hysterics, right around the exact time John would have been sitting down in Los Angeles with Perry Dillon." That laugh again—I thought I saw Ormand wince a bit. "She didn't bother mentioning that she was calling from Perry Dillon's London flat. I found that out from you, back in Boston. And you thought it was Dillon who called me. Jesus."

Another memory, Bree sitting on my hospital bed with the marked call logs in front of her, clearly bewildered, saying she didn't understand, Perry Dillon had never rung her. I thought she'd been telling the truth, and she had been. It had been Cilla who'd rung.

"Did she tell you what had happened?"

"Yes, but she was pretty incoherent. I got the impression that he'd basically got her good and stoned, and got a nice little heap of dirty laundry out of her. That was almost funny. I'd been so freaked about him digging in the dirt and finding out

244

the truth about stuff like me stealing heroin for John from my mother's clinic and my mother taking the blame, and about the backlash against John if they found out I was still underage when we first got together. And here she'd handed him stuff he would never have got his hands on, or even known to look for. She'd made this gigantic mess for everyone around her, and of course she wanted John to fix it. Typical fucking Cilla."

"But Mr. Kinkaid wasn't there."

"No." She sighed suddenly. "Sorry—I haven't had more than an hour's sleep at a time during the past few days. Anyway, I was livid with her. John was just off the road, he was exhausted, and here was this huge steaming pile of shit she was planning on dropping all over everyone. I said I wasn't going to pass it on, John had enough to cope with, she'd made this mess on her own and she could deal with it on her own. So, of course, she promptly flipped out and threatened to kill herself."

Ormand's voice was quiet, steady. "Did you believe her?"

"Why wouldn't I? John's been believing her for years." Her voice was scathing. "She was good at that particular threat. A real pro. She made it sound very convincing. God knows, she had practice. Didn't she, John?"

I closed my eyes. Bring Cilla back to life, I thought, just for one minute, and I'd kill her. I swear I would. I'd wring her bloody neck.

"The point is, that left me no choice at all, except to help her sort it out. Because I sure as hell wasn't going to dump this on John, just to please his insane wife."

"Did you discuss it with Mr. Kinkaid when he arrived home from Los Angeles?"

"No." She reached out and drained a half cup of cold coffee, and made a face. "Not a word. I just surprised and delighted him, I think—first by being so reasonable and philosophical about him slipping up with Dillon, and then by saying I wanted

245

to come to New York for the rehearsals and the Garden show."

She turned and faced me, her mouth trembling. There was something in her face that hadn't been there just a moment before, that might have been a ray of hope. "You *were* delighted. Weren't you, John?"

"You're bloody right I was." I reached out and got hold of one of her hands, lifted it to my lips, and kissed it. "Still am, lady. Next tour, I'm not taking no for an answer. You're coming with me, yeah?"

"Maybe when they let me out of jail." She turned back to Ormand, but she left her hand where it was. "What else do you want to know?"

"Let's move ahead, to about twenty past nine, backstage at Madison Square Garden. You brought the door guard a beer. I gather, from what Mrs. Kinkaid said, that the business with the guest list was prearranged?" She opened her mouth, but he lifted one hand. "No, I don't need background—it's late, we're all tired, and I'd like to get this wrapped up so that I can see what has to be done. Let's just stick with the question. Was it deliberate? Did you know both of them were going to be there?"

Jameson opened his mouth to protest, but she waved him off. "Yes, I knew." Her face was angry. "She'd come to New York because he refused to return her calls. She was freaking out. The guy had fed her heroin and used her and taped her without her knowledge or her permission and then he dumped her and wouldn't talk to her. Perry Dillon was a masterpiece, wasn't he? Certified genuine piece of shit. She wanted to tell him he couldn't do the book, that she'd sue him and she'd win, that she'd get him busted in the U.K. for drug dealing."

"So you agreed to her idea about getting his name on the guest list, with her as a plus-one?" Ormand was speaking slowly, carefully. "And both of them were supposed to show up there at half past nine, or thereabouts? And Mrs. Kinkaid knew that

Perry Dillon was coming, but so far as you're aware, he knew nothing at all?"

There was something strange about the way he'd phrased that. I couldn't quite sort it out—I was very light-headed, really knackered, and things were aching. Whatever it was, Bree seemed to get it, because they were looking at each other, she and Ormand, and her answer was just as careful.

"Yes—that's right. She told me she'd be there around half past nine, and Dillon would as well, and could I fix it, let them both in so she could get him in a situation where he couldn't just blow her off. She said she'd be there a bit early, so he wouldn't know she was there. So I subbed at the door, pencilled Dillon in with a plus-one; she showed up just before half past and I signed her in. I told you the truth about that—about ten different people showed up around the same time she did. He wasn't one of them. Of course, he was late." She was quiet for a moment. "It never occurred to me she'd be calling me from Perry Dillon's cell phone, either. She must have had scrambled eggs where her brains used to be. God, I hate heroin."

I sat there, her hand relaxed in mine, my fingers rubbing lightly over her palm. She felt cold. When we got back to San Francisco, I was going to insist she get some blood work of her own done. Or maybe I'd ring Miranda and get her in on nagging Bree into doing it. . . .

"Did you let Perry Dillon in?" He shot the question at her.

"No. And I still don't know who did—he might have come in after Jerry came back, but when I left, Dillon hadn't shown yet. I left the backstage door and went looking for Cilla. I'd done all I could do about the situation, and I wanted to tell her that. If Dillon didn't show, or didn't get past Jerry, well, not my problem."

Bree was quiet a moment. She was fading—I could hear it in her voice. "It was weird. You know how, if you don't see someone for years and years, you have that picture of them in your head? As if they'd been locked in amber, never changed? That's how it was. I'd only ever seen her once, at a benefit Blacklight played, where I was there as a volunteer for my mother's clinic. I wasn't quite seventeen at that point—John didn't know that, of course; he thought I was in my twenties or something. There was an incident, a girl getting hurt, and John called me over in mid-song, asked me to deal with it. I guess Cilla thought she needed to keep an eye on me, because she made it her business to stand behind me for the rest of the night."

"I see." Ormand's voice was neutral.

"And that's who I remembered, what I remembered." Her voice suddenly shook. "A skinny little starfucker in perfect makeup. Mrs. Kinkaid. The woman who had everything I wanted."

There was something in her voice, something that cut deeper than anything else cut me that night. I must have made some kind of movement, a noise, because she got control of her voice and went on.

"Sorry. Never mind. Anyway—I remembered her as young. And she wasn't. She was in her fifties and she looked about ten years older, raddled—she looked like shit. I wouldn't have recognised her." She swallowed another yawn. "I'm sorry—not trying to be rude, but I'm exhausted."

I wouldn't have recognised Cilla either, I thought. I hadn't recognised the dead woman at the McKinley, not without a second look. I seemed to be fading out, along with Bree; I was dizzy, my head wanting to float off like a child's balloon. Christ, I was tired. . . .

"Anyway, I couldn't find her. I went all over the backstage area, twice—it's huge back there, but it was nearly empty during the show, because Blacklight was on. The roadies and crew were out doing their jobs, and the family and friends were in the wings, and everyone else was in the roped-off guest alcoves just inside the auditorium, watching the band. So I hunted for a while, and I couldn't find her anywhere, and then it occurred to me, I hadn't looked in the band's personal dressing rooms. It would have been just like her, making herself at home in John's personal dressing room; knowing Cilla, she'd have thought, still John's wife, hanging out in his dressing room with his stuff was her right. All the rooms had been open before, but when I went back, the door to John's was shut. That was about half past ten, I think."

She stopped, and swallowed. "I turned the knob, and it opened. And—oh, God."

"You walked in on Perry Dillon's murder?" Ormand's voice was very quiet. The ADA leaned forward. At Bree's side, Jameson suddenly stirred.

"God, no—are you kidding?" She blinked at him. "I wouldn't have kept quiet about that—that would be illegal. If I'd walked in on it, if I'd seen it, I'd have told you. But I didn't. I walked in and found Cilla, standing there with her hands at her mouth and her eyes bugging out of her head. Dillon was on the floor—and one of John's guitar stands was on the floor next to her. It was sort of vibrating, humming, as if it had bounced when it got dropped and hadn't quite stopped bouncing yet. The metal ones do that."

She stopped. It was obvious to me, she was remembering, seeing it. I wondered how many times since opening night at the Garden she'd closed her eyes and seen that picture, just waiting behind her eyes for a chance to give her nightmares.

"Dillon—his throat was just—there was a huge horrible dent in it." Her voice had thinned out. "He was dead. I bent down and checked, pulse, breath, nothing. It was horrible."

"You didn't think she—"

"What I thought doesn't mean shit." She'd interrupted

Ormand. Now she shot a look at Jameson, and I realised this little bit of dirt was one reason their conversation had taken so long. I watched his ears turn pink. "And don't you even try to tell me it was a reasonable inference, that she was guilty. Inferences aren't my job. I didn't see her do it, and that makes anything I could say about it gossip and rumour, not fact."

"That guitar stand was wiped, Ms. Godwin." Ormand's voice was still very quiet, too quiet. "Did you do that?"

"Don't—," Jameson began, but Bree was staring at Ormand, bewildered.

"Hell, no. I didn't touch the damned thing—you couldn't have paid me to touch it. I didn't wipe anything, and I don't think Cilla did, either. She was in no condition to think." Her eyes went wide suddenly. "Oh! Her gloves!"

It was Ormand's turn to blink. "Gloves? In New York? In summer?"

"Little lacy black gloves." I heard my own voice, from a mile away. "Cilla's fashion statement. She loved the damned things, back when we were still a couple. She had drawers full of them. She used to buy them, ten pairs at a time, from this little shop near World's End, in the Fulham Road." I yawned. The room didn't seem to want to stay still; it was the kind of feeling you might get on a boat. "Was she wearing a pair of those, love?"

Bree nodded. "I thought they looked very out of date, very seventies retro, but then again . . . anyway. I guess she might have rubbed with the gloves on, but I didn't see her do it. I said he was dead, and of course she went into screaming hysterics. So I slapped her, good and hard. It made her stop. And then she started babbling, clutching the front of my dress, telling me about how I had to help her get out of it, get her out of New York, get her back to London. Maybe her brains were fried on heroin and maybe they weren't, but she did seem to realise that the only person who could connect her to Perry Dillon was me. She said that John would understand, he wouldn't want her to suffer for this, he'd understand it hadn't been her fault."

"What did you say?" Ormand sounded fascinated. I wondered if he believed her, not so much what she was saying, but the entire situation. The ADA looked pretty slackjawed as well. I'd have bet money that, in their reality, mistresses don't conspire to help wives. They must have thought she was some sort of circus freak.

"I told her no, of course. My own stomach was doing flip-flops. I shoved her out of the dressing room and told her I had to call the police and let them know someone was dead. And then I ran for a bathroom and didn't quite make it. I ruined my dress, throwing up all over it. When I came back out, she was gone. And then I went and found a security guard, and they called you people."

She was sitting up straight, but the effort was visible. She was so tired, every muscle had to be locked up tight. "Is there anything else? Because I'm nearly asleep and John really should have been asleep hours ago."

"Yes, there is." He leaned across the desk. "I want to hear how you came to be in Priscilla Kinkaid's hotel room. I want to know exactly what you've been doing in Mrs. Kinkaid's company for the past few days. And I have to tell you that, without that information, the deal we had is off."

It was right around then that my sleep-deprived, adrenaline-addled brain finally got round to doing a few basic sums and came up with the fact that Ormand already knew what he was going to do. He'd made up his mind how he was going to call it by the time Cilla's suicide message had finished playing. All he wanted were the bits he needed to fill in his picture.

There was something really liberating about that, you

251

know? If he'd already decided, then this was just curiosity, his control thing, a desire to tie up as many of the dangly bits as he could. That being the case, he might as well have the lot.

I couldn't read him so well as I'd have liked—I couldn't tell if he'd believed a word Bree had said. I did, myself, but then again, I know her. Ormand was a different story.

"It was during the show in Miami." Bree sighed, taking a huge breath. Her voice was scratchy. "I'm sorry, Lieutenant, but I'm dry as a bone. Do you have any water—oh, cool, there's still some juice left. Thanks."

Ormand was quiet, just watching her, waiting.

"I wasn't expecting that phone call." Bree leaned back in her chair. "I mean, I'd told her I wasn't going to do any more than I'd done. There was a limit to what she could ask of me. I'd done what I could for her, but that was it. I didn't even know if she was still in New York, or if she'd made it back to London, and honestly, I really didn't much care. John had had two really bad exacerbations and a heart attack. I didn't have any spare energy to think about Cilla. Besides, I'd had my little run-ins with you already. I knew I was top of the charts on your suspect hit parade, and I wasn't worried about it."

"Weren't you?"

Damn. He sounded as if he thought she'd issued some kind of challenge. I leaned forward.

"Why should she be?" I jerked my head at Ormand, making him look at me. "Bree said it best, when I was being worried and she wasn't: You couldn't prove she'd killed Perry Dillon because you can't prove something that never happened."

"Actually, you can." There was that grin he'd given us before, a real one, not the predator look. "But it's a lot of work and a lot of risk and it takes a lot of time and energy and you really have to want a particular result. And in this instance, I don't. Go on, please, Ms. Godwin. You said you'd basically written

Mrs. Kinkaid off, and weren't expecting any more demands from her. What happened during the Miami show?"

"I was dancing in the wings, just offstage. I had my phone in a little antique bag, draped around me like jewelry, and it started vibrating. The band was in midsong and it was really loud, so I backed offstage and pulled the phone out. It was a New York number—I didn't recognise it. If I had . . . damn, I don't know. Maybe I wouldn't have answered it."

"It was Mrs. Kinkaid?"

"Of course it was." She closed her eyes a moment. Stress, exhaustion, a memory that hurt? I wasn't sure. "But I couldn't tell right away. She was completely out of it—dislocation, crying, giggling, fading in and out. My mother's a doctor, and she's worked with junkies for years, so it only took me a minute or two to figure out that Cilla was cold—jonesing, I mean, deep into withdrawal. It was scary."

She turned toward me, just for a moment, the green eyes heavy-lidded with secrecy and exhaustion. Her hair was coming down; I watched a bit come loose from the elastic band. "Besides, I'd seen it up close, once before."

I still had her hand. My own fingers tightened around it.

"She said . . ." Bree's eyes were wide open suddenly. "God. She said—she said she felt like there were things crawling on her. She'd used the last of her stash days before, after Madison Square Garden, and she couldn't get hold of her supplier. She was too sick to hit the street and find what she needed."

I bit down on words, on my own memory, a memory I didn't actually have. Bree leaned forward, her eyes lowered. Something splattered on Ormand's desk: tears.

"She said John was her husband, and he'd run off and left her because of me, and it was my fault, and please would I help? She said she was dying."

I'd heard this before. I'd heard it damned near word for

word. What had Bree said, telling me about the call I'd made to her, the call I couldn't remember?

It was you, but you were crying and you said there were bugs crawling on your arms and you hadn't had any snowball for three days and you said your wife had run off and left you. You remembered my name—you called me by it. You said, "Bree, I'm dying. . . ."

"She started to cry." Bree's voice jerked me back to the present. "She was just wracked with it, in total panic, total despair. I was completely frantic. I didn't know what to do. It was the middle of a gig and I could hardly hear her over Blacklight's PA and I was in Miami and the truth is, I didn't want to help her. I hated the woman, and she hated me, but she'd called me for help and she said John had left her alone and it was my fault. And maybe she wasn't wrong about that, either. Maybe they'd still be together if—"

"*No.*" My own voice was too loud. "Not your fault. Cilla walked out and left me in Seattle. I didn't run off and leave her, Bree—she ran off and left me. And a damned good job she did, because however long we'd have gone on after that, we'd have both been damaged, damaged much worse than either of us were apart. All right? Clear now?"

They were all staring at me, Bree included. I ignored everyone else in the room and bent forward, and took her face between my hands.

"Bree of Arc," I told her. "Sometimes it's very sweet, and mostly it's just really exasperating. But I'm afraid you'll have to do without being burned at the stake for this one, love. Cilla was full of shit. I didn't leave her. She left me. It wasn't your fault. Nothing to do with you, nothing at all."

She started to cry, and I kissed her. I felt her melt into it, her hands closing into mauls on my shoulders, the rest of her relaxing, just letting the fear and the pain and the stress of the past weeks out.

No one moved; no one said anything at all for a moment. I couldn't have cared less, honestly—for that few moments, we were together and safe, while they were gone, invisible, locked out. When we pulled apart, I knew I was smiling.

"Come on, love," I told her. "Tell the nice policemen the rest of the story, so we can blow this place and go get some sleep, yeah?"

"Oh, God, John, it was horrible." The dam broke, at last, words pouring out. "It was completely awful. She said—it was just what you said that night, when you called me at the clinic, and knew my name. I didn't know what to do—I just knew I had to get there. And it's all very well for you to sit there and tell me it wasn't my fault, but damn it, it *felt* like my fault."

"Go on, Ms. Godwin." There was a really peculiar look on Ormand's face. I got this odd vibe off him, just for a moment, that he knew what she was going to say. Maybe he was starting to sort out what my old lady was all about. The ADA kept opening and closing his mouth, like a fish. "What did you do?"

"The only thing I could do. I wasn't going to buy her anything, not snowball, not straight coke or snow either. I got off-stage and I called my mother, and she said that I was clearly insane but if I was determined to play martyr, the best things were sedatives or opiates, because that could be used to get someone through the worst of it. I reminded her that John had that heart attack, and told her they'd given him these big jugs of TyCo, and clonidine to control his blood pressure. She gave me a couple of minutes of hell about how unethical it was for me even to think about helping myself to someone else's prescription."

Another memory, talking to Miranda on the phone. Joan of Arc, she'd called Bree. And what else? Something about how she hadn't been there for Bree once, so now she made it her business to be there. . . .

"She told me people use that for withdrawal control. So I got a cab back to the hotel and took a handful of each one." Bree leaned her cheek against mine for a moment. "I made sure I'd left you plenty, though."

"Let me make sure I've got this straight." Ormand was the only one in the room who wasn't looking at Bree as if she were from Mars. Both lawyers were blinking at her, and the ADA seemed to have decided that everyone on the premises was a nutter, or at least that's the vibe I got off him. "Your—I'm sorry, I don't know the word to use here, and I really don't want to offend anyone. Your lover's wife called you up in Miami. You were already convinced she was responsible for Mr. Dillon's death. She was deep into heroin withdrawal. You and Mrs. Kinkaid hated each other. And you reacted to her plea for help by stealing some of Mr. Kinkaid's medicine to help get his wife through the worst of it?"

"Saint bloody Bree." I heard myself laugh even as I tightened my hold. "Stop looking at her as though you thought she'd just dropped in from another planet, Lieutenant. She's done this sort of thing before. I ought to know—she saved my life once, doing it. And I was on the phone with her mum myself, a couple of days back, and the whole Joan of Arc thing came up. Bree, love, I just want to let you know: If you ever do this to yourself again, I'll beat you like a fucking gong, yeah?"

"Stop laughing, damn it." The words were muffled against my shoulder. "It isn't funny, and anyway, you have no idea why I went. The thing is, I did—I went. I got the concierge at the hotel to get me a flight and some money. I got off at Kennedy and I heard the airport page, you paging me, but I kept going. I took a cab in to the McKinley. When I got there . . ."

She stopped and lifted her head. She'd had her cheek against me, and the bruise looked darker, angrier. "It doesn't matter," she told Ormand. "You don't need details, do you? They aren't important. I broke no laws that I know of. I didn't buy drugs for her or help her obtain any drugs. All I did was hold her hand and bathe her face in cold water and every once in a while, when it got too bad, I gave her a TyCo or a clonidine. That's not illegal, is it? Compassion's not illegal."

"Nope." Ormand was smiling at us, the real thing, a full genuine smile. "Well—giving someone prescription medication that isn't theirs is technically illegal. But beyond that, no. Not illegal, just rather unusual under the circumstances, if those are as you described them. From that bruise on your face, I'm guessing you also restrained her when her reactions to the withdrawal symptoms started getting bad enough for her to hurt herself?"

"I tried to. I didn't really want to touch her—I'd rather have put my hands into a nest of black widows. What she said, in that message, about me hating her as much as she hated me? She was right. I would have loved to watch her die. I've wanted to watch her die for nearly thirty years." Her voice was edged, dark. "Bitch. Evil, manipulative cow. She's done nothing but damage John, and damage me. I hated her. I always have and I always will."

"Then what in sweet bleeding fuck did you think you were doing?" It burst out of me. I knew what state Cilla must have been in. "Are you out of your tiny little mind? Why put yourself through that? Why in hell couldn't you just leave it alone?"

"I don't believe it." She was staring at me, her mouth half-open. "Are you asking me that? You, of all people? You honestly don't know?"

"I understand why you let yourself be guilted into the last few days. God knows I ought to—I guilted you into it myself, once. But why would you protect her in the first place? Why cooperate with her at all? For fuck's sake, Bree, she killed a man. The lieutenant here nailed it: even if you didn't believe it right off, you must have guessed later on. It's not as if you liked her, or had any use for her. Why didn't you just tell her no, sod off, the first time she rang you up? Why would you let her pull you into the shit she was sitting in? Why would you want to help her?"

"Idiot." Bree was in tears. She didn't seem to notice. "My god, you're an idiot. I protected her because I thought you'd want me to. I protected her because you love her."

CHAPTER SIXTEEN

We got back to the Omni, and I knew there were things that needed to be talked about. Problem was, I was too tired to form anything fancier than two-syllable words. I was useless, gone, run off my feet.

Bree was completely silent. The last thing out of her mouth had been to Ormand; there was something going on there as well. He'd told Jameson that he'd have a statement prepared for Bree to sign later in the day, but for right now, we were free to go get some sleep.

"You don't need me to stay here?" I wasn't touching her just then—she didn't seem to want to be touched. "Are you—will there be—I don't—" I knew I'd sort it out later, but for right then, Bree had it sussed and she was dealing, and it would probably be better if I just let her cope.

"I'm not going to recommend any charges be brought against

you, no." He must have heard her intake of breath, because he smiled at her, and for the first time, the smile was actually kind. Man of a Thousand Mouths, Ormand was. "I can't see any possible benefit or reason for continuing this further. We have a recorded confession made under no duress whatsoever. We'll have your statement about her motivations, and about the sequence of events at Madison Square Garden, if we need it. My feeling is that, if Mrs. Kinkaid were still alive, the circumstances would be very different. But since there won't be a main prosecution in this case, any corollary investigation with an eye toward prosecution would be wasting the resources of the State of New York." He turned to the assistant DA. "That's my take. But it's your call."

The bloke nodded. I got the feeling all he really wanted to do was to get away from these crazy people who didn't act or think in any way he could make sense of. If Ormand had suggested that we all get stark and go dance on the roof of the station, he'd probably have gone along with it.

"Really, the only detail that could possibly have led to any kind of inquiry would be the question of who actually phoned Perry Dillon's agent and gave a false name." Ormand dropped his eyes and shuffled some papers on his desk. "That might argue premeditation."

Bree opened her mouth, but before she could say anything, he added, a bit too loudly, "And of course, that would have been Mrs. Kinkaid. So I'd say this is wrapped up."

"Thank you." Her voice was very quiet. I glanced from him to her, and back again. I'd definitely missed something there.

Ormand walked the ADA to the door, spoke for about ten seconds, and ushered the bloke out. When he came back, Bree was still watching him.

"No thanks needed." He looked at her, and there it was, that kindness again. "You know, I'm a big fan of loyalty. I think it's much too rare in this day and age. I like to support it when I see it. And I don't know if I mentioned it, but I'm also a big fan of Blacklight. . . ."

"Any time you want to see a show from the wings, you ring me up." I offered him a hand—a reflex action, really—but he took my hand and shook it. "I'm serious, mate. Permanent guest list. Just ring me up and let me know. You've got my cell number—shit!"

He grinned. "Yes, you can have your cell phone back, Mr. Kinkaid. I wondered if you were going to forget it. If you're ready, I'll have someone get you a cab—give me a couple of minutes to call it out front."

His eyes went back to Bree for a moment. "People are very surprising, sometimes," he said. "It's very easy to forget that. I'll send Mr. Jameson that statement later."

By the time we got back to the Omni, it was just past seven and I was asleep on my feet. I remembered to stop at the desk, to check Bree in, and I remembered to ask for a wake-up call at noon; I was going to need to ring Carla and get her to book us some plane tickets straight to Dallas. Right now, I was on complete autopilot.

Bree just stood there, in the middle of the room, watching me. She didn't say a word. She seemed—I don't know, shy, nervous, diffident. Whatever it was, it was all very un-Bree.

I headed into the loo, took my meds, and brushed my teeth. When I came back out, she was standing just where she'd been. I cocked an eyebrow at her.

"Look, love, are you planning on just standing right there while you sleep? You putting down roots in the carpeting, or something? Because if sleep's next, come to bed."

"I can't."

I stood there and gawked at her. Whatever it was I'd expected to come out of her mouth, it wasn't that; I didn't expect the words and I didn't expect the voice. She sounded terrified, on the edge of tears. Bree, who never cries, had been awfully weepy lately, all things considered. I said the first thing that came into my head.

"Why the hell not?"

"I don't have the right to that bed. Not anymore."

I didn't stop to think too much. I just went over and dropped my arms around her. Purely selfish, that was, because I wanted to stretch out and my legs hurt. I'm a selfish git.

"Bollocks." I tilted her chin down. "Baby, look. I'm *Night of the Living Dead* right now, okay? My brain's not working. I know we need to talk, and we will, I promise. I swear I'm not ducking it, but please, can we do it later? Or at least can we do it lying down?"

"I guess—I mean—if you want me to, I can do that." She had the most bizarre look on her face. "I mean—I know you're tired. I didn't want—I didn't mean to—I just didn't—I wasn't trying to be a drama queen, or anything—"

"What the fuck?" I stepped back then and stared at her. I'd got it now—I sorted it out. She sounded scared. "What in hell's the matter? Hello? Is that Bree in there? Will the little green men who snatched my old lady please give her back?"

She had both hands covering her mouth. Her eyes were enormous.

"Right, that's it." I jerked my head toward the bed. "Let's sit. Come along, love. If the Big Talk's got to be right now, I'm fine with it, but we're doing it sitting."

I took her hand and led her across the room. I sat, pulled her down beside me, and before the bedsprings had stopped creaking she'd started talking, words coming out, and it was a damned good thing I'd made us sit, because what she was saying would have knocked me down, if I'd been standing.

"I blew it. I blew it, I blew it so bad." She was nearly choking, a stream that wouldn't stop. "I let her die, John. I could have called the cops, 911, anything. I got there and she was a wreck; all I had to do was call someone, but no, not me. I hated her fucking guts and I stayed there and watched her, she was suffering and what did I do, did I get her a doctor, did I get her taken care of by someone who knew what the hell they were doing? No, not me. What did I do? I washed her fucking *face!*"

"Bree—"

Out of nowhere, she beat against my chest with both fists. I got hold of both hands and pushed them back down, and held as hard as I could—she was usually as strong as I was, if not a bit stronger, but this was all new territory. She was shaky and uncoordinated, her breath was full of pathetic hitches, and she seemed to be trying not to scream under her breath. All sorts of things I'd never seen Bree do before were front and centre this morning. This was the first time I'd ever seen her in bona fide hysterics.

In a way, I suppose it was lucky we were both so wiped out. If either of us had been more on top of it, we probably would have had all the usual defenses in place, all the usual call-and-response patterns of what made us a couple, twenty-five years' worth of them, all set up and ready to go. I would have gone tired and frail; she'd have gone nurturing and protective. Just like old times, you know?

But there was something inside my head, a little voice with a little message playing for me, over and over: *new ground, get it sorted out now, new ground, get it sorted out now.* And I got it, and the message was spot on. I knew it, bone deep. We couldn't snap back into the old pattern, not completely.

"Okay." I blotted her cheeks with my fingertips. "Your face is a mess, and your nose is pink—ah, here we go, take a tissue. Stop a minute, take a deep breath, blow your nose and then talk to me. I mean it, Bree—not the rubbish you've just been talking."

"I'm not—"

"Yeah, you are. It's rubbish. So you feel guilty, right. And you feel responsible, okay. And you feel you let me down, yeah, I get it. For what it's worth, you didn't. You're the only person on the planet who has never once let me down. If you don't believe

263

that, then you're the idiot, not me, and pot calling the kettle black, all that, you know?"

"John—"

"I want to know what set this off. And you're going to tell me." I didn't know I could sound quite that implacable, but then, I didn't think I could feel that implacable, so I suppose it was reasonable, really. "Something happened, didn't it? Something you didn't tell Ormand? Something you weren't planning to tell me?"

I saw her face change, and I knew I'd hit the bull's-eye. I pulled her close. "There are days—seriously—when I'd like to take a stick to you. Now lose the Brave Little Woman bit, and just dish, love. What happened?"

It came out then. First the words were disjointed and then they were nearly incoherent and the longer I listened, the more I felt my skin wanting to crawl. The old familiar feeling, of being helpless, of not being able to deal, was right there between us, waiting. Thing is, if I let it, we were back at square one. And square one wasn't going to wash, not anymore.

". . . she called me a thief, a robber. She said I'd broken into her world and taken the only thing she'd ever had that was ever worth anything. I was washing her face, she had a nosebleed, a really bad one, and it got all over everything, her blood on my hands, and she saw it and said it was my fault, all of it, but the one thing I wouldn't ever be able to take away was her power over you, because you still loved her and that was why you'd never wanted to take your name back from her, and her blood was all over my hands and she started laughing, she was leaning back against my arm and she called me Lady Macbeth. . . ."

"It's okay, love, honestly, it's all right, don't cry, or, no, sod that, cry all you need to, it's okay . . ." Helpless, useless—or maybe not. Maybe I was being of some use after all, crooning the sort of soothing words at her that seemed to be the best I could do, because they seemed to be having some effect. Anyway, just for a nice bit of difference, I was the adult. I was the one offering comfort.

"She told me she'd got you to go back to London, go back to her, just to see if you'd do it. She was so weak, she couldn't move on her own, I had to help her sit up to get half a TyCo down her throat, she was leaning up against my arm like a baby, and she said, 'does it make you feel better, me being this wrecked?'" Bree began to shake. "She was right. It did make me feel better, being stronger than she was. And God, John, I wanted to just kill her. I didn't know I hated her that much—it was like a black hole. She'd fall asleep for half an hour and I couldn't sleep, I couldn't eat, all I could do was sit there and fucking remember those times you left, when you went back to her, you went away, there was nothing I could do and there was nothing I should have even tried to do. And then I'd sit there hating you, hating me, because how could you love her all this time, how could you love her more than you loved me, what had I done, what hadn't I done, and then I'd have to tell myself it wasn't your fault, it wasn't anybody's fault, you couldn't help who you loved. . . ."

"Christ." Memory is a bitch and a whore, I swear. The words came back to me, spoken on a dreary San Francisco afternoon, as clear as yesterday: *Don't do this to me. Don't do this to us. We're too—we're so new.*

"She was right. She was right about all of it." Bree was quiet now, her voice deadened, somehow still. "I've spent all these years in what should have been her house, with the man who married her, not me. This—it isn't my bed. I don't have any claim to it. She was right. I was so busy resenting her, seeing her as the Big Bad Evil Usurper and spoiler of my happiness, I forgot the reality. I was the usurper, not Cilla. You married her. You stayed married to her. You loved her."

She looked at me. "And I let her die. I let her sucker me into leaving her alone. She was right about that, too—I wanted to get out of there, get away from her for an hour. So I left her alone. I'm sorry, John. I'm so sorry."

"Some of that's true, I suppose." I had no idea what was about to come out of my own mouth, but fuck it, in for a penny, in for a pound, yeah? She'd just let it out. My turn to do the same. "Well—not completely true. See, you're mistaking love for laziness."

She blinked at me. I went on, easy, conversational.

"I'm not dissing the stuff you're afraid of. But honestly, Bree, if you mean what you're saying, then what in the name of sweet bleeding Jesus have we been up to for the past quarter century? Of course this is your bed. You're my entire life." I shook my head at her. "You let her die? You kept her alive, and she shit all over you by way of saying thank you. And I know you love the drama, but honestly, Bree, you've got to stop wallowing and believing every bit of rubbish you're told, so long as it feeds your guilt. It's making you crazy, and I won't have it."

She was smiling, or at least she was trying not to smile—I couldn't tell. But she looked alive, somehow. Not so defeated.

"You keep protecting me," I told her. She was letting me talk and I needed it; I needed that space, that way of sorting it out. "And that's brilliant. I love that you protect me—I need you to do that for me. But you have this thing you do, you cut me slack when you ought to be nailing me on my shit. And I let you do it. What did Domitra call me—a dimwit or a dick? Bloody hell, she has no clue how right she is."

I looked at Bree. "We got unlucky once, with timing. The timing couldn't have been worse. You called me on Cilla once, and it was the wrong time, the only time when I had no choice at all. I had to go back that first time, Bree. She had that much right to my loyalty."

"Don't you think I knew that?" Bree's hands were back in her lap, together, tight, defensive. *No*, I thought, *not this time.* Not now, and never again. I reached out and pulled her hands apart, and hung on.

"No, I don't think you knew that. Not in your heart, love. You were so young, then—still covered in down, basically. If I'd had any clue just how young you really were, I would have killed myself staying away—but I never stopped to consider the potential for damaging you. I couldn't see past my own feelings. The fact that I loved you as much as I did—as I do—well. Fucking Rock of Gibraltar. Blocks out the sun."

She was quiet. I went on talking, letting it out.

"The thing is, you never called me on it again. Inertia's really easy, love. Painless. Cilla was active—ringing me up, making demands, forcing me to act, even the suicide threats. You? You went the other way, and stayed passive. Saint Bree and her magic invisibility button. It gets really old, you know?"

"What the *hell*? Are you daring to sit there and tell me that you stayed married to Cilla all these years because I didn't tell you not to?"

She was staring at me, and unless I was reading her completely wrong, she was about to lose her temper. Good. Off balance was what we both needed right now. I'd got a bit of second wind, but it wasn't going to last, and I wanted us back together, because I knew what I was about to say.

"Partly, yeah." I grinned at her. "You know how lazy I am. And there's something else you didn't do, as well."

She was good and furious now, cheeks flying red rage. She opened her mouth to blast me.

"You never said you wanted to marry me." I took her face

between my hands and caught her eyes, holding them to mine.

"That light's always on, Bree." I spoke quietly. "It's always burning. I have no idea how to turn it off."

"Good evening, Oakland!"

We stood in the wings, me and Luke, waiting for the lights to go down. Across the stage, in the shadows, Stu and Calvin were waiting for their cue, as well.

There were a few different faces in the wings at the Oakland Arena tonight. It was a nice familiar mix, just one reason I love playing at home, the way the rest of the band loves ending up the European legs in London. Of course, the fact that we can climb into the car, and Bree can drive us across the Bay Bridge and we can see the lights of the city if they aren't buried under the fog, that's another reason. Knowing that the cats were curled up on various sofas and cushions, waiting for us, that was one more reason. It's always good to get home.

I was tired as hell, and my legs were sore. A lot of that wasn't being ill, though—the last two weeks of the tour had been completely insane. The story had broken just before the Dallas show, and of course the media had descended on us, hordes of press. The show had been a fucking zoo. I'd stopped reading the papers entirely at that point—even a lifelong passion for wanting to know what's going on in the world couldn't hold up against the shit they were printing, and it sure as hell couldn't hold up against the complete shitstorm of press.

At least two people actually had enjoyed the insanity before and after the Dallas gig, even though it had been for some really interesting personal reasons. Domitra, of course, loves being given a good reason to leave people who hassle Mac in serious pain. There weren't that many media people out there stupid enough to try it with her standing there, but a few must have needed glasses or their minds checked, because they tried bulling their way past her. The Bunker Brothers were there for one of those encounters; Stu told us later that Dom had got herself a lovely workout. Personally, I'd call that Darwinism at its finest.

And if we're talking about sheer mind-boggling stupidity? Luke, heading in for the preshow sound check, had actually been manhandled by a reporter from a tabloid. The bloke had grabbed his arm, and what was more, he'd done it in front of about ten onlookers, including a local cop. I'd heard all about it later, from Carla; she told me Luke had started out curt but polite, the bloke tightened his grip instead of letting go, and then put the cherry on top of the stupidity cake by asking if it was true Solange had been kicked out of school for drugs.

Luke hadn't hit him. But he'd got the reporter hard up against the building wall and held him there, telling him in no uncertain terms what an asshole he was, and what Luke was planning on doing to him if he ever got within fifty light-years of the band again. The bloke had hung there, terrified and pinned, until venue security and Phil McDermott's staff could get there and hustle the bloke away. I was sorry I'd missed it.

So we had some ducking to do, the rest of the tour. Ormand had done a decent job of keeping things fairly quiet and low-key, but all the elements were there, megastar band, dead sleaze bashed with a guitar stand, guitarist's estranged wife guilty, suicide, confession. You had to expect the press would be relentless, and they were.

I'd come in for the brunt of it, of course. Carla had been splendid, keeping them out of my face. Right after I'd given Bree her new sandals—those lemon-yellow sandals I'd bought at Jimmy Choo—I'd presented both Carla and Dom with their prezzies. That was just before the news about Cilla broke, but

Carla would have done it anyway. I'd had to release a statement, a nice little bit of nonsense, designed to tone things down—Carla and Bree both helped me write it.

And I owed Ormand one particular bit of thanks: He'd kept Bree out of it completely, not one word anywhere in the media that she'd been involved in any way at all. I owed him for something else, as well, since I'd finally got enough sleep to understand that weird bit of byplay between Bree and Ormand, about who had made that phone call to Dillon's agent.

"... *the Oakland Arena is proud to present* ... "

Bree had been front and centre the entire time. A lot of it was protectiveness, the old reflex I valued so much, but there were times when I watched her dealing with it, and I could see a huge difference. There was the woman trash-telly reporter who'd somehow scammed her way in backstage in Detroit, for instance; the woman headed for me, started her questions, and before anyone could do anything, Bree had a death grip on her and was strong-arming her out the backstage door, offering to kick the woman's ass in twelve different places the entire time she was dealing with it. I knew just how badly she wanted to press the magic button, and disappear. But she never did. She was there, you know? All the way there. She'd become visible.

Kris and Tony were both here tonight, along with their wives; they were going to be sitting in for a song. The surprise of the day, though, that had come about a week earlier. Patrick Ormand had startled the living shit out of me by ringing my cell phone the morning after we played Denver to mention casually that he was planning to be out in the Bay Area on business, nothing to do with the recent unpleasantness, but his visit coincided with the Oakland show, and was that offer of permanent guest list still open? I'd said yeah, of course, once I got over the shock of him ringing me in the first place.

So he was there, deep in conversation with Bree—he seemed

to have taken quite a fancy to her. He didn't look anything like a cop, either. There's something about a pair of jeans and a T featuring an airbrushed photo of a prominent conservative talk show host with a red line through his face that pretty much abolishes any feeling of official cop cred, you know?

"... *put your hands together, girls and boys* ... "

"JP?" Carla had come up next to me. She was dressed to the nines, which surprised me for a minute. A gig, for Carla, is part of her job, and she's usually pared down for action as needed. It took me a look at her feet before I sorted out that she'd probably dressed to do justice to the pricey pair of Jimmy Choo heels she was wearing. "Just a reminder, I'll need the entire band backstage in the dressing room just before the encore; there's a publicity thing arranged; it'll only take a minute. Okay?"

"Right." I caught Luke's eye, and rolled my own eyes a bit. He grinned at me, and shook his head, before looking around for Solange—he'd flown his daughter out from London, to look at California universities.

Everyone was looking forward to the day after tomorrow. The entire band had broken with a lifelong tradition; instead of heading for the airport, everyone was staying in the Bay Area to decompress for a few days. Bree had suggested a massive party at our place, and announced that she was going to cook for it. I thought she was out of her mind, and said so, but everyone else seemed to think it was a fabulous idea, so I was stuck. I mean, after giving her shit for demanding invisibility all these years, I could hardly give her shit for offering hospitality, especially to my mates, yeah?

"... *give it up* ... "

Mac breezed over, dancing in place, warming up. Domitra was right behind him. She was in work shoes, her Docs; she let her eyes flicker to Carla's feet, caught Carla's eye, and stuck her tongue out. Those shoes had definitely rung some chimes, you know? Mac grinned at me and slipped out onstage, as the houselights went down and the stage shone under the sudden pool of gold and ink.

"Hey, baby." Bree was up behind me, patting me lightly on the bum, slipping her hand between my thighs, squeezing once. She'd done that at every gig since Dallas. She was in white velvet, a new dress, one I hadn't seen. Unusual colour for her, white, but she carried it off. It had the usual buttons. Her face was energised, and even in the shadows, her eyes were bright green. If they stayed that colour the rest of the night, I was in for some brilliant sex. "Right here."

"... *BLACKLIGHT!*"

The last gig of a tour is always special—it has a kind of energy to it, a settling of accounts, the knowledge that, for a good long while to come, these people don't have a shot at seeing you play and you don't have a shot at giving them what they've come for. Tony once compared it to the last game of the World Series: throw everything you've got at it, because tomorrow isn't an option. I'm not into baseball, but that makes sense, that comparison.

There were some really memorable moments during the Oakland show. We'd arranged for Tony and Kris and another friend of ours, a local harp player named Jack Carter, to sit in on one song, and since all the local fans have known and loved these blokes for decades, of course they went nuts. I had one totally surreal moment, when I glanced into the wings during a particularly hot guitar solo of Luke's and saw Bree dancing with Ormand. I suppose life can get weirder than that, but that was quite weird enough for me.

Two hours, two hours twenty. The show went longer than usual, which is another thing you come to expect on closing nights; after all, it's not as if you have to save anything for the next show, you know? But finally, offstage and into the wings, a ten-minute breather before the encore . . .

Bree wasn't there.

I'm not really sure what went through my head at that moment, but it wasn't pretty. Before I could flip my shit, though, Carla had me by the arm.

"Dressing room," she reminded me. "Hurry. We only have ten minutes max, and then encore."

I found myself surrounded by the band, herded by Carla and Ian down the ramp toward the dressing rooms. The crowd was chanting, stamping; tiny points of flame, Bic lighters, flickered like fireworks. We walked into the dressing room, and everyone stopped, and stepped away from me.

Bree was standing there by herself. She had her hands clasped in front of her, as if she were planning on praying or something. There was no one else in there—no media, no press, no publicity people.

Luke got behind me and gave me a push.

"What . . ."

She took a step forward. Behind me, between me and the door, the band waited. Luke was there, and Kris; I saw Ian leaning against the door, grinning, and Patrick Ormand, of all people, looking amused in one corner.

Yeah, so, I'm dim. It took that long for it to dawn on me that I'd been set up for something.

"You told me, back in New York, that I'd never said I wanted to marry you." She was in front of me now, eye to eye. She seemed to be having a bit of difficulty with her voice. "So I figure the ball's in my court."

She held out her hands to me. In the palm of each one was a thin gold band. Dead simple; dead elegant. Bree has taste. The white velvet suddenly made a world of sense, you know? And so did the huge party she'd been planning.

"Marry me." The room was perfectly quiet, the stamping and crowd noise dim and muffled. "Please?"

"Oh, hell yeah," I managed, and even though I was pretty much drowned out by the cheers that went up from the evil bastards behind me, who'd known this was bloody coming and hadn't bothered to warn me, she heard me. "Too right I will."

I reached out and gathered her in.

EPILOGUE

"Good evening, San Francisco, and welcome to the Fillmore."

"Nice crowd out there tonight." Tony flexed his fingers. "Full house?"

"Yeah, looks like." We'd cracked the door to the dressing room open, and I peered out. "A thousand, maybe a bit more."

"We're delighted to have with us tonight a group of musicians you all know and love . . ."

I reached out and snagged a mouthful of nachos. No bubbly backstage here, no catered spread, no list of what the band requires as part of the craft services contract. We'd got nachos and sandwiches from the house restaurant, the Poster Room.

Playing at the Fillmore was always a kind of homecoming for these blokes, and I loved the place, the feel of it, the photos and classic posters of gigs from decades gone by that lined the walls.

Some of the gigs and people were before my time—I was a kid in the mid-sixties, on another continent. So I had a few fannish moments of my own, every time I walked past some of those posters in the lobby, saw some of those names.

" . . . *Tony Mancuso, Kris Corcoran, Billy DuMont, Jack Carter and JP kinkaid . . . *"

"Right." I gulped down a mouthful of water—I only ever sing backup with Blacklight, but tonight I had a few numbers I'd be singing lead on. I'm not the world's strongest singer, but this wasn't an arena or a stadium, it was a local club, and this wasn't Blacklight, it was just a few local blokes, getting together to play some blues and rock. "Showtime."

We got the dressing room door open and stepped out, waiting. Bree had commandeered a small table near the front, the ones they reserve for the band's friends and family, and was parked there with Sandra and Katia. She saw me and waved. She was in leather jeans tonight and a black velvet blouse, with the prerequisite buttons at the back, from neck to hem. Bree was always more casual at smaller gigs.

". . . *a warm San Francisco welcome, please, for our very own Fog City Geezers!*"

The house lights went down and we walked out onstage, to a lovely thunderous roll of applause, hoots, our names being called out from the back of the house.

First thing I did was to check for my usual stool. The roadies—two very nice blokes from the Bombardiers—had set it out for me. I made a mental note to thank them from the stage, during the show. Good roadies are worth their weight in gold. The size of the band doesn't matter, or the size of the venue; roadies make a musician's life possible.

"Right." I picked up my 345, slung it over my shoulder, and stepped up to the mic. "A very good evening to you all, and thanks for coming. We're going to give you a couple of hours of old music, new music, just music in general. If you want nosh, you can get it any time during the show, and the same for liquid—and if you're broke and just want a bit of a munch, there's a big basket of free apples out in the lobby. Also, the cool people who run the Fillmore asked us to make a special announcement: If you're not broke and can spare a bit, we're asking that you please put what you can in the Red Cross hurricane rescue collection jars out there—Hurricane Katrina relief needs whatever you've got, right now. Every penny helps. Oh, in case you're wondering, or were out eating apples when we came on? We're just a bunch of cranky old sods, and we're called the Fog City Geezers."

Hooting, stamping, a few friendly things called out from the darkened club. If anyone here knew about the murder of Perry Dillon, or my wife's suicide, or gave a toss, they weren't saying so. I love playing San Francisco. Good people.

I grinned out into the darkness. "Right, so, this first number is an old Rufus Thomas song. I'm doing the singing, and singing—well, it's not my strong point, you know? So I'll try not to mangle it too badly—the vocal, that is. And I want to dedicate it, as well. This one's for my old lady, because she's got an eye for good clothes."

More cheerful hoots and encouragement. I'd been watching her, knowing where the table was, and in the darkness I saw her head whip around. "Here we go," I told the audience, and grinned toward Bree. "It's called 'Walkin' the Dog.'"

We went into it, full-throttle rocking blues. Eight bars, and then I stepped up to the mic, and sang:

"*Baby's back, all dressed in black, silver buttons up and down her back. . . .*"

I saw Bree's hair swinging and then she was dancing, swallowed up in the crowd. By the time we got to the third or fourth number, Katia and Sandra would be out dancing, as well. You're never too old to rock and roll.

Kris and Tony came in, doing backup vocals:

"High, low, tipsy-toe, she broke a needle and she can't sew. . . ."

We'd give the people what they'd come for, play our hearts out and our arses off, hang about afterwards if we weren't too tired, talk about guitars and history and food and politics and music, music, music.

And later, after that, we'd put the two guitar cases into the back of the car. I'd climb in and Bree would get behind the wheel. We'd drive for a few minutes, up to Clay Street, park the car in the garage, and we wouldn't worry about the guitars until morning. The cats would curl around our feet, glad to see us. Bree would remember that I hadn't eaten in a few hours and she'd pull out something she'd made earlier, so that we could have something before I took my night meds. I'd remind myself to set up a Geezers gig at the Boom Boom Room, just across the street from the Fillmore. By morning, I'd forget about it.

"If you don't know how to do it . . ."

I caught Tony's eye, and he grinned at me. Jack was wailing away on the harmonica, burning it up, burning it down, stitching a call and response with Kris's bass. The place was cooking, just the way it should be. It's what it's about, yeah?

". . . I'll show you how to walk the dog."

Sometimes I think there's no escape from rock and roll. But I'm damned if I'd have it any other way.